THE ABDUCTION OF ADRIENNE BERG

CHERI KRUEGER

Black Rose Writing | Texas

The author grants the final approval for this literary material.

First printing

This is a work of fiction. Names, characters, businesses, places, events, and incidents are
either the products of the author's imagination or used in a fictitious manner. Any
resemblance to actual persons, living or dead, or actual events is purely coincidental.

ISBN: 978-1-68513-285-9
PUBLISHED BY BLACK ROSE WRITING
www.blackrosewriting.com

Printed in the United States of America
Suggested Retail Price (SRP) $21.95

The Abduction of Adrienne Berg is printed in Garamond Premier Pro

*As a planet-friendly publisher, Black Rose Writing does its best to eliminate unnecessary waste to
reduce paper usage and energy costs, while never compromising the reading experience. As a result,
the final word count vs. page count may not meet common expectations.

THE ABDUCTION
OF ADRIENNE BERG

Love is the ultimate outlaw. It just won't adhere to any rules.
The most any of us can do is sign on as its accomplice.
~ Tom Robbins

CHAPTER ONE
DANGEROUS

Adrienne knelt in her rose garden, gripping a shiny trowel in both hands high above her head. With a strangled samurai cry she stabbed the tool deep in her husband's throat, expelling a low grunt as the metal bit and buried to the hilt. The soil was as reluctantly yielding as human flesh, the image bright in her brain. Vibrations from the tool sinking into the earth resonated in her fingers, in the bones and tendons, calling up a bloody memory that made her shudder and slam a mental door. She focused on her breathing, substituting visions of murder for a calming exercise some therapist from her past suggested: write down what you cannot change and throw it away. *Let it go.* She drew in the dirt:

I want

I need

Sweeping her hand across the words, she scattered them into oblivion, embarrassed even in the privacy of her own thoughts that she didn't know what she wanted or needed. What she did not need was Dustin's glib reply to her idea of a vacation. "A vacation from what?" His sneer echoed in her brain and kept her anger boiling, a reminder that her wants and needs are irrelevant.

Loosening the trowel, she dropped it to one side and yanked a feathery weed from the bed of mulch. The smell of damp earth layered with the musk of red roses was usually calming, but she could not quiet her thoughts.

Furious with Dustin, and impatient with herself for expecting anything else from him. Why be angry at a dog for behaving like a dog? A waste of energy.

Dustin had left for work hours before she woke up, and the crunch of footsteps on decomposed granite did not compel Adrienne to turn around; he amused himself by sneaking up on her and she played her part by acting surprised. He would apologize for the heated discussion (nothing so passionate as an argument) of the night before, not quite sure why he was apologizing, but feeling it was required—and life would go on as it had for years.

A hand fell heavy on her shoulder; Adrienne turned with a ready false smile, expecting bland blue eyes but seeing pale green-gold hazel. She rose, stumbling on the knee pad.

"Gabriel." Her voice breathy with surprise.

"Hello, Mrs. Berg."

"Please, call me Adrienne," she said automatically. "Did you bring Dustin home?"

"I dropped Dustin and his crew in Santa Barbara. They expect me to fly them back this afternoon."

Adrienne shaded her eyes and craned her neck to see his face. She had only met Gabriel once, at a cocktail party a few days before. He was out of context in her backyard. Surreal. Electrifying.

*   *   *

The night they met, Adrienne was doing her practiced best to avoid conversation. Positioned at the fringe of a large group, she was close enough that no one felt obligated to rescue her, but far enough that she could feign interest without active participation. Eyes scanning the room, she paused on a man leaning in a shadowed doorway—a big man, broad-shouldered and tall. When her gaze landed on him, they locked eyes and a jolt shook her, as if she had touched her tongue to a lightning bolt. He had the clean-shaven jawline of a marble statue, a craggy nose that had been broken at least once, and a hint of curl in his black hair; light hazel eyes glowed in the olive of his skin. His mouth curled in a slow smile and Adrienne's heart skipped a beat, butterflies took flight in her lower belly. She jerked her attention elsewhere.

When she looked back, he was gone. She had time to feel simultaneous frissons of relief and disappointment before a presence loomed over her. Even before she turned, Adrienne knew it was that man. The man with the golden eyes. He radiated heat, his scent earthy, warm and spicy. Dark chocolate and peppercorns.

"I know what you're up to," he murmured in a voice like rough silk.

Her skin hummed like a tuning fork. Adrienne half-turned and raised an eyebrow. "Am I so obvious?"

"You look bored," he said, with that lazy curl of a smile. His lips were nearly a parody of the perfect mouth, marred only by a purple scar in the divot of his top lip. "Let's make up stories about these people."

"I know all their stories." Adrienne took a sip of her drink. "They're all boring." She looked him up and down and turned back to her restless scan of the room. "Tell me your story."

"Nah, you'll probably think I'm boring, too. You have that look."

"What look?" She narrowed eyes briefly before smoothing her face to social neutral.

"Like you are often bored."

A puff of amusement escaped her. "Things I find interesting are usually done alone."

"Please tell me what you do alone that is so interesting?" His smile was an eloquent smirk.

"Reading, writing, painting, gardening." Adrienne opened her mouth as if to add something and sipped her drink instead, avoiding his mischievous eyes. She was keenly aware that she attracted cattiness; there were people here who would waste no time gossiping about Dustin Berg's wife flirting openly at the Marin Civic Center fundraiser. "Now you know everything about me," she said. "Your turn, whoever you are."

"I'm Gabriel. Lawrence Fife's chauffeur." He shrugged. "See? Boring. And poor."

She flicked a glance at his perfectly tailored Armani suit. "Hello Gabriel, I'm Adrienne. Does Mr. Fife buy your clothes, you poor man?"

He flashed a quick grin that showed strong white teeth and a crooked right incisor. "You know your labels."

"It's part of my job." She waved her glass in a brief salute to the room.

Gabriel slipped his hand under hers and brought the martini glass to his mouth. She was too surprised to stop him. The contrast of his thick, dark fingers, big-knuckled and calloused, against her thin, smooth white hand was provocative, elemental and raw as a Mapplethorpe photo or O'Keeffe painting. Shaken, she could not take her eyes from him.

"Straight vodka?"

Adrienne took a sip from the same spot where his lips touched. "It appears so." She moved a step away; the heat of his body was overpowering, and she knew her cheeks were flushed. "What do you drive for Mr. Fife? Does he have any interesting cars or just boring old limousines?"

"A Bentley, a limo, and a Cessna."

"Ooh, you're a pilot. That's interesting."

"Not really, the chauffeur only sees the airports." He cast a roving eye across the room before returning his heavy-lidded gaze to her.

"You've probably met my husband, Dustin Berg."

"Yes, I know him." Gabriel's eyes shifted and he shot her a quick smile. "Sorry to throw you to the wolves but I have to go." He slipped away before she could form a reply.

Mystified, Adrienne scanned the vicinity to see Dustin headed her way with Lawrence Fife in tow. She had met Fife a few times and was not a fan; his smiles never reached his muddy eyes, and she couldn't bring herself to call him Lawrence no matter how many times he insisted. She pasted on an appropriate smile, noting a number of baby sharks in Fife's wake, and she was soon surrounded by cutthroat young men in designer suits.

Dustin claimed his trophy with a possessive hand on the small of her back while Adrienne fluttered at his side, a canary in a gilded cage, pretty and pointless. The men talked in vague terms about an upcoming business trip and Gabriel's name was mentioned. Dustin didn't always share his schedule with her, and she didn't really care where he went, but she actively avoided looking ignorant, so she didn't ask where they were flying. She scanned the room with surreptitious glances over the top of her martini glass, but she never saw Gabriel again.

Until now.

"Why are you here?" At his stony expression, her bubble of inappropriate lust burst, and a quick clench of fear knotted Adrienne's stomach. She didn't know this man and she was home alone, the backyard secluded. Perfectly private.

Gabriel tucked something in his back pocket. "Your husband has a gym bag in his closet. Please take me to it." He gestured towards the house.

Confusion creased her brow. "You flew all the way back here for his gym bag? I didn't know Dustin owned a gym bag. He doesn't go to the gym."

"Please, Mrs. Berg." Gabriel gestured again and moved close enough to press the tips of his fingers against her spine.

"You wait here and I'll bring it to you." Adrienne quickened her step but he easily kept up, his one stride to her two. She stopped at the back door. "Please wait here."

He looked at her with regret darkening his eyes. "I'm coming with you."

The light pressure of his hand turned into a push and the ball of fear in her guts grew greasy, thorny. "Gabriel, I'm really uncomfortable right now. I would rather you wait outside." She used her most authoritative voice, painfully aware of how weak she sounded.

"I don't want to hurt you, Adrienne, but you are about to become more uncomfortable." He reached around her to open the door and pushed her inside. She let out a startled cry and pushed back; he clapped his hand over her mouth and a heavily muscled arm around her waist. "There's no point in fighting me," he growled, muffling her screams as she struggled in his arms. "Please, Mrs. Berg. Please don't make me hurt you. I have a gag and I don't want to use it. No yelling." Her body gradually relaxed. He released her and motioned towards the stairs. "Where is Dustin's bedroom?"

Thoughts racing and her eyes darting around the room, frantically scoping out escape routes, Adrienne planted her feet like a sprinter poised for flight. "Find it yourself, asshole."

Gabriel clutched her elbow and uncoiled a thin rope from his back pocket—it was about three feet long and fashioned into a noose. "Do I need to put you on a leash?"

"Let go, you're hurting me." When he released his grip, Adrienne rubbed her elbow. "Take what you came for and go the fuck away."

Silent, he gestured upstairs, his mouth a thin line.

She ran up the stairs, two at a time, she could hear him thundering behind her. At the top of the stairs, Adrienne abruptly whirled around; fists clenched and roaring in anger, she pushed against Gabriel's chest with all her strength. It was like pushing a tree.

"Please, Mrs. Berg." His expression regretful, amused and stubborn.

She slammed her elbow into his rock-hard stomach and he gave her another push, this one not so gentle. Stumbling, Adrienne spat a string of undecipherable curse words and turned right at the landing. Her suite was to the left; after ten years of marriage, the Bergs agreed that sleeping in the same room was not an option, one of the few aspects of their life where she put her foot down. Another was the choice to not have hired help; Adrienne remembered too well her resentful days of being a maid. In theory, Dustin took care of his own bedroom and bathroom. Adrienne kept the rest of the house clean and didn't care if her husband wallowed in his own filth. She could not remember the last time she opened his bedroom door and was not surprised to find it locked.

She shrugged. "Sorry, I don't have a key," she said and staggered when Gabriel pushed her to one side and kicked the door open. "Jesus! What the fuck?"

He spun on his heel and gripped her shoulders. "Please sit down and be quiet," he said, shoving her backwards until her knees hit the edge of the bed. "Stay." He pressed hard on her shoulders. "Understand? Do not move a muscle."

Adrienne shot daggers from her eyes, but his back was to her as he headed to the closet. The double doors opened to a space almost as large as the enormous bedroom. Gabriel rifled through the hanging clothes, ducking to look underneath, opened drawers, checking her with constant, quick glances. She measured the distance to the door; she would have to run past him to get out and she was certain she couldn't outrun him, but every muscle in her body was tensed and ready to leap if an opportunity showed itself.

Gabriel pulled a long black duffel bag out of a tall cupboard. "Gotcha." He carried it to the bed and dropped it at her feet. "Exactly where the stupid fucker said it would be."

"What is that? What's in there?" She stared into his eyes, his face unreadable, and looked away. "Never mind, I don't care. Just take it and go."

He opened the zipper with a snaky hiss. "Three million in unmarked, one-hundred-dollar bills."

Adrienne stared at the money, feeling windless and dizzy like she had been punched in the gut; her mind raced with possible reasons for that much cash to be in Dustin's closet. Off-balance, lightheaded, she gripped the edge of the bed and pondered the enormous gap—the Grand Canyon—that suddenly appeared between who she thought Dustin was, and who her husband might be. On the heels of that, a bizarre feeling of lightness and euphoria came over her, imagining a life without Dustin that this money could give her. *Freedom.* She raised her eyes to Gabriel's and tightened her jaw. "Now what?"

"I'm stealing this. And you're my hostage."

She sprang to her feet, but he snagged her around the waist before she took a step. He tossed her on the bed like she weighed nothing and straddled her, holding both her fists with one of his hands and covering her screaming mouth with the other. Leaning close to her face, he said in a low, soft voice, "This is happening. The more you fight, the more I'm going to hurt you." The sorrow in his expression and his calm, quiet voice clashed with his savage words.

His weight squeezed every molecule of oxygen from her lungs, but she managed to bite his hand. When he jerked away in surprise, she croaked, "Swear you won't rape me."

He leaped off the bed. "Fuck, no, I won't rape you. But I will hurt you if you push me. Do you understand? I'm taking this money and no one can stop me."

"I won't try to stop you. Take it and go. I swear I won't tell anyone you were here. I don't care about the money," she babbled breathlessly. "You don't need me, just take it and go."

Gabriel pulled a knife from his front pocket, pushed a release on the side and a long, slim blade popped out with a sibilant snick. Adrienne pushed herself upright on the bed, scrambling until she hit the headboard, kicking at him with her dirty gardening shoes. He grabbed the front of her shirt and pulled her back against his chest, sitting her between his legs on the edge of the bed and gripping her with his tree-trunk thighs. "Stop it, be still." He squeezed her until she went limp, airless.

"You will record a message for your husband." He pulled a small black device from his pocket. "When I say go, you say they will kill me if you try to find us. Got it? You say Dusty, let them have the money and they will let me go in two weeks."

"Two weeks!" Panting, she squirmed, trying to see his face. *This is not happening. This cannot be happening.* He held her tight against his body, silent, solid and immovable as a boulder. "I'm not going with you for two weeks," she sputtered, stalling, "and I never call him Dusty."

With a swift stroke, Gabriel ran the edge of the knife along the sharp jut of her jawbone. Adrienne screamed in quicksilver bright pain, blood trickled hot on her throat, spattered her shirt and dripped dime-sized droplets on the bed. He held the knife to her throat with his right hand, tape recorder in his left. "Don't look for us for two weeks or they will kill me. Say it."

She howled, frantically swiping at the blood snaking down her neck, wiping her bloody fingers on the bedspread. "Dustin! He's fucking crazy!" she screamed. "Let him have the money!" She screamed again at the pressure against her throat. "Two weeks! He says I'll be home in two weeks! Don't try to find us!" The knife bit again, this time her collarbone. She shrieked, the sound of an animal caught in the jaws of a steel trap. "Stop cutting me!" Adrienne sobbed.

"Perfect." Gabriel pushed her to one side, tapped a button on the recorder, and wiped the knife on the bed. He grabbed a pillow and pressed it to her face while she bellowed in rage and terror, pounding him with her fists and kicking frantically, futilely.

"Hold still," he said. "I'm wiping off the blood."

She struggled another moment before flopping bonelessly back on the bed, choking down sobs. Tears trickled into her ears and down her jaw to mix with the blood.

"I'm sorry, I'm sorry, I'm sorry." Gabriel pulled the pillow away. The cut on her jaw was still weeping and he pressed the pillow against the blood. "I'm so sorry. I didn't want to hurt you, but it needed to sound real. And you don't scare easy."

He looked close to tears himself, and his expression surprised her into silence. She stared at him while he checked her wound again. The next time they locked eyes, she spoke through gritted teeth. "Are you going to kill me?"

"We need to go." Gabriel shouldered the bag of money and pulled her to her feet.

"Can I change my clothes?" She used the edge of her sleeve to wipe her nose, refusing to look at him. "I have blood all over my shirt."

He blew a harsh whoosh. "Hurry, change and bring the clothes with you. Nothing else. We can't let this look like you're in on it or they won't care if you die."

"In on it? Dustin would never believe I helped you plan this. When he hears that recording, he'll call the police."

Gabriel gave her a somber look, his eyes filled with pity. "Dustin stole this money and he's not alone. Do you think he wants to explain to the cops why someone would kidnap his wife? Or why he has three million dollars in a gym bag?" He waved his hand impatiently. "If you want to change clothes, you have one minute. Starting now."

She stood on trembling legs and forced her knees to stiffen. "My clothes are in the other bedroom."

He hoisted the gym bag over his shoulder, and kept one hand on her shoulder as they crossed the landing. He waited at the closed bedroom door, arms folded across his chest, watching her every move. Adrienne grabbed clean clothes from her closet and dashed to the bathroom, closing and locking the door. Using a wet washcloth, she roughly wiped away crusty, drying blood while scrambling through the drawers for a weapon. She jolted at a loud thud on the door.

"Hurry up, get your clothes on and open the door."

"Give me a damn minute." Every muscle tense and shaking, Adrienne changed into jeans and a black t-shirt. She flung open the door and shoved the bundle of dirty clothes at him. "If you're keeping me for two weeks, I'm packing a bag."

He shoved the clothes back in her arms. "You can wash these. It won't look like you're leaving against your will if you pack like you're going on vacation."

"Can I bring my toothbrush?" She fidgeted while he patted her down; he found tweezers in her front pocket, a nail file in her back pocket and a Lady Bic disposable razor in her sock.

Gabriel tossed her puny weapons in a drawer. "I'll buy you a toothbrush."

She snatched a yellow pill bottle by the sink. "I have to bring my thyroid pills."

"He'll notice them missing."

"Listen, I have no thyroid function at all. If I don't have my medicine, my body will start to fall apart and that's not how I want to die." Adrienne shook out a handful of pills, wrapped them in a tissue and stuck them in her pocket. "I'll leave the bottle here."

Gabriel settled the bag of money over his shoulder. "Fine. Now go, go, let's go." Downstairs, she darted for the front door and he grabbed her by a handful of t-shirt. She wrenched away from him, scowling, fists clenched.

"Do not make me chase you," he barked. "Use the kitchen door, my van is parked on the side." He hulked over her as she stalked across the room. "No funny business. You'll see the van, walk fast and do not make a sound."

Tucked against the side of the house, hidden from the neighbors by a screen of thick bamboo, was a white van with a spray of delphiniums and **Larkspur Flower Company** painted on the side. Gabriel herded her with a firm hand on her shoulder, opened the sliding side door, and tossed in the bag of money. An air mattress covered most of the floor, an empty metal shelf was bolted to the side and a set of open handcuffs dangled from one narrow beam.

Adrienne backed away, bumping into his bulk. "Gabriel, you don't have to do this. I don't need handcuffs. Please don't put me in handcuffs. I'll be good. I'll be still. I promise."

"Get in and be quiet. I'm serious, I will gag you." Grabbing her around the waist, he lifted her squealing into the van and climbed in behind her. "Hush!" He hugged her hard to his chest, forcing the air from her lungs. Tossing her gasping onto the air mattress, he swiftly cuffed both hands above her head to the metal shelf, reached into a red cloth bag by the sliding door, and pulled out a ball gag. "You think you're uncomfortable now?" He shook the gag at her. "Don't make me use this."

Rattling the chains, breathing in quick gasps, Adrienne said, "I'm telling you, I don't need to be restrained. I want to come with you."

"What are you talking about?"

"I won't fight you. A two-week vacation from Dustin is fine with me." She spoke fast and low, urgently. "He can see what it feels like to miss me. Or he can go to jail. I don't care. This is the most excitement I've had in years," she panted, heart racing. "I want to go with you." She rattled the handcuffs again. "You don't need these."

"Nice try." He pulled a hypodermic needle from the red bag. "But I don't believe you."

Gabriel knelt, squeezed the breath from her struggling body and sank the needle into her vein. After a few seconds, she went still and limp. He unlocked the handcuffs and positioned her gently on the air mattress. "I'm so sorry."

CHAPTER TWO
ECHOES DOWN THE CANYON

Adrienne's return to consciousness was slow, syrupy, like surfacing from muddy water after a deep dive. Disoriented, her cheek stuck to plastic in a way that reminded her of sweaty legs scorching on hot vinyl. Her head throbbed in rhythm with her thumping heart, and it hurt to swallow. She squeezed her eyes tighter as reality hit: she was in a parked van, evoking grim days of living in a car. Only this time she was a hostage of more than poverty-stricken circumstances. She opened one eye a slit and inhaled sharply, wincing as she peeled her sticky cheek off the air mattress. Gabriel crouched next to her, staring intently, the glow from a small flashlight heightened the stark angles of his face.

He handed her a bottle of water. "Can you sit up?"

Struggling upright, she grabbed the bottle and took long, thirsty gulps, water dribbling from the corners of her mouth. The water hit her stomach and for a moment, she thought it would come right back up. Closing her eyes to the wave of nausea, her body swayed and bumped the empty handcuffs. The rattling chains reignited her fear and anger. She touched the bony line of her jaw where he cut her skin and felt a bandage, smelled the distinct odor of hand sanitizer. "What did you drug me with?" Her words came out hoarse, scratchy.

Gabriel half-stood, hunchbacked in the short van. "Hungry? I've got fruit, granola bars, jerky."

"Where are we?" The interior gloom was only minimally diminished by the flashlight. A thick blanket stretched across the wire cage that separated the back of the van from the cab and the two windows on the back doors were blocked with squares of cardboard. "Is it day or night?"

He dropped a paper grocery sack at her feet and sat cross legged on the floor next to her. "Oreos? Pop-Tarts? How about a tangerine?"

Adrienne frowned in his direction, but he was too busy rooting in the bag of junk food to notice. "I'm not hungry." She rubbed her wrists and peered at the tiny black hole in the bend of her arm. "How long was I asleep? Where are we?" The residue of drugs in her system made her feel goofy, like Alice in Wonderland, like this was all a dream or a book she was reading. "Are you really keeping me two weeks?"

"Stop." Gabriel slapped his hand on the metal floor; it sounded like a gunshot. "Please. Stop asking questions. You're like a child with all your questions."

Reacting without thinking, she lashed out and smacked the paper sack. "You're like a child with your junk food. I don't eat this crap."

"I suggest you lower your standards or you might starve. You won't be eating hot food any time soon." He picked up the flashlight and pointed to an ice chest in the corner. "Cold hot dogs? I have buns, mustard..."

"I'm not hungry." She wrapped her arms around her knees, holding herself tightly together, fists and jaw clenched. Angry tears trickled unbidden; she blotted her eyes on her jeans and refused to look his way. She *was* hungry. Tired, sore, scared, angry, and hungry. "I hate mustard," she said under her breath. "What if I have to use the bathroom?" she said louder.

He pointed the flashlight to the corner opposite the ice chest where a tall orange bucket seemed to grin cheerily. "That's our toilet for the next few hours. See the sheet? Just unhook that corner and hook it over there for privacy." He popped a whole Oreo in his mouth and chewed while staring at her.

"You have got to be kidding me." Adrienne turned her back to him and made herself into a ball. "I'm feeling very claustrophobic. I might have a panic attack."

"I can put you back to sleep."

"No!" She scrambled on her butt away from him, kicking out and landing a solid hit on his thigh. She was barefoot and it felt like she had kicked a brick. He didn't even blink. "No more needles, no more handcuffs. Why won't you believe me? I don't want to run away from you. I'm fine with a two-week vacation from my life."

"I didn't get that impression when I found all those sharp objects in your pockets."

"I won't apologize for defending myself, but I've had time to think and I accept being gone from home for two weeks. I won't try to escape."

"Great. We're camping, relax and enjoy it."

"What happens in two weeks?"

"No questions."

Clenching her fists until her nails cut her palms, grinding her teeth in frustration, she dropped cross-legged on the air mattress. Her stomach growled, loudly, and it felt like something was in there with teeth. Adrienne grabbed the paper sack and pulled out a mesh bag of tangerines, dug around again and came up with a Three Musketeers bar. Peeling back the silver wrapper, she chomped on the candy bar and bared her chocolate-covered teeth at him. Gabriel opened his mouth to show a chewed-up mush of cookie and startled a bark of laughter from her.

"Classy," she muttered, peeling a tangerine and wolfing it down. Her body welcomed the energy. *When did I eat last?* With no sense of time, Adrienne could only judge by the growl in her belly and the pressure of her bladder that she had been asleep for several hours. *Not asleep, drugged unconscious.* She finished the tangerine, watching him with narrow eyes, gaze locked. She refused to blink first.

His eyes dropped to the bandage on her face. "I'm sorry for hurting you."

"Why did you do it?"

"I told you, I needed it to sound real."

"No, I mean why did you steal the money? How did you know it was there?"

He looked away. "Dustin and Jarrett have big, fat mouths. I heard them talking about this bag of money, joking with me about it like I was an idiot.

I just wanted to take it from them." His pale eyes were amber in the dim light. "Dustin is more stupid and greedy than evil but still, not a good guy."

"I think you just described yourself." She tossed back a handful of Cheez-its and wiped her hands on her jeans. "Please don't make me use the bucket. If we're camping, we're far away from people, right? In the woods or something? Let me jump out and use the bushes."

He chewed the inside of his cheek. "I'll have to handcuff you."

"How am I supposed to pee in the bushes with handcuffs? I told you, I won't run." She tried to decipher his expression. After an intense stare-down, she said, "Should I be afraid of you?"

"I don't want to hurt you. But I won't let you get in my way either."

"I'm afraid of you, trust me, I know what men are capable of. You don't have to worry about me escaping. Please don't make me pee in the bucket."

Gabriel rubbed his cheek, the scratch of his whiskers against his palm was like sandpaper in the silence. "I swear to god if you make me run after you..."

"I won't, I won't, I promise. Do you have any paper?" She flinched when he opened the red bag.

"Here you go. Bury what you use." He reached for the back door, paused and removed the cover from the dome light, unscrewing the bulb. "Don't make a sound." He opened the door and hopped out, reaching for Adrienne's hand to help her.

She stood on wobbly legs and looked around her in the pitch-dark night; the air smelled fresh and the outdoors felt extravagantly roomy after the close quarters of the van. The trees that surrounded them were the tallest redwoods she had ever seen, and so close together they blocked nearly all the star-filled sky. The chill damp of fog and the smell of the ocean filled the air.

"Don't make me chase you in the dark, both of us will get hurt."

Adrienne ignored him and hurried behind the nearest bush. The dark was so thick and silent it seemed to have physical weight, a velvet cloak. She shimmied her jeans down and released a stream with an involuntary sigh. The noise was loud in the stark silence and went on for an embarrassingly long time. She stepped out from behind the bushes. "Oh, what a relief it is," she whisper-sang.

"Shhh."

Her eyes adjusted to the dark and she could see a sprinkle of faint stars through the tall trees. The forest was eerily, spookily beautiful, the damp chill felt like tiny crystals on her skin. Stalling, she walked in baby steps as he gestured to the van. She mouthed silently, with great exaggeration, "Don't make me go back in there."

Frowning, he gently guided her with a big hand on the small of her back. "Don't push your luck," he said close to her ear.

She climbed inside and moved as far from him as she could. "It's no coincidence that you talked to me that night at the civic center."

"Obviously."

"I'm such a fool. I thought you were flirting." She resumed eating Cheez-its with grim determination.

"I was flirting but that's not why I talked to you."

"Why did you talk to me?"

Gabriel didn't answer for a long beat. "I don't know why. I only intended to watch you."

"Someone saw us together," she said. "Someone must have seen us together."

"I can be like a ghost when I want to be. No one saw us."

She stared at him, chewed, swallowed. "How long are you keeping me in this van?"

"I'll answer this question and that's it. At first light we walk to a cabin. It's not much bigger than the van but there is an outhouse and a well."

"And we're staying there for two weeks?"

"Yes. Please, no more questions, Adrienne, please. The less you know the better. Okay? I'll tell you what you need to know when you need to know. Now go to sleep."

"Go to sleep? I just woke up, remember?" She waved at the air mattress. "Are both of us supposed to sleep on that?"

"It's just for a few hours." Gabriel pulled the sheet from the orange bucket area and laid it over the plastic bed, handing her the blanket from the front cage. "If you can't sleep, can you be still and quiet? And promise not to stab me? I need to sleep, and I don't want to drug you again."

"Don't fucking touch me." She made herself small, back in the corner and knees drawn up.

"Don't try..."

"I know, I know!" she snapped, overwrought, and feeling something like a sick hangover from the drugs, junk food, and spent adrenaline. "Don't try anything. Don't run, don't scream. Gotcha. You're a big scary man and I'm a helpless little woman. I'm scared, okay? Happy?"

"Yes, thank you." Gabriel positioned the air mattress in front of the sliding door, pillowed his head on his arms and facing her, he closed his eyes.

Hugging her knees, she watched him through slitted eyes. Starlight glittered weakly through the windshield, filtered through wire diamonds. He shifted on the mattress and his shirt hiked up on one side, baring a brown triangle of skin more erotic than if he wasn't wearing a shirt at all. The tight jeans cupped his butt and hugged his thighs. She thought about that night at the civic center, when they locked eyes and she felt that lightning bolt of attraction. She thought he was intriguing. *Why lie to myself, I thought he was sexy as hell.* And now? After he had cut her and dragged her who knows where? The attraction was palpable as a river running under her hand, a buzzing electric current, a rumbling engine. *I should be afraid of him. What's wrong with me?*

She dozed and jolted awake as her body tipped over. Gabriel was sprawled like a starfish and snoring. Adrienne curled on her side, and for the first time in hours she thought about Dustin. Where did he get that money? Gabriel claims Dustin stole it, which means he might not call the police. What did he think when he saw her blood, and heard the recording? She tried to imagine herself in Dustin's shoes, but it was impossible to picture a scenario where she would have three million dollars, where someone would kidnap her husband and record his screams. *I don't know Dustin at all.* As she considered this, Adrienne clenched her fists and her jaw, feeling foolish and ignorant, taking deep breaths to stem the rising tide of red-fury. *He probably laughed at me when he stashed that money in his closet.*

Pushing aside her questions about the money, and the very real possibility that Dustin had other secrets and lies, shoving down ten years of hurt and disappointment...*accept the things I cannot change*...she mentally surrendered to her raw desire for the man who held her captive and conjured a happier place, where she sipped fruity cocktails with Gabriel, swinging in hammocks over a white sand beach with swaying palm trees above them and not another person in sight. *Take the money and run* dream-Adrienne whispered.

CHAPTER THREE
SHADOWS AND TALL TREES

At some point during the night, she half-woke, grumbling as Gabriel scooped her up and laid her on the air mattress. The next time Adrienne became aware of her surroundings, he had curled around her in a protective shell, his solid bulk almost touching her back, heat radiating from his body. His right hand rested on the curve of her hip. She fought the urge to move closer. *Do I want to fuck him?* If he had asked the night they met, she would have turned him down flat. Although her attraction to Gabriel was powerful, Adrienne had never cheated. Not even ten years with self-absorbed, nearly sexless Dustin Berg—Iceberg, she called him—made her consider cheating. She traded a life of poverty and insecurity for material comfort, and the fact that Dustin wasn't interested in sex was tolerable; her vows seemed a fair trade for stability. Adrienne tried to convince herself stability was all she needed.

Gabriel's spicy smell, the radiant heat of his body, and the pressure of his heavy hand on her hip had butterflies whirling and tickling her insides. She inhaled a shaky breath, exhaled in a soundless sigh, and moved away to test his reaction—which was a firmer grip on her hip.

"Where do you think you're going?" Husky voiced, his breath ruffled the short blond hairs framing her face.

She tried again to move away but his fingers cupped her hipbone for leverage. "I need take my pill and water a bush," she said. His grip loosened and she scooted to the edge of the mattress, grabbing her shoes. "Are you going to follow me?"

"Go ahead, I'll be right behind you. Don't run. I'm serious, don't test me."

Opening the back door to the pale gray dawn, she jumped out of the van and her eyes widened; for a moment, she forgot her bizarre circumstances. They were parked in an enchanted forest, magical in the mist. The trees were skyscrapers and so close together the sunlight struggled to reach the forest floor. The craggy, blood-red bark of the trunks made a dramatic backdrop for the riot of greens—airy ferns, puffy moss, spiky bushes. She could not see any bare dirt; the earth was hidden beneath a thick layer of undisturbed needles and other forest debris that made a deep cushion of compost under her feet, spongy with moisture. Fog chilled the air, pungent with rot and fresh growth.

Squatting behind a bush, she relieved herself, eyes constantly moving, scanning the area around her vulnerable bare butt. Adrienne pulled up her jeans and did some stretches while waiting for Gabriel to appear. He jumped out of the van holding plastic bottles of water and hand sanitizer.

"You'll want this," he said, handing her the bottles. "I'll be over here."

Adrienne walked to the far side of the van, took a pill from her pocket and gulped down half the bottle of water without stopping for breath. The front of the van pointed into a deep gully, a dry riverbed, the left side of the bank higher than the van. She took a few steps down the gully and it became narrower and deeper, choked with baby redwoods and rhododendron. At the sound of running footsteps, she turned around.

"Where do you think you're going?" Gabriel hissed.

"You already asked me that today. I'm not going anywhere." He motioned for her to lower her voice, and in a ferocious whisper, she said, "See? See me staying here? Even though you won't answer my questions or tell me a damn thing like what's for breakfast or do we have any coffee?" She put her hands on her hips. "This is not how Clyde would have treated Bonnie."

"We are *not* Bonnie and Clyde. Don't jinx us. I don't want to die from a hundred bullet holes. And to answer your coffee question, I have espresso in a can. Breakfast options are the same as last night's dinner options. May I recommend the Oreos?"

She tilted her chin at him. "I want to know what happens next."

"We move out after breakfast. It's a hike, eat something so we can pack up."

He pulled small cans of coffee icy cold and dripping from the cooler. Adrienne chugged hers down and finished the Oreos while Gabriel polished off the Cheez-its. After breakfast, he squeezed the air out of the mattress, layered the sheet and blanket on top, then the grocery bags. He rolled it up and used bungee cords to hold it together.

"Can you please carry this?" He held the bundle out. "Tell me if it's too heavy."

She eyed him for a long beat, his arrogance was astonishing. *He wants his hostage to help?* Taking the bag from his hand, she hefted it a couple of times. "It's not too heavy."

"It doesn't feel too heavy yet but you'll be carrying it about a mile."

Adrienne looked at the cords digging divots in her arms. "I got this."

"I'm moving the van. Don't run. You'll get lost, I'll find you and I *will* be angry."

She flipped him a casual middle finger. Adrienne had decided she would not be afraid of Gabriel, at least, she wouldn't let him see her fear. Showing fear brings out the worst in people, she had learned that lesson young. Constant fear was exhausting, and frankly, his 'big bad man' thing was wearing thin. If Gabriel wanted to hurt her, he would, and she could not do a damn thing to stop him. She had lived this long by adapting and watching for opportunities, and today was no different.

He drove the van deeper into the gully. Branches scraped the metal in outraged squeals, sending birds squawking and reeling. The van rolled until bushes closed in behind it, and Gabriel squeezed himself out the back door. He held up his hands in a silencing gesture. In moments the sounds of the forest resumed to bugs buzzing and birds chirping. He adjusted some bushes behind the van, picked up a branch and used it to blur the tire tracks from the dirt.

"Is the van stolen?" Adrienne ventured a question.

"Borrowed." He shouldered the bag of money that looked like it weighed as much as she did and lifted the ice chest that was probably another fifty pounds. "Grab your stuff and be quiet."

"You don't have to be a jerk," she said, slinging the bundle over her back.

"Quiet. Save your breath."

"You could say please you know."

He gave her a solemn stare. "Please swear to me you won't run. I don't want to use the leash."

"Try it, motherfucker." She narrowed her eyes and saw him suppressing a smirk as he turned away. "You think that's funny?" He didn't respond. "Jerk," she said under her breath.

They plodded steadily uphill, her bundle heavier with each step. Thick layers of dead needles and chunks of bark grabbed at her shoes, dead branches appeared from nowhere to bite her ankles. Rolling the ice chest was noisy and Gabriel had to carry it, stopping for frequent breaks. Adrienne watched him struggle for a long time, she didn't mind seeing him suffer, but they obviously had a destination, and she would rather be anywhere but stumbling through the forest, carrying a heavy load, and slapping mosquitos.

"Let me help you," she said. "I take a handle, you take a handle." When he gave her skinny arms a dubious glance, she flexed her biceps. "Let me help as much as I can."

They made their laborious way through the forest; even without an obvious path, Gabriel seemed to know exactly where they were going. They came to a fork where a deep ravine cut between a low hill rising on the left and the forest slanting down on the right. A narrow rocky ledge ran up the side of the hill and soon revealed itself to be a trail of wooden steps pressed into the clay-like earth, wet and dried so many times it was like concrete.

"We're climbing that?" Adrienne lowered her bundle to the ground and rolled her shoulders, rubbing the back of her neck.

Gabriel dropped the gym bag, shook out his hands and stretched his arms high, exposing his hairy stomach. "Let's take a break and eat something. And be extra quiet, sound echoes down the canyon." He opened the ice chest and pulled out a package of hot dogs and a bag of buns crushed inside a ziplock bag. "They won't be pretty but we can scarf down a couple of dogs. Sure you don't want mustard?"

"Positive." She peeled a squished bun apart and folded it around an ice-cold hot dog, munching morosely and washing it down with a fresh bottle of water, unable to take her eyes off the steep, narrow footpath; the trees blocked her view of the top so she couldn't see where the trail ended. "Is this how I die? Falling off the edge of that cliff?"

"You probably wouldn't die, the trees would break your fall. But it would throw a monkey wrench in my plan."

"You mean *our* plan, we're on the same team." She tossed a chunk of hot dog at him.

It bounced off his arm, he caught it and popped it into his mouth. "Don't litter. This is evidence. And it's *my* plan, not our plan. You're my hostage."

"Whatever you have to tell yourself to make it through the day." She took a big bite from her second hot dog, ignoring him as she eyeballed the steep path.

They rested until Gabriel stood with a soft groan, shouldering the bag of money. "Let's get this over with. Be careful and be quiet." He shot her a crooked smile. "Please."

One glance down the ravine was enough. Heart thumping, hand braced on the hillside, Adrienne kept her eyes on the ground, planting one foot at a time on the gritty wooden steps. Gabriel pulled the ice chest, and she lifted the wheels over the edge of the steps behind him. Every crunch and scrape were amplified. She didn't raise her eyes to see where the steps ended but she could feel in her aching thighs when the path leveled, and soon it widened to a plateau. In a small clearing sat a building about the size of a single car garage. It was made of redwood, with a tilted rusty tin roof, so mossy and weathered and covered in ferns it looked like it had sprung from the ground organically.

"We're here," Gabriel said.

CHAPTER FOUR
I CAN'T TELL YOU WHY

Dustin Berg and Jarrett Austin huddled in the corner of the airport office, watching from a safe distance as Lawrence Fife erupted, spewing expletive lava that scorched the eardrums. Their boss ranted and raved, waving at the emptiness where his private plane should be, the empty spot where his chauffeur should be standing by to welcome them aboard.

"What was Gabriel thinking? Fife is going to kill him," Jarrett said. "Or have him killed. Fife won't do anything he can pay someone else to do."

"Do you think Fife found out about the money?" Dustin's eyes went wide. "Maybe he's using this to distract us until the police come?"

"If Fife knew what we did, we wouldn't be having this conversation," said Jarrett. "He would have ripped out our throats." He flinched and ducked as Fife screamed at the manager.

"My pilot had no right to take my plane without permission!" Fife was nearly purple with rage.

"He told me one of your guys forgot something important at home," the manager said. "He filed a flight plan for Buchanan Field and back, boom boom, quick turnaround, see?"

Fife waved off the paper with a rude sputter. "He has no reason to go to Concord. This is insane. Why would Gabriel do this? Can you track my plane and tell me where he is?"

"Let me check." The manager tapped a screen. "Hmm, I'm not seeing the transponder." He cut anxious eyes at Lawrence Fife's sweaty red face. "I'll alert the authorities."

"No!" Fife barked. "I don't want the police involved. Gabriel could have a perfectly valid reason for this behavior." The prospect of the media finding out sent his blood pressure spiking.

Fife called his insurance company, and they were able to use their hidden tracking device to find his plane sitting on a farmer's private airstrip in Martinez, a scant five miles from Buchanan Field. The insurance company was even more eager to call the police, but money talks and Fife paid them to shut up. He would not file a claim until his employee had a chance to explain.

"And it better be good," Fife gritted. His phone sprang to life, a quick glance at the screen was followed by a grimace of pain. Sighing, he answered, "Hello, Bridget."

"My sister called. Cindy is missing."

"Cindy?" Fife rubbed his forehead. He had a plethora of pain-in-the-ass family members. "Which one is Cindy?"

"Lawrence! Cindy is Barbara's daughter. Cynthia? Our niece? Our niece is missing and you can't even remember her name?"

"What am I supposed to do?"

"Barbara told me Cindy was fooling around with your chauffeur. She ordered Cindy to stay away from that man and next thing you know, she's gone. Barbara hasn't been able to reach her for two days."

Lawrence stumbled to a hard plastic chair against a cinder block wall. "Gabriel and Cindy?" They were introduced when Gabriel flew the family from San Rafael to Anaheim, but the prospect of his prep-school-princess niece dating his chauffeur was inconceivable. "When was that Disneyland trip?"

"That was for Cindy's college graduation, early April."

"They've been seeing each other a couple of months," Fife mused aloud. "and now Cindy is missing and Gabriel hijacked my plane."

"What?" Bridget squawked. "Hijacked your plane? Do you think Cindy is with him? Barbara will have a heart attack, her only daughter throwing away her future for a Mexican laborer."

"For god's sake, Bridget, listen to yourself." Fife rubbed his aching head. "I can't talk about this right now. I'm pissed off and tired and you're not helping." He ended the call abruptly and snapped his fingers at the herd of his employees cowering in the corner. "Over here now and tell me everything you know about Gabriel Navarro and Cindy Moore."

They scuttled over. Dustin began with, "Who is Cindy Moore? This is the first time I've heard Gabriel's last name."

"His name is on your paperwork every time we fly, Berg." Fife closed his eyes and held up one hand to stop the babble of nonsense that all boiled down to the same thing, these guys were a bunch of idiots. "I got it, none of you know anything." He threw his hands in the air and stomped back to the manager's desk to charter a plane back to San Rafael. If Gabriel and Cindy had run off together, they should be easy to find; Cindy was as smart as a box of rocks, and if Gabriel was willing to throw away his life for her, he wasn't any smarter.

* * *

The chartered flight home was a silent two-and-a-half hours. Dustin tried several times to reach Adrienne, but she wasn't answering her phone. That wasn't unusual, she was known for losing her phone in random places around the house, usually with the ringer off, or letting it die completely. But it was the cherry of annoyance on top of a thoroughly frustrating day as Dustin was hoping his wife would pick him up from the airport. He shared a taxi with his co-workers and arrived home after midnight, hours after Adrienne's regular bedtime.

Dustin stopped in the kitchen for a glass of water before trudging upstairs, not bothering to be quiet since the house had the best soundproofing money could buy. He stumbled to a halt in front of his bedroom door that should not be open, and reached around the door frame to flip the light switch. He screamed and dropped the glass; it bounced on the plush blue carpet and splashed water in a thick spray, mimicking the pattern of blood on the decorative pillow. He ran to the bed, casting his eyes around wildly. A streak of dried blood with sharp edges was stark against the white sheet. Drops of blood on the bedspread neatly blended with the abstract maroon and navy pattern. "Adrienne!" he screamed, clutching his hair with both hands.

He ran to the closet and screamed again when he saw the money was gone, money he and Jarrett had been skimming from Fife Industries for the past several months. Their method was based on the movie 'Office Space', and they were quite smug with their perceived level of genius. The plan was to leave the brutal world of Bay Area real estate, set up a money-laundering business like in 'Breaking Bad' and gradually trickle the stolen money into their lifestyle. They were going through the final steps: Remove program that steals Fife's money. Empty Cayman account. Retire early. Jarrett said it was a brilliant plan. It almost worked.

Dustin ran across the landing to Adrienne's bedroom, calling her name. He scanned her closet, but he couldn't tell if anything was missing. He checked the bathroom and saw a washcloth draped over the faucet, dried stiff. Reaching for it, he knocked over an orange pill bottle and noticed there were only four pills inside. "She must have another bottle somewhere," he said, peering at the label. "She never lets herself get this low." He unfolded the washcloth and whimpered when he saw dried blood.

He ran back to his bedroom and saw a black device on his nightstand; it didn't belong there, and it looked as coldly evil as a loaded gun or a coiled snake. Dustin turned it over in his hands, found a Play button and jabbed it with a finger frozen stiff in shock. When he heard Adrienne scream, he screamed along with her. He played it again, hands shaking, and the second time he heard her howl 'stop cutting me' he burst into tears. Maybe he didn't love his wife the best he could, like a husband should, but he didn't want anyone to hurt her.

"What a shitstorm," he sniffled, scrolling his recent contacts. "Jarrett, I know it's late but we need to talk. Come to my house and hurry."

* * *

Jarrett paced the bedroom, incandescent with rage, his already bulky body seemed to swell, and his face turned as red as his hair. "Gabriel knew about the money. Your wife knew about the money. She stole the money and ran off with Gabriel."

"I thought he ran off with Cindy?" Before Jarrett said his name, Dustin had no idea who might have made Adrienne scream on the recording, but now he felt stupid. Of course it was Gabriel. Last week, he flew them to the Caymans, with blessings from the boss to enjoy a short vacation at his private getaway. The trip was to withdraw their 'retirement fund'. They joked with the pilot that the bag he helped them load on the plane was full of cash. And when he asked where they got it, they told him their entire brilliant plan. Hiding in plain sight, Jarrett said. It was a goddam joke. Gabriel wasn't supposed to believe them. "Maybe he took Cindy *and* Adrienne? Maybe he's trafficking them?"

"More likely he's fucking them," Jarrett spat. "The three of them are drinking margaritas and banging each other in the Bahamas by now."

"No, Adrienne wouldn't do that. She's never met Gabriel. Besides, there's blood everywhere." Dustin gestured over his shoulder at the bed, he couldn't look at it. "And listen to that recording again, she's terrified."

"Or a really good actress." Jarrett waved off the tape recorder. "I don't want to hear it again. It gives me the creeps. I always thought Gabriel was shifty."

"You said he looked like a Chippendale's dancer."

"Both statements can be true. He's a shifty stripper who stole our money and your wife."

"What do we do?" Dustin looked bravely into his friend's stormy eyes. "We can't tell anyone. Not the cops and definitely not Fife. He'll have us killed to set an example."

"Well, boy genius, we're not riding off into the sunset with our retirement fund, so we can only hope Fife doesn't find out we stole three million of his dollars." Jarrett's voice rose on each syllable until he was screeching.

"Maybe we should polish our resumes, just in case."

"Sometimes I want to punch you." Jarrett cracked his knuckles. "We need to find them. We need a private investigator."

"That sounds expensive, could we steal more of Fife's money?"

"Your face is looking more punchable by the minute," Jarrett snarled. "Gabriel won't get away with this. I don't even care about the money. He won't make me look like a fool."

"I don't care about the money. I need to find my wife! You heard that recording."

Jarrett grabbed him by the shoulders. "You need to prepare yourself. Adrienne is probably involved. She might be banging Gabriel, or she might already be dead."

Dustin shoved Jarrett backwards. "Don't say that. Don't even think it. My wife will not die for this money. That can't happen."

"Maybe we won't have to spend any money." Jarrett paced, palms laced behind his head, arms like wings, red hair gone wild. He looked a bit like a parrot. "Fife's wife is nagging him to track down his niece and Gabriel will be with her. We'll ask Fife to keep us in the loop and when they find him, we'll give Gabriel a good ass-beating on his behalf. Fife's really pissed at him for abandoning the plane in Martinez."

Dustin gave his manicured hands a dubious once-over. "I've never beaten anyone up before. I'm pretty sure if I hit Gabriel, it would hurt me more than him."

Jarrett scoffed. "So don't use your hands. Use a tire iron or a baseball bat."

CHAPTER FIVE
VOICES CARRY

Gabriel motioned for Adrienne to go in the cabin ahead of him. He hurled the money bag inside and dragged the cooler over the threshold, shut the door and groaned, twisting his body right and left, spine crackling.

Adrienne dropped her bundle with a thunk and rubbed at the grooves in her arms caused by the bungee cords. Glancing curiously around the small cabin, she drifted towards a scatter of boxes and bags along one wall. "Is this for your torture dungeon, mister kidnapper?"

"I'll show you all that stuff later. Just chill for a minute." Gabriel rinsed two short glasses in a white porcelain sink that used a pump handle instead of a faucet. Next to the sink was a large metal cabinet. Other than plywood cupboards, the square room was made entirely of redwood: floors, walls and ceiling. A folding blue card table with scratched metal legs, stained padded top, and four matching chairs were the only furniture.

He opened the ice chest. "I brought vodka to celebrate making it this far."

"Would you be celebrating if I had fought you?"

"I wouldn't have let you hurt yourself by fighting me. I'd have knocked you out and carried you." He chuckled at her indignant expression and showed her the two glasses. "Do you want a shot? Or do you plan to fight me?"

She waved a hand. "I'll have a shot. Don't give me a reason to fight you."

"Let's take it outside." He carried a folding chair and a glass containing three fingers of Grey Goose to a spot of dappled shade near the front door. Adrienne followed, settling her chair near his. Heaving an almost audible sigh, Gabriel's shoulders sagged.

Adrienne slumped in the chair, drawing her arms close to her side. She trickled icy cold vodka on her tongue and held it in her mouth, savoring the notes of vanilla and citrus that wafted into her sinuses, complemented by the astringent scent of freshly crushed redwood needles under her feet. Closing her eyes, she picked out the whisper of high branches trembling in the breeze, the brrrr of bugs, the trill and caw of birds. The wind shifted direction, a pinecone thumped to the ground, and she heard music.

"Gimme three steps?" she whispered.

Gabriel nodded and whispered back, "Probably farther away than you think but sometimes it's hard to tell. Sounds travel different here, that's why we have to be quiet. The last thing we need is a nosy neighbor."

They sat outside for at least an hour, resting and sipping, before Gabriel rose. He grimaced an 'oh my aching back' expression and motioned for her to follow. She stood, wincing at her stiff muscles. Inside the cabin, Adrienne dug in the red bag for the roll of toilet paper.

"You said there's an outhouse? I can't wait for a tour."

"This way."

She followed him out the front door. "Is this the only way out?"

"There's the window but don't try it."

Adrienne did not dignify that with a response. The privy was several steps into the forest, they followed a dirty yellow nylon rope that ran limply from the cabin to a tree near the outhouse. She gingerly pulled on the handle with one finger and peeked inside. "It doesn't smell as bad as I expected."

"Give it time. If you sprinkle lime after each, uh...event, it helps." Gabriel pointed to a large metal flour sifter on the floor. "Don't get it on your skin."

Peering into the corners and checking overhead, she said, "Snakes? Spiders?"

"Sometimes." He bit the inside of his cheek to hide a smile.

"Sucks being your hostage. What about hostage rights? Next hideout I want a real bathroom."

He turned his back. After she stepped out, he said, "My turn," and held out the rope. "Back up against this tree. I don't want you running off while I have my dick in my hand."

Adrienne shook her head rapidly. "Nope. You are not tying me to a tree."

"Yes. I. Am." He gave her his fiercest glare and pushed her backwards, pulled her hands behind the tree and tied them together, disregarding her struggles and death threats. After he exited the outhouse, he untied her in silence, and ignored her curses until they reached the front door. He turned to her and snapped, "You keep forgetting you're my hostage."

Flinging open the door, he motioned her ahead of him, closed the door, and walked directly to the scatter of bags and boxes, squatting without looking her way. "This is not for a torture dungeon. This is for you. Clothes, toothbrush, tampons, shampoo." He piled stuff on the floor. "Hairbrush, underwear, socks."

Adrienne crouched beside him, still fuming over the indignity of him treating her as a hostage when she had been very clear she wasn't trying to escape. She sifted through the clothing: track pants, t-shirts and hoodies in dark gray and navy. The underwear was boxer briefs. White athletic socks, no-name tennis shoes. "Boy clothes?"

"The sizes are easier. And if someone sees you, it's better you look like a boy. If anyone is looking for us, they're looking for a man and a woman."

She waved a black sports bra, thick with spandex. "This is for my breast binding I suppose?"

"You're welcome." Gabriel flashed a crooked smile.

"What's in here?" She picked up a plastic bag and jumped away when he tried to yank it from her hand. "Hair color in medium auburn. Is this for a disguise? Oh, I know...you could tell me but then you'd have to kill me." She scrutinized a small blue and white box. "Colored contacts, dark brown. In two weeks you'll have a beard. It is a disguise. Where are you going? You can tell me. I won't tell anyone." Her eyes shifted from his intense gaze to his sculpted lips, back and forth like a tennis match, his babbled words about her being his hostage registered on some dim level. *On the run. Hiding. Disguises. My life has become a movie.* But this is real. She touched the bandage on her face and watched his expression shift. He looked vulnerable, so she pressed. "You can't tell me anything?"

He walked away and opened a shallow cupboard. "I tried to make this stay comfortable for you. I have another air mattress, blankets, pillows, playing cards, games, and books. Lots of books."

"How long have you been planning this?" Adrienne gestured at the stuff strewn about. "How many trips up the hill?"

He gave her a sideways look. "Most of this has always been here. What I bought for you I carried in one trip. The day after we met."

Adrienne's stomach did a slow roll. Remembering that night, the lightning bolt of lust, his dark hand on hers, her mouth where his lips had touched, him smiling in her eyes and all the while he knew she would soon be his captive. The memory made Gabriel seem monstrous and made her desire for him monstrous. As monstrous as it was undeniable. She wanted him and she would have him. She didn't consider it cheating, she didn't think of her yearning for Gabriel in connection with her other life at all. Their destiny was unavoidable, the path of a meteor set in motion eons ago.

"Do you know how I feel when I think of our first conversation? I thought you were hitting on me, but you were planning to kidnap me."

"You'll be back home before you know it." His voice gruff, he avoided her eyes.

"Two weeks is soon enough." She walked closer and put one hand on the center of his chest. He gazed past her, eyes blank. "I told you, this is exciting." She stroked her palm across the ridge of his pectorals. "You're exciting."

Gabriel brushed her hand away. "You are my hostage. Don't mistake kindness for weakness." He stalked past her to the metal cabinet. "This is a bear box. The food goes in here before we go to sleep. Please bring me the bags from that bundle."

Adrienne's face burned from his rejection. She did as he asked with her lips pressed in a hard line, flinging the bungee cords across the room and yanking the bags of junk food out of the rolled-up air mattress.

"Please try not to make noise." Gabriel took the bags without looking at her.

"Please go fuck yourself." She glanced inside the metal cabinet and did a double take. "Don't tell me you hauled all that food up here in one trip?"

He flicked her a glance. "This has been used before as a place to hide."

"How do you know about this place?"

He shook his head. "No questions."

"God, you're such a jerk." Adrienne reached over his shoulder and snagged a bucket of red licorice. "No black licorice? Hostages need choices, you know. Not everyone likes red licorice."

"I didn't buy that for you."

"Too bad, I'm eating it."

He shuffled cans and boxes without speaking, organizing the supplies before closing the door. "Come here, let me show you how this handle works."

She watched as he explained the mechanism created to thwart crafty bear hands. "Do you really worry about bears?"

"Did you notice we're in a forest? You need to worry about bears."

"You're just trying to scare me again."

"You should fear bears far more than you fear me." Gabriel carried the ice chest to the metal cabinet and set it on the lowest shelf. "Is that it?"

"Everything except the licorice." She passed the container. "Are you locking up the vodka?"

"I'd like to get organized before we any drunker. Then the waiting begins."

"This is where I ask, 'waiting for what' and you stop talking to me." She dragged the air mattress to the far-left corner. "Can this be where I sleep?"

He grabbed the box with the new air mattress and the foot pump. "This is where we both sleep."

"I have to sleep next to you?"

"I'm sleeping between you and the door."

"I told you I won't try to escape." Adrienne gestured an elaborate shrug. "There's bears, remember? Why would I run through a bear-infested forest in the dark?"

Gabriel set up the foot pump to inflate the air mattress. "Why don't you move the table next to the window? We can play cards or cribbage until dark, no lights allowed."

"Not even to go to the outhouse?"

"One last trip before dark, then the door gets locked. You can use the sink."

"Gross."

"I left the orange bucket behind."

"Even more disgusting. Is the pump hard to work?"

"It's noisy. Don't touch it."

She made a growling noise. "We're playing cribbage? I'm gonna kick your ass."

CHAPTER SIX
GAMES PEOPLE PLAY

They set up the cribbage board and Adrienne dug through her memory for the rules and strategy. Gabriel was ruthless, taking every point she missed and skunking her the first game.

"Who taught you how to play?"

"No questions. Play your crib."

She blew a raspberry and threw down two cards.

"You remember this crib is mine?"

"I know how to play the game, Gabby."

He added two cards to hers and pushed them to one side. "I don't really like Gabby."

"I don't really care."

He laid a card on the table. "Two."

"Where are you taking the money? Are you leaving the country? I bet you're getting a fake ID. What's your new name?" She said this fast, in a hissing whisper.

His face in a beam of late afternoon sun, Gabriel captured her gaze with his glowing green-gold eyes. "Adrienne," he breathed, almost silently. "Try to relax." He folded the cards into his hand and leaned towards her on his elbows. "Please stop asking questions. It's hurting our hostage kidnapper relationship." His small smile widened at her quick snort of laughter. "Can we just play cards?"

* * *

They played until the sun slipped behind the low hills, commenting on the birds and squirrels darting in the dappled shadows of the forest. Just before dark, they trekked to the toilet and back. Gabriel tied her hands in front of her in a half-ass gesture of dominance before he used the privy. Adrienne walked back to the cabin without him, a half-ass gesture of defiance. He untied her hands with a pretend scowl and a crooked smirk.

The fingernail moon hung just outside the frame of the window, leaving the cabin in nearly complete darkness. Gabriel turned his back while Adrienne changed for bed, but she propped herself up on one elbow and brazenly watched him undress. Pearlescent moonglow emphasized the play of his muscles in light and shadow, his body a sculpture come to life. He stripped down to boxer briefs, watching her face, and slid under the thin cotton blanket.

She rolled to face him in the dark. The pillow was flat and smelled of storage, but this was a better sleeping arrangement than the night before, crammed in the van and sharing one mattress. *That wasn't so terrible, being smooshed together.* The air mattresses touched along one side and his jostling for position made her bed shake. "Settle down over there," she grumbled.

"Be quiet over there."

The moon offered enough light to see Gabriel lying on his side, facing her, one arm curled under his pillow. Just enough light to see the shine on his open eyes.

"You don't have to be mean to me," she said.

"You don't always get the last word." An edge of unfurled laughter in his whisper.

"Word." She poked his shoulder.

He poked her back, gently, his index finger landed on bare skin where her too-big shirt slipped over the curve of her clavicle. His touch lingered on her skin and turned into a brief caress. He rolled away without a word, leaving her to stare at his broad back and straining her eyes to follow the curves and planes of his body. The urge to reach for him was so strong she clenched the pillow with both hands. In her mind, the moment played again and again: her hand reaches out, strokes the valley of his spine, he turns to her, gathers her in his arms, kisses her, hot exploring kisses. She rolled over with a silent moan, angry at him for rejecting her. Angry with herself because she ached for his touch. An ache unlike any she had felt before, accompanied by the firm conviction that she was completely fucked-up in the head.

*   *   *

She woke in the morning with his back pressed to her, butt to butt between blankets. Listening to Gabriel's breathing, she couldn't tell if he was awake or asleep, but his warmth was welcome in the chill, and the rise and fall of his body relaxed her like a massage. She had almost dozed off when he shifted, and his hand cupped her shoulder.

"Are you cold?" His low voice rumbled close to her ear.

"A little."

He crawled out of bed and draped his blanket over her. She rolled over to watch him pull on his pants with her unblinking gaze on his bulge.

"You could give me some privacy," he said, zipping his jeans.

"I'm your prisoner. I don't think I owe you anything."

He shrugged into his shirt. "Lounge in bed all you want, prisoner. I'm making coffee."

"Really?" She wriggled upright. "Hot coffee?"

"It's instant but yes, hot coffee. I have a one-burner propane cooker we can use for coffee, and to heat soup and such."

After a breakfast of canned peaches and oatmeal, they carried their coffee outside and walked in a circle around the cabin for exercise and fresh air. They didn't speak, focusing on their feet to avoid broken branches and things that crunch.

Adrienne was stiff from their climb to the cabin; she massaged her sore arms and rubbed her back muscles while they strolled, her mind as blank as she could make it. *Two-week vacation* was her mantra as she walked in slow, deliberate steps. Not *I'm a prisoner* or *I can't believe the bastard cut my face* or *what the fuck Dustin?* From an early age she had learned to adapt, to accept what she cannot change, and prepare to pivot when she had the opportunity. To hide her true self, to become someone else. This was just another situation to work through and wait out. *If he tries to hurt me again, I will draw blood. Screams will echo down the canyon.* "Two-week vacation." Her whisper was next to inaudible, for her own ears only.

Gabriel halted and held up one hand in his imperious gesture for silence. "It's our neighbor, the Lynyrd Skynyrd fan."

Cocking her head, she listened for a moment and said, "Simple Man. I love this song." She turned her head from side to side, trying to determine where the music was coming from, but the capricious breezes tossed the sounds against the trees and hills, scattering the music so it seemed to come from many directions.

"This would be a good time to pump some water, while our neighbor has his music cranked up." Gabriel headed towards the open cabin door, motioning her to follow. "Come on, I'm not leaving you out here alone."

She followed with dragging feet. The cabin was stuffy while the forest was cool and smelled of freedom. "Can I stand here?" She stopped at the open doorway. "I swear I won't run."

"Why do you push me?" He gestured at the open doorway. "Come inside. Take a nap or find something to read."

"Bossy. I should run just to make you chase me."

Inside the cupboard she found a stack of paperbacks next to the cribbage game, along with Scrabble, a baggie of dice, notepads, pens, pencils, Mad Libs, coloring books, crayons—a time capsule of things people used for entertainment before electronics. Adrienne chose the fattest paperback, a well-worn copy of 'Swan Song', even though she had read it before. She sat on the air mattress with her back against the wall and stared at the first sentence without seeing it, observing him over the top of the book, flicking her eyes down whenever he glanced her way.

Gabriel held a thick black plastic bag in the sink, water gushing. The pump was noisy, the rush of water was noisy, and it took several minutes to fill the bag. He lifted it, muscles straining, and carried it outside.

She jumped up to follow him. Two wooden walls—about five feet tall and four feet wide—stuck out from the back of the cabin. Using a ladder, Gabriel hung the bag above the walls and screwed a dangling spray nozzle to the threaded opening. A dark blue plastic curtain with a sailboat motif stretched between the two walls.

"I'm setting the bag in the sun so we can shower with warm water."

"Shower?" Scowling, she added, "I hope you don't think I can shower in handcuffs."

"No, but when I shower, you'll be in handcuffs."

Adrienne's jaw dropped and she scanned his unreadable face. "Gabriel, listen to the words I am saying. I will fight you so hard. I will scream, believe me. I will scream. I'll scream loud enough for every neighbor to hear. Don't even try to put me in handcuffs."

"We'll talk about this later." He pointed to the front door.

"No fucking way, we're talking about it now." She planted her feet and crossed her arms. "I'm not taking another step until you swear. Swear to me now. No handcuffs."

He waved his hand. "Okay, I swear. No handcuffs."

She eyed him warily. "Promise? You're not trying to trick me?"

"I promise. No handcuffs." His face seemed suddenly older. "I won't hurt you again."

*   *   *

They spent the next several hours reading, Adrienne on the mattress, Gabriel at the table. The silence was heavy, as if the cabin were holding its breath. She caught his gaze one too many times and refused to look again, concentrating on the printed page so intensely the words blurred. *Two weeks like this? Two weeks of unknowns, instant coffee and outdoor bathroom facilities...exciting? Yes. In a weird way, yes.* This world was otherworldly: a cramped, two-person drama, a stage play, while her other life went on without her—the other world, that included everyone but the two of them. What was happening in that world? Someone could have found the van. Someone could be climbing the steps right now. *Are the police looking? Is*

Fife looking? Is Dustin looking? All of the above? None of the above? Better to push aside the other world and tackle a more immediate, manageable challenge: convincing Gabriel to trust her, to stop treating her like a prisoner and start treating her like a woman.

* * *

Adrienne used her fingernail to mark the floor by her bed and counted the days, three lines on the day when she took her first shower, Gabriel's back discreetly turned but directly in front of the flimsy shower curtain. When he showered, he kept his eyes on her. She sat on a stump and looked at her book, turning a page now and then to make him think she was reading. The shower wall covered her to the eyebrows but only covered Gabriel to mid-chest; she took advantage of the situation and stealthily stared. He had the most beautiful body she had ever seen in the flesh.

Days went by. Gabriel's beard grew longer and his patience shorter. If she asked about his plan, he would snap 'no questions' and each time it would take longer for him to talk about anything at all. Hours of games, hours of reading, hours of silence. He made a routine of sit-ups, push-ups, planks and squats. She followed along when she felt like it but preferred to watch. Short bursts of activity revolved around meals, the most anticipated times of the day, even with their limited food choices. They played cards or read, went to bed when it was too dark to see, and woke at dawn, often touching back-to-back. They didn't talk about that either.

What he did talk about was a village, his ultimate destination. Gabriel's silky words in the dark were released slowly, deliberately, as he checked each sentence for clues. He would not say the name of the village or give any indication where it was in the world. But he would talk about the clean air and the quiet, the quality of light, the fresh food. The fruits and flowers. The rugged remoteness and sense of history. The welcoming people. Adrienne often fell asleep to the low, slow rumble of his voice.

By the seventh night, she could not see herself living in Dustin's life. The thought of facing her husband and the rest of the world made her stomach clench in greasy knots. The excuses and lies Dustin would tell to her face first, then in court. Cops and questions. Prison. They might lose their house. Adrienne listened to Gabriel's husky-voiced dreams of his future and imagined herself in this magical village, far from anyone she knows. *A place where I decide who I am.*

"Take me with you," she said on the eighth night. The moon glowed hazy through clouds; she curled on her side, facing him and the window. He was lying on his back with his hands laced under his head, looking straight up and didn't turn her way when he answered.

"You wouldn't like it."

"Why do you say that? It sounds wonderful."

"You wouldn't like it," he repeated and turned his back to her.

She asked him again on the ninth night and the tenth. They did not discuss this or the village in the light of day, it was only in the dark she would urgently whisper, "Take me with you. Don't leave me here. Don't make me go back to Dustin. I'm not asking to be your girlfriend or your partner. I don't want any of the money. Just take me with you."

On the eleventh night, while playing an exceptionally giggly game of Scrabble, inventing new words and silly definitions, Gabriel said, "Why do you want to come with me?"

Adrienne narrowed her eyes. "Don't you listen? I hate my life. I don't want to live with Dustin anymore."

"Divorce him."

"I don't want to go back there," she said. "I never want to see his face again."

He stroked his beard, eyes distant. "You could travel as a man."

"Excuse me?"

"I have been listening, and I've been thinking. If you come with me, we could disguise you as a man. People will be looking for a man with a woman."

Her eyebrows shot up. "A man? How's that going to work?" His eyes raked her up and down, pausing at her breasts. She crossed her arms and tucked her fists in her armpits. "Maybe it's easier for me to pass as a man than someone more blessed in the boob department, but I don't look like a man. Maybe a boy."

"Cut your hair short like a boy," he mused, looking past her. "There's enough hair dye for both of us, two sets of contacts, this could work."

"I don't look like a boy. And you want to cut my hair? If I wanted to fight you, this would be the time." Her smile faded. "But if this is the only way I can come with you, cut my hair. I trust you." She held herself still when he reached towards her face.

Touching her jaw near the knife slice that was now a flaking scab, he said, "Why would you trust a man who did this to you?"

Looking him square in the eye, Adrienne said, "Fuck if I know. I shouldn't trust you. I should be afraid of you. I should hate you. I don't know why I don't hate you. But my life before you no longer seems real. What would I go back to? Dustin? I would rather be your captive than his. Wherever you're going, I want to go."

"You would let me cut your hair?"

"How short?" She ran her fingers through the chin length strands.

"Short enough to look like a boy."

She squinted at him. "If you make a mess, do you have a hat?"

"Sure, I have a hat." He opened a cupboard and pulled out clear spectacles with black plastic frames. "And these, you can use these for your disguise."

She settled the glasses on her frowning face. "Why do I have to be a dork? Can't I have a boy band look? Justin Bieber or Harry Styles?"

"You're too pretty for a pretty boy disguise to work. You need to be plain." He reached out and his expression shifted when she flinched from his hand. "Adrienne." He tucked her hair behind one ear. "You're too pretty to be a boy but we'll do the best we can."

"Now will you tell me where we're going?"

His lips curled in a lazy smile. "Mexico."

CHAPTER SEVEN
COME SPY WITH ME

Mr. Hanks—the expensive private investigator that Lawrence Fife hired—found Cindy's trail within a day, and even though he didn't have to work very hard to find her, Fife considered the money well spent. The sooner he was uninvolved with Cindy, the better.

"It doesn't appear she's trying to hide," said Hanks on the phone. "She bought a one-way plane ticket to Puerto Vallarta with her credit card and used the card again to check into a condo six blocks from the Malecon. I confirmed with the rental agency that she picked up keys."

"What about checking Gabriel's credit cards?"

"With her mother involved, we can use the concerned relative angle to access Cindy's records, but for Gabriel we would need a court order."

"It doesn't matter. They're together." Fife blew a harsh breath. "Cindy is an adult, if she wants to run off to Mexico without telling her mother, why is that my problem?"

"Terrible, terrible," Hanks said. "Anything else, sir?"

"Thank you again for your help. Just bill my office." Fife ended the call and leaned back in his chair. When Austin and Berg approached him with their display of righteous indignation, Fife knew they were brown-nosing. Couple of suck-ups. They claimed to take Gabriel's betrayal personally, a big 'fuck you' to all the guys, not just the company. They worked cheaper than Hanks, and it would keep this idiotic Romeo and Juliet bullshit contained. Fife called Berg and Austin in for a meeting.

"You wanna kick Gabriel's ass?" Fife looked from one idiot to the other with his typical angry scowl. "Cindy is pregnant, and her mother said if she had that baby she was cut off." Barbara used the words 'that Mexican's baby' but Fife didn't believe it was his ethnicity that infuriated bigoted Barbara as much as Gabriel's lack of social status. A chauffeur, even if he did know how to fly a plane, was not good enough for her Ivy-League-sorority-girl daughter. Cindy and her mother argued, Barbara pushed hard for abortion and Cindy left. It seemed completely reasonable that Cindy would want to get away from her mother. If Devon Moore were alive, he would be wrangling his wayward daughter, but since he died, Fife had become his sister-in-law's surrogate husband. It was a burden he did not bear gracefully, only doing what was necessary to keep peace in his own house. "Gabriel's ass is probably in Mexico with Cindy."

Dustin's stomach crawled into his throat. "Mexico!" He clamped his mouth shut before the fountain of secrets spilled over. He cleared his throat. "Why would Cindy be in Mexico?"

"She's hiding from her mother. I don't know why Cindy chose Puerto Vallarta of all the places in the world but that's where she went. She left her phone behind, and her mother won't stop nagging me. I want you guys to go knock on her door and tell her princess ass to come home."

Fife handed each of them a sheet of paper. "I'm not sending you on an all-expenses-paid trip to Puerto Vallarta without profiting from it somehow. These are potential investment properties. If anyone asks why you're going to Mexico, this is why. Understand? I don't want any further office gossip about Gabriel and Cindy." Fife pointed at Jarrett; he seemed the more violent of the two. "If you want to beat the shit out of Gabriel, wait until Cindy talks to her mother. After that, I don't care what happens to him."

"When do you want us to go?" Dustin asked.

"Now, today, get your tickets booked." Fife stood and gestured at them to leave. "I want this goddam soap opera to end."

They hurried down the hall with Dustin whispering, "Fuck! I don't want to go to Mexico." He followed Jarrett into his office and shut the door. "I need to stay here and wait for Adrienne. She's supposed to be home in a few days."

Jarrett raised skeptical eyebrows. "Let's say the two-week thing is true. You don't need to wait here, you can wait in Mexico." He rubbed his hands together. "I can't wait to get my hands on Gabriel."

"How could he be in Mexico? He has Adrienne."

"You know he's with Cindy. Maybe he used a private plane?"

Dustin facepalmed. "That makes sense. He stole Fife's plane, so he has no problem stealing planes."

"Or money, or wives, or daughters." Jarrett paced the office. "Man, it aggravates me, the shit good-looking guys get away with. Women get hypnotized or something when they see a guy like that. Follow him around, break laws. Why do women like bad guys?"

"My wife is not hypnotized, she was kidnapped." Dustin stood in front of Jarrett and poked him in the chest. "She is not fucking Gabriel and you better stop implying that she is or I'm going to kick *your* ass." He gave Jarrett another poke for good measure.

Jarrett sneered. "With those soft hands?"

"I'll use a tire iron or a baseball bat," Dustin said around tight lips. He looked at the list Fife gave him and shook his head in dismay. He just wanted to find Adrienne and now he had dozens of hotels to inspect. He alternated between extreme worrying, extreme terror, and extreme fury over the past days since his wife, his money and that fucking pilot disappeared. Cindy obviously hadn't disappeared; the spoiled brat just didn't want to phone home. His wife was an unwilling victim, and he was terribly afraid that the two weeks Adrienne had screamed about was a lie she had been forced to tell. Gabriel had always seemed like a pleasant enough guy, friendly and polite, but he had a look about him—the look of a man capable of violence. He had no logical reason to keep her alive and Dustin was sick with the very real possibility that his greed and arrogance got his wife killed.

* * *

Jarrett and Dustin boarded a plane the next day, nonstop from San Francisco to Puerto Vallarta. A taxi dropped them in the arts district near Pipi's, a local landmark, blocks from the Malecon and the Pacific Ocean, and within sight of Cindy's vacation rental. Fife put them up in a decent condo with two ensuite bedrooms and mini-splits in every room; they had to dodge the dripping condensation coming and going through the only exit door, but it was the closest place to Cindy's they could snag at the last minute.

After they settled in the condo, Dustin and Jarrett walked to the unit where Cindy had checked in, knocked on her door, and received no answer. They made a rough schedule, taking turns watching Cindy's apartment and scouting properties, with some down time—after all, a man needs to relax after a stressful day of wheeling, dealing, and spying. If they had no sightings of Cindy within forty-eight hours, they would ask the rental agency for a welfare check.

They did not watch her apartment as closely as they discussed, but they told Fife the truth when he called two days later—no sign of Cindy. Fife arranged for the property manager to meet Berg and Austin at Cindy's place.

The realtor, Lorena, was grateful for their discretion in calling her before contacting the authorities. "The police force is spread quite thin in the area," she chattered, unlocking the door after knocking and getting no answer. "It might be days before they could check. Young girls are always wandering off and finding their way back in Vallarta." She ushered them inside the apartment that had the same basic layout as the men's condo. Lorena hurried to the closed bedroom door on the right, rapped on it sharply and waited for a count of three before knocking again, louder. "Cindy? I'm opening the door." The room was empty and the bed undisturbed. Lorena repeated this at the other bedroom door while Dustin and Jarrett roamed the living room and kitchen, finding no sign of occupancy.

Lorena walked into the living room frowning, hands on hips. "So strange. I gave her the keys myself, but I can't see that she stayed here at all."

"That is strange," Jarrett agreed and handed her a business card. "If you see her, please call me. Her folks are worried."

Jarrett called Fife to report their findings and held the phone away from his head so Dustin could hear Fife yelling. When the screams subsided, Jarrett continued, "I don't know, boss, it may be time to do some research on Gabriel. Far as I can tell, Cindy's trail is…" Jarrett started to say 'dead' and bit his tongue. "Cindy's trail is cold."

"You two stay there and keep an eye on her condo," Fife said. "She may be craftier than I gave her credit for. I'll pull Gabriel's employee record and call his emergency contact. And find some goddam properties to buy, you're not on vacation," he barked and ended the call.

"Such an angry man," Jarrett said.

"Now what?" Dustin said.

"We watch for her," Jarrett said. "Cindy is with Gabriel and they have our money. They're probably still in town and using that condo as a decoy. I say we go to the Malecon and have a stakeout. Everyone ends up on the Malecon at some point in the day."

"Stakeout? You mean sit on the beach and drink beer."

"And people watch. It's a legitimate spy thing to do."

Because Dustin had no better ideas, he let Jarrett talk him into drinking beer on the beach.

*　*　*

Fife headed for the office; he could call someone to pull the file for him, but it was bad enough that Austin and Berg knew about his embarrassing family. Gabriel had worked at Fife Industries for two years and his file only held his new hire paperwork. The emergency contact was Billy Jones, marked as 'friend'; Billy's phone number with a 510 area code was disconnected. There were no beneficiaries listed on his insurance, he hadn't signed up for the 401k. His mailing address was a UPS store drop box. Fife flipped through the thin sheaf of papers again. Nothing. One dead phone number, one worthless address.

Fife wasn't excited about digging into Gabriel's past, the more questions that were asked, the more people who knew about this, the higher the odds of the press latching on and from there his embarrassment could go viral. He skimmed Gabriel's application. Two years at community college in Oakland, two years at San Francisco State, graduated with a business degree. Eight years in the Navy flying planes as a junior officer before an honorable discharge. In the three-year gap between his military service and his start at Fife Industries, Gabriel had written 'sabbatical'. "That's right," Fife said to the empty room. "He told me he had to go hiking and find himself, some such hippie shit. Must be nice to walk around for three years and not make any money." He tossed the thin file on his desk. "Where the fuck are you, Gabriel? Who the fuck are you?"

CHAPTER EIGHT
DESPERADO

"Mexico? You're crossing the border with three million cash and a hostage?"

"I thought you were an accomplice?"

Adrienne shot him a look. "Have I officially been granted accomplice status? No more talk of handcuffs?"

"No more talk of handcuffs. Our life becomes more difficult when we leave this place and I don't want to fight you. I want to trust you." Gabriel touched her chin with one finger, directing her eyes to his. "But believe me when I say this, I am a desperate man. I don't want to hurt you, but I won't let you stop me."

She met his piercing gaze with her own stubborn expression. "I have no reason to stop you."

"I need to make a phone call." Gabriel pulled a flip phone from his pocket.

He was full of surprises. "They'll check your phone records."

"It's a burner." He walked away and talked for several minutes while pacing the clearing. When he came back, he said, "It's all set. Are you sure you want to do this? Positive? Okay, let's get to work on our disguises."

Adrienne sat in a chair outside and armed with only a pair of scissors, Gabriel worked on her boy haircut. He cut the back and sides almost skin close, with the top only slightly longer. Fickle winds blew clumps and strands in every direction. The breeze tickled the newly bare skin of

Adrienne's neck and she felt changed with each snip, transforming, an actor cast in a new role.

After he was satisfied with the cut, she colored his hair and he colored hers. They washed off the auburn dye with the shower nozzle, unsuccessfully attempting to rinse their hair without getting their clothes wet. It turned into an almost silent water fight with them both drenched and crying tears of laughter. Back in dry clothes, they stuck in the brown contact lenses and stood side-by-side to check their disguises in a mirror.

"I do not look like a boy," Adrienne insisted. "But I do like this haircut, Gabby. I may keep it like this." Words came to her: elfin, pixie-ish, sprite-like. No more beauty parlors. No more designer dresses and uncomfortable shoes. She would go barefoot and braless. She would learn to make tamales from scratch with food she grew in her own garden. Adrienne's skin tingled and her nerves buzzed with anticipation, ready to leave this cabin and this country to start her new life in the tiny magical village Gabriel whispered about in the dark.

"Where in Mexico?" Her eyes caught his in the mirror.

"I'm sorry, Adrienne." He turned away from the mirror to look her in the eye. "It's best you don't know just yet."

She opened her mouth to argue and snapped it shut, turning her fake-brown eyes back to the mirror. "Tell me our new names, Gabby. I'm calling you Gabby until you do."

"Me, Lazaro Cardenas, forty-two years old. You are my cousin, Andrew Cardenas, age twenty-two. Both born in the States. We're traveling through Mexico on a road trip vacation, on a six-month visa. It's rare to get your car searched going into Mexico, and I have no intention of coming out, at least not until I know people have stopped looking for us." His eyes scanned her face. "Are you sure this is what you want to do?"

"Yes, I've told you a million times. I don't want to go back to that life. I *can't* go back." Adrienne showed her teeth in a grim smile. "If you try to leave me behind, I'll follow you."

"We need to work on lowering your voice." Gabriel crossed his arms and widened his stance.

"Is that an instinctual man thing? Making yourself bigger?" She mimicked him, spreading her legs shoulder-width apart and crossing her arms into awkward wings. He stuck out his chin, she mirrored him. "How much 'manning' will I have to do? Just long enough to cross the border?"

"We have a long drive, so you'll need to be Andy for a few days."

Adrienne's past lives had not included nicknames or terms of endearment, and hearing 'Andy' in his silky voice made her fluttery inside. "What happens next? When do we leave?" She closed the space between them, watching his face.

"A man will be here tomorrow to make our passports and to drop off a car with insurance and registration in the name Lazaro Cardenas. He was supposed to take you from here but when you said you wanted to come, I called him to make you a passport."

"You were going to leave me with this man?" she said, incredulous. "What if he's a rapist or something, what if he planned to sell me?"

"We've known each other since we were eight years old. He was going to drive you somewhere safe and drop you off."

"How much of the three million is his?"

"None of your business."

"Being an accomplice feels the same as being a hostage." She sidled close enough to lay her hand on his chest. "Are you going to reject my accomplice advances the way you rejected me as your prisoner?"

Gabriel glided from under her hand and walked to the bear box. "Let's have that last bit of vodka."

She hugged herself, cheeks burning. "You're not attracted to me at all, are you? Are you gay? I sometimes wonder if Dustin might be gay."

"I'm not gay, but you might be on to something about your husband." Gabriel busied himself pouring the vodka in equal amounts, handed her a glass with two fingers of clear booze. "To us, may we have a long and beautiful friendship."

"That means you think I'm ugly."

"Not even in the ugly ballpark." He motioned to the card table. "Sit with me?"

"What choice do I have." Her face was fiery hot, she kept her head down to hide it. He leaned across the table and tapped her hand; she jerked away without looking up.

"I'm very attracted to you." His voice was a husky murmur.

"Obviously," she drawled. "You can't keep your hands off me."

"There's a woman waiting for me in Mexico."

That made her look up. "You have a girlfriend? A wife?"

His gaze dropped to his drink. "Not a wife."

"Okay, so a girlfriend. Great. You have a girlfriend waiting for us in this new life. The three of us. Gabriel, Adrienne and?" She raised a questioning eyebrow.

"Cindy."

"Cindy and Gabriel with me as the third wheel."

He rubbed a hand across his face. "I didn't want a girlfriend, but she's pregnant, and I will be a father to my child. I will be in his life, every day of his life."

"But why do you need three million dollars? Why run away to Mexico?"

"Her mother hates me." Gabriel clenched his jaw. "She hates me so much. If we're together, Cindy loses her allowance and her inheritance." He lowered his voice, as if talking to himself. "The day we met, we found out we had both visited this remote village in Mexico and it seemed like an odd thing to have in common. Like a sign, you know? When she told her mother she was pregnant and her mother went berserk, we planned to go there with our little bit of savings because money goes farther in Mexico. But your idiot husband joked that his heavy bag was full of money. And idiot me believed him."

He paused for so long she looked up to meet his eye.

"I couldn't stop thinking about how to get in your house to look inside that bag. I knew you probably would be home, so I prepared myself. I practiced what I would do and say. If the bag of money was a lie, I would have brought you here while I waited for my friend and left tomorrow with a new passport and no money. I prepared for that possibility. When I saw the bag and the money inside, I stepped outside myself, like my body was on autopilot. None of what happened seemed real."

"That's a lame excuse," she said. "It wasn't me, your honor, I was on autopilot."

"It's no excuse. I'm telling you how I felt. Cindy left for Mexico before I took the money so if the plan goes sideways, she has a solid alibi."

Adrienne straightened in her chair. "She knows about me?"

"I told her the same thing I tell you, sometimes it's better you don't know. I pray her part of the plan has gone well. We haven't spoken since before I borrowed the plane."

"Stole the plane," she interjected.

He twisted the glass in a sunbeam on the table. "I know where she's supposed to be, but I won't know for sure until I see her."

"You're in love with her?"

Leaning back in his chair, Gabriel sipped his vodka and gazed out the window. "Love doesn't matter. We're having a child together."

Cold resentment replaced the heat of embarrassed rejection. Cindy changed everything. Daydreams of barefoot-gardener-chef Andy always included having sex with Gabriel. Adrienne assumed that would eventually happen, she *counted* on it. Hours and days of watching his body, whispering together, laughing together, sleeping together, surrounded by his scent. In her dreams she reached for him, over and over, and in her dreams, he turned to her and took her in his arms. *That will happen. One way or another, that will happen.*

She clenched her fists under the table, nails biting into her palms. "Let me see if I understand your moral code. It's okay to steal, torture and kidnap but infidelity is crossing the line?"

He tightened his jaw. "Everything I did, I did for my child."

"I don't believe that," she said, biting each word. "You stole the money for yourself because your rich girlfriend is losing her gravy train."

"My child will never know poverty. I won't allow it." The setting sun cast harsh shadows under his cheekbones, carving his expression into granite.

She bent her head, missing the swing of her hair that used to hide her face. "Where do I fit in? What if Cindy doesn't want me around? I can't go back to Dustin."

"We'll make it work. You can be auntie to my son."

She sputtered. "Of course you think it's a boy. Will I be auntie or uncle Andy?"

"When the road trip is over, when we're safe in our new home, you can be anyone you want to be. It's important that you are happy, Adrienne. I changed the course of your life. I did this to you and I'm responsible for your happiness."

"No, I absolve you of that responsibility. I'm in charge of my own happiness, you're in charge of my safety. I don't want to end up shot or in a Mexican prison." *Or any prison.* "Who are we hiding from besides Dustin and Jarrett? Cindy's mom? Fife may have found out about the stolen money and called the cops. Dustin could be in jail right now. We have no idea what is going on out there." Adrienne swept her arm across the rapidly darkening window view.

"We'll know by tomorrow. Try not to worry, you need a good night's sleep."

When the cabin was too dark to play games or read, they would go to bed, because they had nothing left to do. Tonight, she would reach for him. Before it's too late.

CHAPTER NINE
DON'T FORGET TO REMEMBER

That night, Gabriel dragged his mattress across the room. "You can have your space."

That's what he said, but she knew why he stayed away from her—so there would be no touching. Adrienne stared sightlessly into the thick, satiny dark. No sign of the moon on this overcast night; the stars hid behind clouds, the blackness in the cabin complete. Gabriel tussled with his pillow and blankets, then settled, and the silence became as complete as the darkness. She strained to hear his breathing, holding her own breath. Time passed, soft snores reached her ears, the clouds shifted outside the window and weak starshine outlined the curve of Gabriel's bare shoulder. She rose from her bed as if his skin had called to her.

Lifting the blanket, she slid in next to him, curving against his back, molding herself to him, shushing his sounds of protest. "Go to sleep, I just want to hold you." *Liar. You're hoping he can't control himself.* She breathed the spicy scent of his skin, her right hand resting on his hip. The tenseness of his body gradually relaxed. She touched her lips to his naked back— stealthy, lighter than a butterfly. His breathing deepened. She moved her hand from his hip, where his skin was covered by underwear, to the bare skin of his waist. Hot. So hot. She listened for snoring, let her hand slide to his stomach. His hand grabbed hers and pressed it against his furry belly, hard muscles and soft skin. Not a word was spoken. She fell asleep holding his hand.

* * *

Gabriel was making coffee when she woke, the morning light bright on her closed lids.

"Rise and shine. We have a busy day."

Adrienne kicked off the covers and stretched, giving him ample opportunity to peek at her in her underwear. He turned his back and busied himself at the bear box.

"We're leaving today for sure?" At his affirmative nod, she thought...*shit is about to get real.* They were leaping back into the other world; a world with news and noise and police, possibly bad guys lying in wait. She eased out of bed and slipped on her shorts and shoes before crossing the room to pour coffee. "Are we taking all this stuff with us?"

"Only our clothes. We'll leave the mattress and cooler here for the next person."

"Whose house is this?"

"It's complicated. Different people use it for different reasons. I slept here the first time when I was ten." Gabriel twisted his lips in a wry smile. "After breakfast we'll take a walk, there's a view I want to show you."

"When do you expect your friend?"

"Early afternoon. We have plenty of time." He sipped his coffee, eyeing her over the rim of his mug. "Are you nervous?"

"A little. Aren't you?"

"A little," he echoed. "My friend is bringing a smartphone. Once we're out of the trees and can get a better signal, I'll check the news. Then I'll know how nervous we need to be."

After breakfast, Gabriel said they were taking a hike. "Short but strenuous" were his words. Behind the cabin was a steep hill, almost straight up; they struggled to the top while the morning fog chilled the air, and every surface was still slippery with dew. Gabriel topped the rise first and helped her over the last stony outcrop. Adrienne straightened, peering through the trees.

"I don't believe it," her voice was hoarse from days of forced whispering, and full of wonder. "That's the fucking Golden Gate Bridge. That's Oakland. That's Tiburon. I can practically see my house from here." She looked Gabriel up and down, as if seeing him for the first time. "Where are we?"

"Canyon. It's an old community but not many people know about it. I only know about Canyon because almost everyone uses propane, and my dad drives a propane truck. This is on his route." He walked a few steps away and looked over the edge. "When I was eight, my mom left us. I rode with my dad any time I wasn't in school."

"Your mom left?" His expression indicated the subject was closed. Adrienne, personally familiar with less-than-stellar mothers and sharing his reticence to talk about them, let it drop.

"I've been to almost every house in Canyon. My friend Billy grew up here, his dad grew up here. His grandpa or great-grandpa was one of the first settlers. Loggers. They cut down nearly every tree." He gestured at the towering redwoods. "All second growth and protected now."

The cabin had felt so very far away from everything, an island in the middle of the widest ocean, another planet or another dimension, a place with no past or future, only the present. Adrienne was overwhelmed at the immediacy of the 'normal' world—if 'normal' is sitting in a car for hours before chaining yourself to a cubicle for more hours in a pointless race to buy as much stuff as you can before you die. A cabin in the forest seemed light years closer to what 'normal' should be, for the madness across the bay to be so close felt like a rip in time.

The elegant orange bridge stretching across the blue-gray sky had always been a part of Adrienne's world. Growing up in Oakland, the bridge was an orange smudge through dingy windows in a series of rent-subsidized apartments or old cars. Crossing the bridge to her life with Dustin was a Cinderella story, but her expansive, expensive view of the bridge from Marin didn't change the fact that she was a fake, a phony, a paper doll. Everything authentic and real snuffed out and stuffed into expensive clothes and uncomfortable heels. Painted into a candy-colored shell. Alive but not living. A prison of her own making.

Standing in the cool forest, she cast her gaze across the bay and the freeways, the bustling hive of cars and ships and people and buildings. Today they would leave asphalt and steel and concrete to live the simple life in Gabriel's magical village. *I may never see the bridge again.* She looked inside herself for anything that felt like regret, sorrow, homesickness, and felt nothing but a wistful affection for the beauty of the bridge itself, and restless anticipation—the bridge was a symbol for new beginnings, a literal crossing from one side to another.

"Another minute and we should go back to the cabin," Gabriel said. "I want to be packed up to leave as soon as the passports are ready."

"I'm ready," she said, peering down the hill. "Don't break a leg."

"Stop saying things like that," he groaned. "Now that you've jinxed us, be extra careful going down. Slow and easy."

"I'm unjinxing us. If you talk about the bad things that might happen, it prevents them from happening."

"That is the most illogical superstition I've ever heard. Please be careful. I'll wait here until you're all the way down."

Adrienne was extra careful, and still ended up sliding in the loose clay and crumbling rock, scraping her bare knees, palms and forearms, cussing and spitting in a controlled monotone on the way down. At the bottom, she dusted herself off, grimacing in pain, and after a closer inspection of her shredded flesh, she made her way to the shower nozzle to wash off. Toeing off her shoes, she hesitated only briefly before pulling off her top and shorts, setting the water flow to a trickle. By the time Gabriel appeared at her side, she had rinsed off the embedded dirt and gravel from her bleeding wounds.

"I told you to be careful." He squatted to inspect her banged up knees. "We'll need to do some first aid on this mess before it gets infected."

Adrienne heard noises coming from him but was distracted by his face being so close, with only her underwear between them. She could almost feel her fingers twining in his thick, once-black-now-reddish-brown hair and pulling his face tight against her. She threaded her fingers together before they took on a life of their own.

He stood to inspect her arms. "That's not too bad. Your knees, though...can you walk?"

"I walked over here," she snipped, gathering her clothes. "Where's the first aid kit?"

"I'll get it for you." He followed her inside and opened the bear box.

She collapsed into a folding chair, wincing at every bend of her knees. Gabriel pulled a chair in front of her, manspreading like mad, engulfing her elfin self in his looming bulk.

"Let me see your arm." He motioned to her, a command.

"I can do it myself."

"Please." Gabriel took her hand and held it when she tried to pull away. "Let me help, I feel responsible." His lips quirked in a smile. "Even though you jinxed yourself."

Before she could stop him, he poured hydrogen peroxide on her scrape. Adrienne hissed in pain and her eyes filled with sudden tears. "Just rub salt in it why don't you?"

"We need to keep it clean." He dabbed the scrape with antibacterial ointment, intense concentration lined his face. "Other arm." He waggled his fingers, another of his imperious, arrogant gestures, as if non-cooperation were out of the question.

Gabriel was gentle but detached. Jittery with frustration, Adrienne watched his impersonal hands on her body, eyes stinging, blinking furiously, feeling crushed by a sense of profound loss, the loss of something that she never had. *He doesn't want me. He doesn't desire me at all.* An image flashed in her mind, of Gabriel holding another woman in his arms, kissing her. Her throat closed. *Accept what I cannot change.*

She popped four extra-strength ibuprofen and repacked the first aid kit while Gabriel sorted through the bear box. After two weeks without supplies, anything perishable was long gone and the food that was left didn't look appetizing, but they shoveled down some canned chili with the last of the saltines. They packed their clothes, squished the air out of the mattresses and rolled them in a corner, put the blankets and pillows and games back in the cupboard.

Two backpacks sat by the door, along with two weeks accumulation of trash in a single garbage bag, and the gym bag full of money. They used towels to wipe down all the surfaces, not because Gabriel thought the police would find the cabin but to give themselves a job to do while waiting for the knock on the door. The sun was low in the sky when the knock finally came. Gabriel leaped to his feet, glanced out the window and flung open the door.

"Billy, am I glad to see you." The man Gabriel embraced was very tall and thin with a port wine stain that covered his right eye and spilled down his cheek to his top lip. He hugged Gabriel with one arm, the other hand gripped a steel briefcase.

"You're late," Gabriel said. "Is everything okay? Adrienne, this is Billy." Nerves had his voice crackling. "Is everything okay?" he repeated.

"Hi Adrienne, yes, everything is fine." Billy dropped the briefcase on the card table. "Let's get this done. I'm running behind. Adrienne, stand over there for your photo. Yes, you can look in the mirror first. No glasses. No smile. Ready." And flash. "Gabriel let's do this. That's the beard you're going with? That mouth mullet?"

"It's called a goatee." Gabriel chuckled. "And yes, I grew it for the photo. I think it changes the shape of my face more than a full beard."

Billy laughed and rattled off some rapid Spanish.

"English, Billy. Adrienne doesn't speak Spanish."

"She needs to learn if she wants to be happy in Mexico."

"She'll learn," Adrienne said. "Gabriel could have been teaching me."

"You're right, I fucked up." He raised his hands in surrender. "I've had a lot on my mind and didn't think of every detail."

"Not thinking of every detail could get us in trouble." *What else is he missing? What else is he hiding? Everything. He hides everything.*

Billy produced passport cards that would get them into Mexico, and a California driver's license for Lazaro Cardenas in case they got pulled over. "These are the real deal," he said. "There should be no reason for anyone to question their authenticity."

Adrienne ran her thumb back and forth across her passport: new name, new look, new identity. In each chapter of her life, she had a different name. Adrienne Cook was on her birth certificate, a scared and angry girl, nearly feral. Adrienne Berg was on her driver's license, a privileged woman with the means to do almost anything but who did almost nothing, more a prop than a person. Andrew Cardenas was on her passport. A third life as a criminal.

A thief and a liar. Not much different than her mother, except her mother was dead and Adrienne was alive. Truly alive, instead of just existing. As Andy in Mexico, her name would not be recorded anywhere, and she could be anyone.

"It's time." Gabriel hoisted the gym bag to his shoulder. "Grab the backpacks, Adrienne."

They moved carefully down the wooden steps, hurrying to beat the cloak of night, mindful of the treacherous trail. It was easier going down than up; gravity was on their side, and they had less to carry. Gabriel and Billy took turns leading them on the winding, unmarked path through the forest, a path that constantly tried to trip her. Adrienne concentrated on her feet so intently that she took a step onto blacktop before realizing the forest had ended.

"Your car is over there." Billy picked up the pace, his voice an urgent whisper. He unlocked the driver's door of the nondescript dark sedan and popped the lock manually to open the back door. "Press this latch here, the back seat tilts forward and your bag will fit in here. There's a tent and sleeping bags in the trunk."

Gabriel hefted the money into the open space, unzipped the bag and pulled out a cloth sack before dropping the seat. "This is yours, brother. Thanks for everything."

They shared a hard, fast hug. Adrienne tossed the backpacks in the car and settled into the passenger seat. Billy tipped one finger in a salute and ran down the two-lane road carrying their bag of trash in one hand and his bag of money in the other, into the night and out of sight.

Gabriel gave Adrienne a long look from the driver's seat. "Last chance to change your mind. Billy can take you somewhere safe and you can find your way home."

"My home isn't here," she said.

He smiled and his teeth gleamed in the dark. Starting the car, he flipped on the headlights and eased down the empty road. "The journey begins."

"Can we get a room tonight? Have a real shower and sleep in a real bed?"

"Tonight we get as far south as I can drive. And hotels want credit cards. We'll find a campground with pay showers."

"With hot water," she grumbled. The outdoor shower was better than nothing, but the water was only lukewarm. Adrienne craved a shower of scalding water almost as much as she craved Gabriel's hands on her body.

"In the glove box should be a smartphone and charger. When you have signal, check the news."

She powered up the cheap phone, opened a browser and found a local media website. She scrolled through today's headlines and local news. "I'm not finding anything in the news, do you think it's safe to do a search on this phone?"

"We need to know who is looking for us. Clear your browser when you're done."

Instead of using the pre-loaded browser, she downloaded an app and searched for her name, Gabriel's name, Fife Industries. "What's Cindy's last name?"

"Moore."

She tapped the screen, shook her head. "Nothing. There's nothing. Nothing about you, nothing about Cindy. Nothing about me. Dustin didn't tell anyone." Adrienne felt sick with disbelief that her husband had remained silent.

"It's two weeks today, maybe he plans to tell someone tomorrow."

"Would you wait for two weeks? If you came home to find your wife missing, saw her blood, heard her screams? Would you wait to call the police if it was Cindy? Or your baby?"

Gabriel cut his eyes from the road to look at her face. "No," he said, his voice rough. "I would have called the police, then hunted down the kidnapper myself."

"He's more concerned with his own neck than mine." Adrienne cleared the search history, deleted the app, powered off the phone and put it away. Fingers numb, she moved through these tasks mindlessly and turned to the passing scenery: trees, trees, trees, rolling at a sedate fifty miles per hour on two-lane blacktop. *I made the right choice. Dustin doesn't deserve me.*

CHAPTER TEN
BREAKING THE LAW

"Where the fuck is my fucking money, you fucking cocksucker?"

Dustin's jaw dropped, he stared at Jarrett with cold fear in his bulging eyes. "Mr. Fife...what...what are you talking about?"

"Five million dollars is missing from the general account! You and that other cocksucker stole it! Don't try to deny it!"

Fife's screams pierced his eardrum; Dustin held the phone at arm's length and shook it at Jarrett. "He knows!" Dustin said. "Why is he saying five million?"

"How should I know?" Jarrett shifted his eyes.

"You two are dead meat." Fife was no longer yelling; his voice had gone steely. "I would hunt you down and kill you myself except the shit has hit the fucking fan here. Some twat in accounting noticed the missing money and went to the feds instead of coming to me. And now the cops and the fucking press are asking where you two shitbirds are." Fife shouted, "By the way, dumbfuck, where is your wife?"

With no activity on Cindy's phone, credit cards or passport in over two weeks, Barbara Moore had grown impatient waiting for her daughter to contact her and filed a missing person report. The police could not locate Gabriel Navarro, Cindy's alleged boyfriend, and found no activity on his phone, credit cards or passport. But they found no sign of foul play. The police gave Barbara the same information as the private detective—Cindy flew to Puerto Vallarta, rented a room that she never used, and hasn't been seen since. The officers who spoke with Mrs. Moore conferred and agreed; if she was their mother, they would have also skipped town.

Different authorities were notified about the missing money. They traced the Cayman account, noted the withdrawal of three million cash and coupled with Fife's private plane flight records, those authorities viewed Adrienne, Dustin and Jarrett as alleged embezzlers who stole alleged money and left town. Possibly with the pilot. No one was interested in looking for them; they had more important cases than hunting down people who stole from a rich man. Because of the company-funded trip to the Caymans where the alleged money originated, Fife had been questioned extensively by the FBI and he was in a rage at the implication he had been involved.

"Where's the money, asswipe?" Fife took deep, calming breaths, the last thing he needed was another heart attack over a few million dollars. It was the embarrassment, the scandal that infuriated him. He valued his privacy above all, paid dearly for privacy; these two idiots screwed him over, then the weasel in accounting tattled to the cops. His privacy was violated. No loyalty left in society, no matter how much you pay people. Trust no one. "Start talking. Where's the cash? Where's your wife? Is she with you? Is Gabriel with you?"

Dustin tried handing the phone to Jarrett who jumped back with both hands in the air. "Tell him, it was your idea. You wrote the code." Dustin was talking to thin air; Jarrett had left the room. "Well, Mr. Fife, have you ever seen the movie Office Space?"

"Everyone knows how you stole the money, dipshit, where's the cash? That's the only answer I need from you right now."

"Gabriel stole it from my house and kidnapped Adrienne so I wouldn't tell," Dustin blurted.

"Kidnapped? When did this happen?"

Dustin gulped and searched his brain for the date. "Two weeks ago. I was told to wait two weeks before I called the police. I was planning to call them tomorrow." He actually had no intention of calling the police; he and Jarrett had argued extensively over the subject and concluded that no good could come of that phone call.

"Why do you think she was kidnapped? Maybe she's Gabriel's sidepiece?"

Dustin aimed a dirty look at the phone. "I found evidence that she was taken by force. I'd rather not talk about it, what I found was quite disturbing." He heaved a ragged sigh.

"Your wife was taken by force and you didn't say anything? No one noticed?"

"Um, well, Adrienne doesn't have close friends or a job. She mostly stays home."

"You're quite the asshole, Berg."

"Yes, sir. Are the police coming for us?"

"They sure are." The police were not coming for them, Mexican authorities were not interested in Fife's problems, but Fife was not paying for that condo another night. "You have one chance to redeem yourself. Maybe you'll live long enough to go to jail. Find Cindy before the cops do and I'll ask the judge to go easy on you. If you make me come looking for you in Mexico, I will kill you. I'm thinking machete, slice you right in half, nice and quiet. What do you think, Berg?"

Dustin gagged, swallowed bile, and cleared his throat. "I'll take jail. What can we do?"

"Someone saw Cindy in Puerto Vallarta. She bought a candy bar or a Starbucks or a dress, something. Someone will remember her. Find Cindy, and you'll find your wife, Gabriel, and the money." Fife released a harsh growl of frustration. "You have no idea how lucky you are to be so far away. If you were standing in my office, I would chuck you out the window."

Another elevator delivery of bile rose in Dustin's throat—Fife's office was on the thirtieth floor, downtown San Francisco. "I do know how lucky I am, sir, and I won't let you down. We'll find Adrienne and Cindy and your money." And a tire iron or baseball bat for Gabriel.

"God, I could just strangle the lot of you. Loyalty... horseshit," Fife barked. "A messenger will be there within the hour with photos of Cindy. Show her picture to everyone, everywhere. Get the fuck out of that room as soon as that packet arrives and don't call me again until you have news. If you want to live, get me news fast, comprende?"

Dustin stared at the now thankfully silent phone, frozen and hot all at once, stomach churning, acid burning the lining of his throat. "Jarrett!" he croaked. "Fife is pissed." He walked across the living room. "Are you seriously hiding in your bedroom?" He knocked, no answer, opened the door to Jarrett lying on the bed with earbuds, eyes closed. Dustin grabbed his foot. Jarrett leaped off the bed and his cell phone went flying with the earbuds attached.

"What the fuck, Dustin!"

"We don't have time for this shit. Fife wants to kill us. He wants to cut me in half with a machete and throw you out the office window."

"Christ, the man is a psycho. For a measly five mill?" Jarrett scratched his head and yawned.

"We need to get out of this room. Fife wants us to find Cindy before the cops do and if we do, we might get off easy. He's sending someone with photos, and we're supposed to go around to shops and ask if anyone remembers seeing her."

"I think we should make a run for it, just get on a plane and go to the Caymans. The other two million is sitting in our retirement account waiting for us."

"You didn't turn off the program when you said you did?" Dustin glared fiery sparks at Jarrett's sheepish face. "They're looking for us, they know we did it. Our passports won't get us anywhere. And I don't want to run. I need to know that Adrienne is okay. I need to know I didn't get her killed. Or worse." Dustin brushed a tear from his cheek. "I wish we'd never done this."

"Grow up for fuck's sake. Turn yourself in if you want. Maybe Fife will do you a favor and use a bullet instead of a machete."

"What are you going to do?" Dustin blotted his eyes with the neck of his shirt.

"I'm going to find Cindy. She's with Gabriel, Gabriel has our money. If I'm hiding from Fife and the cops the rest of my life, I want the damn money I stole. It's rightfully mine." He saw the look on Dustin's face. "Ours, the money is ours. We'll find them, get our money and find a place to hunker down. I know this sweet little town by Lake Chapala."

Thirty minutes later, a messenger delivered a manila envelope with a dozen eight by ten color glossies of Cindy Moore. There were also copies of the information Barbara Moore gave to the police: Cindy's contact list from her phone, social media accounts, places she had visited before in Mexico. The messenger recommended a cheaper motel a few blocks away.

Dustin and Jarrett walked, suitcases rolling noisily on the cobblestones, barking blame at each other until they arrived at the drab, single story cement block of a motel.

"This room is disgusting." Jarrett's lip curled. "Twin beds? Bathroom down the hall?"

"Fife cut us off, we're paying for everything now."

"So? We have money in the bank."

"You mean in our frozen accounts? We're wanted for embezzlement, remember?"

"Wait, you're saying the only money we have is the cash in our pockets?"

"We could try our credit cards but even if they work that leaves a trail for the cops."

"Let's at least try an ATM." Jarrett ran his finger across the greasy dresser and grimaced at the filth on his finger.

"One that's not too close, in case the cops are watching our accounts."

"Good plan." Jarrett pulled out his phone. "I think there's a Santander about a mile from here."

"You can't use your location, the cops will find us for sure."

"Come on, the Mexican cops don't care about a couple of gringos who stole money from a richer gringo. They'll knock on the door and when they find us gone, they'll go have a siesta. Fife is trying to scare you."

"In the movies the bad guys use burner phones," Dustin said, a stubborn set to his jaw.

Jarrett frowned. "We're not the bad guys. And I'm not giving up my phone, it has all my numbers and pictures and stuff."

And he was supposed to be the smarter man. Dustin dropped the subject but turned off his location and powered off his phone. The only person whose phone call he wanted was Adrienne's and he had a sick feeling that she wouldn't be calling him.

They walked a humid, sweaty mile to an ATM that swallowed Jarrett's card. "Fuck," he spat. "Try yours."

"I'll try a different machine, we passed a Scotiabank back there." Where Dustin's card was promptly eaten. "Let's sit in the shade for a minute."

A tiny square was set into a side street, four stone benches around a bushy cypress. Dustin looked around, waited for two bros in madras shorts to pass, and pulled out his wallet. "How much money do you have?"

Jarrett whipped his head around in all directions before hissing, "Put that away before you get robbed."

Dustin ignored him, counting under his breath. "I have four hundred and sixty-three American dollars and a couple hundred pesos. Another thousand US in my money belt."

"I'll count mine when we're in a safe place."

"You mean that high security motel room? Let me see what's in your wallet, we're a team."

"Two thousand, two hundred and eighty-four dollars," Jarrett intoned. "I always know exactly how much money is in my wallet. Except the pesos, I don't count them."

"Okay, that's good. This gives us some time." Dustin heaved to his feet. "Let's grab some tacos and beer and chill on the Malecon. We deserve a break after this horrible day."

* * *

The next morning, with mild headaches and acid reflux, they hit the streets with Cindy's photo. First stop: Waldo's—if you needed a dress or a mango or an aspirin, you could buy it at Waldo's. They showed Cindy's photo to the woman running the cash register, respectfully waiting until she had no one in line.

"Buenos dias, senorita," Dustin said, with not even the vaguest Spanish accent. "Have you ever this girl? This chica?"

"The word is mujer, she's a woman not a little girl." Jarrett smugly showed off his Spanish vocabulary.

The woman took the photo in both hands. "She looks familiar. Is she famous? A movie star?"

They would get similar responses from almost everyone who took time to look at the photo. Cindy's professional head shot, coupled with her classic California-girl bone structure made everyone feel like they had seen her somewhere before.

"She's a model, si?"

"I saw her in a magazine."

"Is she on that one Netflix show?"

"I think I saw her on American Idol or The Voice. She looks so familiar."

People who didn't make those types of comments were more likely to take brief glance, shake their heads, and hurry on. Girls are always going missing, no one wants to be involved in that.

Dustin suggested taking the city bus to Walmart. When they stepped onboard, Jarrett showed the driver the photo. He expected the driver to wave him on and was surprised when the man took the photo and studied it.

"Is she very tall?" the driver asked, raising one hand high above his head.

"Yes," Dustin blurted, eyes hopeful. "Do you remember her?"

The driver's accent was heavy, his English fluent. "It was many days ago, but I remember her. She missed the Walmart stop and was very embarrassed. I made a special stop so she wouldn't have to walk so far and she gave me twenty US dollars. Pretty girls are easy to forget, kind girls I remember."

"Looks like we're going to Walmart," said Dustin.

"She's not still there, dude." Jarrett rolled his eyes.

"Maybe someone who works there will remember her, dude." Dustin shoved him towards a seat. "We can show her picture there all day in air conditioning. Everyone goes to Walmart."

CHAPTER ELEVEN
AS THE WORLD GETS SMALLER

Gabriel dashed inside a local bodega for road trip snacks and to break a hundred-dollar-bill. He came out with jerky, a giant bag of Fritos, bean dip, powdered sugar mini donuts, chocolate milk, two large coffees and a map of California.

"When we get there, I'm eating nothing but salads for a week." Adrienne brushed at the drift of sugar on her shirt. "People cannot live on junk food alone, you know."

"Cindy might have a garden started already," Gabriel said through a mouthful of doughnut. "She loves to garden and cook and eat healthy. You two have a lot in common." He shot her a quick glance. "I think you'll like her."

Adrienne made a noncommittal noise. She despised Cindy and had never laid eyes on the girl. And she was a girl, twenty-two to Adrienne's thirty-two, and spoiled rotten. Raised and educated in ivory towers. Cindy had never slept in a car or eaten food from a dumpster. Or fought for her life. Adrienne resented Cindy's hold on Gabriel, she had trapped him with an unplanned baby. And surely it was unplanned, Gabriel is hot but he's not in the same league as Cindy. That woman was the reason Gabriel wouldn't touch her and Adrienne hated Cindy with the white-hot passion of a thousand fiery suns.

They stayed on Highway 5 all the way south, cruise control set at one mile under the speed limit. North of Carlsbad, Gabriel jogged east, following signs to Rustic Oaks Campground, where they offered RV and tent camping, a general store and pay showers. The grounds were neat and clean, shaded by ancient oaks and cooled by a rushing stream. It was after midnight and the welcome booth was closed but he found a self-pay station. Gabriel paid for two nights, and they made their way slowly down the dirt road, headlights off. At a tent site with no close neighbors, they parked sideways to make a protective shield, and for a quick getaway.

Gabriel turned off the key and leaned his head back with a low groan. Adrienne's window was down a few inches, she breathed in the thick scent of rotting oak leaves and damp earth. The stream was a low rustle, almost indistinguishable from the branches shaking in the breeze. Bugs whirred and chirped. Her body felt like it was still moving. Gabriel climbed out and she met him at the trunk to unload the camping gear—a two-person umbrella tent and two sleeping bags, all brand new. They had backpacks with clothes and toiletries, snack food, and something slightly less than three million dollars cash to unload from the car. They set up their meager camp in drained silence; after two weeks in the cabin and nine plus hours in the car, all safe topics of conversation had been beaten to death.

Lying atop the sleeping bag, using her rolled up clothes as a pillow, Gabriel inches away, Adrienne was reminded of that claustrophobic night in the van. She remembered how it felt to watch him sleep, overwhelmed with dark emotions. Confusion, fear, anger, betrayal. Lust. Shameful, undeniable lust. The lust was still there, and the answering reverberation emanated from his bare skin, but she was too exhausted to act on it.

He broke the silence, voice slurred with fatigue, "Is the phone still in the glove box?"

"Yes. I turned it off."

"I meant to look at the news again but I can't keep my eyes open another minute."

"Try closing your mouth, too."

He aimed a weak kick at her. "Good night, Andy."

"Good night, cousin." His chuckle was the last thing she heard before falling asleep.

* * *

Trees behind their tent framed the rising sun, waking Adrienne at dawn and heating the nylon tent that was so thin she could see rising steam from sun-heated dew. She and Gabriel were pressed back-to-back, and she eased her body away from his snores to push the sleeping bag down, muggy in this tiny space. This time tomorrow they would drive through the border crossing at San Ysidro. She still didn't know how far into the country they were going but Gabriel said he would tell her after they made it through customs. In case she changed her mind. She would not change her mind, and she would not think about what would happen if they got caught. She would only think about a sleepy, sunny village with kind people and fertile soil. Light that was perfect for painting. A hammock for reading. A rocking chair on a wooden porch for writing. Neighbors who greet you instead of averting their eyes to avoid conversation. Adrienne had no reason to believe any of her fantasies were possible, but she had to dream about something, and this dream made her happy, to believe the magical village might be a place she could belong.

Gabriel stretched and yawned, she grabbed her pants and slipped them on before rising. "I'm going to the bathroom, do you want me to wait for you?"

"No, go on, I don't want to leave our stuff here unguarded. Don't forget you're a boy."

She looked down at her track pants, sneakers and hoodie. "You think this is too feminine?"

He gave her a sleepy smile and waved her off. "I'll check the news on the phone and go the bathroom when you get back."

It was early, just after five, but other campers were already stirring. Adrienne smelled bacon and her stomach clenched in longing, with visions of an enormous hot breakfast dancing in her head: waffles drenched in syrup and butter with a pile of bacon for dipping. *No chance of that today.* She hurried down the winding dirt road to the bathrooms, thankfully clean, private and unisex, as were the showers—which she planned to use after coffee. She strolled back to the campsite, heart light, arms swinging. They had all day to rest, she had a hot shower to look forward to, and the border was only a few more miles away.

She rounded a corner to see the campsite and Gabriel pacing by the car, looking at the phone. He caught sight of her and stomped to her side.

"I thought you said you found nothing in the news?" He handed her the phone, looking both scared and angry.

Adrienne read a headline that stopped her heart.

MAN WANTED FOR QUESTIONING IN THE DISAPPEARANCE OF TWO BAY AREA WOMEN.

The police are looking for any information regarding the whereabouts of Gabriel Navarro, age 35, of San Rafael. He is a person of interest in two separate cases of missing women, also from San Rafael. Ms. Cindy Moore has a romantic relationship with Mr. Navarro. He is also believed to be the last person to see Mrs. Adrienne Berg. Police urge anyone with information to come forward.

There were photos: Gabriel's employee photo from Fife Industries, grainy and resembling a mugshot. A full-length press photo of Adrienne, looking both polished and ill-at-ease. She recognized the venue as a Soroptimist event that featured shirtless waitstaff. She saw Cindy's face for the first time in the glamorous head shot the article used. Adrienne's hate grew like a wildfire fueled by gasoline.

"This was *not* online when I checked. See the time stamp? This was posted after we went to bed." Adrienne touched his shoulder. "Gabriel, this is serious. It's like they think you killed us. And if they think you're a killer, they might not hesitate to shoot you. You should let me call someone so they know I'm okay."

"No," he barked. "Nothing changes." He paced in a tight circle. "We need to remember, we are Andy and Laz. I wasn't around when you were growing up and this trip is for us to bond. That's why we don't know much about each other."

"Where are we from?"

"My license says Davis, let's say you grew up in Fresno. Your mother starved you as an infant and that's why the cousin of a six-foot-two man is five feet tall." Gabriel's shaky laugh lessened the tension.

Adrienne gestured down her body. "Right? You didn't think about that when you made me a man. You should have put my age down as twelve." Her smile changed swiftly to a frown. "I'm worried, Gab...Laz. This is not worth dying for. If anyone pulls a gun, you stick your hands way in the air, okay?"

"Absolutely. But no one is going to point a gun at me. Stop talking about bad stuff, please? I'm shutting off the phone and I don't want to look at the news again until tomorrow."

After alternating between long, hot showers and guarding the campsite, they sat at their picnic table, pretending to read. Gabriel was visibly tense, he stared unfocused at the same page for minutes without blinking and in her peripheral vision, Adrienne saw his hands tremble. His nerves were making her nervous. She wanted to go for a walk but what if something happened while they were separated? *If he is arrested, I need to be by his side. They need to know I'm an accomplice and not a victim.*

She laid her book face down on the splintered wood and stood to pace the road, as far as she could go without losing sight of him. She practiced her 'man-walk', pointing her feet straight at each step to avoid any hint of a feminine sway. On her fourth pass, he rose to join her.

"We should try to sleep as soon as it's dark. Tomorrow is another long day of driving."

She nodded, no need for a reply as they had already discussed this. But to be contrary, she said, "Why wait? Let's just leave now."

"I want an early start so the lines are shorter, and we can cross most of the country in one day. We can't drive in the dark. It's not safe. We cross the border at dawn and soon we'll be home."

"Home? I can't wait to hear the name of my new home." Adrienne gave him a meaningful, pointless glare. He wouldn't say it until he was ready. Gabriel might be the only person she had ever met more stubborn than herself.

They were in bed by dark, the cell phone by Gabriel's head with the alarm set for four AM. They lay awake but still. Not fidgeting, not talking. Adrienne wore her travel clothes, black track pants and t-shirt. She lay on her back, hands clasped across her stomach, staring up. She would remember she was trying to fall asleep and close her eyes, only to have them pop open again. She lay her arms down at her side, focusing on the breathing tricks that helped her fall asleep, flinching, then relaxing when Gabriel's fingers curled gently into hers. Not so much holding hands as simply touching, and that was enough to calm her.

CHAPTER TWELVE
NEW WORLD IN MY VIEW

Adrienne was awake when the cell phone chimed its alarm. Gabriel must have also been awake because the noise stopped instantly. They rose together and broke camp in silence, the tension crackling between them felt like electric shocks every time they touched. They choked down an energy bar with a warm bottle of water as they rolled out of the campground.

Less than an hour later, they idled in line at the port of entry. It reminded Adrienne of the sprawling toll plaza on the Bay Bridge, and how many hours of her life she had lost trying to cross the various bridges in California. Even at five AM, the wait at the border was nerve-wracking. Dull gray sky brightened to pink and blue, German Shepherds skulked, and machine-gun-toting border guards were in constant motion, looking as suspicious and mean as the dogs.

Finally, it was their turn at the red light/green light. All their wishes, prayers, crossed fingers and toes failed—they got a red light. "No big deal, we're fine, no need to panic." Gabriel steered the car to one side.

"I'm not panicking, you're panicking," Adrienne hissed from the side of her mouth.

A short, skinny man with deeply bronzed skin and a bushy mustache approached the driver's window. His name tag said Rodriguez. Unsmiling, he said, "Good morning, may I see your passports, license, registration and proof of insurance." His brisk voice made this a statement instead of a question.

Gabriel passed over the documents.

"Anything to declare?" asked Rodriguez, flipping through the paperwork. "Animals, drugs, more than ten thousand dollars in cash?"

"No, sir."

"Purpose for entering Mexico?"

"Vacation."

"Can you unlock the back door, please. And the trunk."

Gabriel complied. He looked straight ahead, keeping his hands in plain sight on top of the steering wheel. Adrienne sat ramrod straight, trying to look taller and manly. Rodriquez squeezed both backpacks before opening them. After a cursory look inside, he dropped them in the back seat and moved around to the trunk. The sounds of the border guard opening the well for the spare tire were as terrifying as footsteps from inside a house where you thought you were alone. He closed the trunk and came back to the window.

"Camping?"

"We hope not, the tent is for emergencies."

"You can't pitch a tent on the side of the highway, you know? It can be dangerous at night."

"Yes, sir. If we had to camp we would find a safe spot."

Rodriguez nodded and looked at the passport cards in his hand. "Andrew?" He leaned down to get a better look.

"Yes, sir?" in a cracked whisper. Adrienne put her hand to her throat. In a husky, low voice, she croaked. "Sore throat, sorry."

"Is he sick?" Rodriguez said to Gabriel.

"No, sir. He was sick last week. It's a sore throat from coughing."

"He's quite small for twenty-two," Rodriguez frowned at passport.

Gabriel leaned towards the open window and cupped his hand around his mouth to murmur, "He's very sensitive about that, sir."

He gave Adrienne a long searching stare. She kept her face somber and her eyes squinted slightly. Rodriguez handed the stack of documents back to Gabriel. Gabriel clasped them and Rodriguez—still gripping the papers—said, "Did you vote for Trump?"

Gabriel's eyes went round, startled. "No, he's a horrible man."

Rodriguez scowled. "I like him." After a heavy silence, he laughed and released his hold on the papers. "Just kidding, everyone hates that fat fool. Enjoy your vacation." He waved them on.

And just like that, they were in Mexico.

Adrienne turned on the phone to find the first Pemex station outside of Tijuana, Gabriel wanted out of the busy town before stopping for gas. Even with baseball caps and sunglasses they felt exposed, and the fewer eyeballs on them the better. She opened a map app. "I have to know where we're going, down Baja or the mainland?"

"Mainland."

"When are you going to tell me the name of the town?"

"After we get gas. I want to buy a paper map so we can leave the phone off."

She glared at him. "It's always 'after this I'll tell you' and 'after that I'll tell you' and I don't know how we're supposed to trust each other when you hide everything from me. You leave me in the dark and feed me bullshit as if I were a brainless mushroom." It came out in a furious burst and had no effect; Gabriel kept his gaze roaming across the crowded streets. Adrienne stabbed at the phone screen. "Stay on Highway Twenty until you get out of town, about ten miles," she said. "The street view shows a market around the corner, maybe we can find some hot food." Tamales, enchiladas, chile relleno, something hot and fresh and not from a can.

Before she powered down the phone, Adrienne did an internet search for Gabriel's name. The article had been picked up by the national wires and was trending on Twitter and Reddit where posts mentioned the stolen money and theories had gone wild. The most popular theory: three people stole a bag of money from two other thieves and ran off to Mexico. "People think we're a throuple." Adrienne said through clenched teeth. It was fine if the world thought she was fucking Gabriel, but not Cindy. *I wouldn't touch that woman with a ten-foot pole.* "As usual, the media gets the facts wrong."

"A throuple?" Gabriel flashed her a quick grin. "I prefer people think of me as a man having sex with two beautiful women as opposed to a serial killer."

"Shut up and drive." Adrienne glanced from her phone to the street signs. "Your stop is right there. Do you want to use the phone before I shut it off?"

"No, I need to keep an eye on this guy pumping our gas. Can you search for a money changing kiosk? We need to stock up on pesos."

The station attendant was happy to take their US dollars. This close to the border, American money was not unusual, but they definitely did not get the best exchange rate. The tank took most of a hundred-dollar-bill that Gabriel produced from his shoe, drying it on the sunny dashboard before handing the limp greenback to the attendant.

"There's a place called The Money Center a kilometer or so down on your right. Turn at Gustavo Salinas." Adrienne powered off the phone and tucked it away. "Now I suppose you can't tell me the name of the town until we have pesos."

"After I get my change, I will park over there because it looks like a spot with no cameras. Then I will go inside to buy a map. I'll show you on the map when I come back." Gabriel spoke slowly and carefully, as if talking to a child, and clutched his shoulder when she punched him. "Hey! Don't hit your favorite cousin."

"Don't get too caught up in this role play, cuz," Adrienne drawled.

Gabriel tipped the attendant, leaning towards generous but not enough to be memorable. He drove to the far side of the gas station and parked near a rickety fence.

"Wait here. Don't try to escape," he said with a smirk.

"Go buy a damn map." Adrienne locked the door behind him and kept her eyes moving, scanning the bustling service station parking lot, the busy streets and crowded sidewalks. "Come on, come on, come on," she said under her breath when it seemed he had been gone too long. Finally, Gabriel appeared, ambling casually across the parking lot, carrying a greasy white paper sack. She popped the lock on the driver's door.

He slid in, closed and locked the door. "They don't sell maps, I had to walk around the corner." He dropped the map in his lap and handed her the warm bag as the smells reached her nose.

"I smell bacon." Her mouth filled with saliva, and she reached inside the bag with a whimper.

"Ginormous breakfast burritos." Gabriel grinned. "You won't have to eat again for a week."

"Sweet Jesus, and a cold soda. Did we die? Am I in heaven?" Adrienne took an enormous chomp; the burrito was filled with bacon, sausage, scrambled eggs, fried potatoes and cheese. It was mind-blowingly delicious. While chewing, she pointed at the map. "Show me."

Gabriel carefully set aside his two-hander of a burrito, wiped his hands on a tissue-thin napkin, and unfolded the map, keeping it below the window line. He refolded the map until all of Mexico was hidden except the western coastline of the mainland, even Baja was folded under. He tapped the top of the folded rectangle. "We are here, between Tijuana and Mexicali. We're going here." He traced his finger down Highway 15, down, down, down, south past Mazatlán and stopped on Puerto Vallarta.

"Puerto Vallarta is not a tiny Mexican village," Adrienne said. "Do you have to lie about everything?"

"I've never lied to you. Look closer." Gabriel folded the map and held it higher. He tapped a dot east of Vallarta. "San Sebastian del Oeste." The Spanish words rolled off his tongue like music. "An official pueblos magicos, a magical town. Remote, but with enough tourism for gringos to blend in. It's truly a magical place."

She traced her finger down the lengthy map distance from where they sat to where they were going. "How far is that? It looks really far."

"About two thousand kilometers."

"In American, please."

"Fourteen hundred miles. It will take two long days, possibly three. We can only drive during daylight.

"Two or three more days in the car?" Adrienne moaned. She took another hefty bite of her burrito which had lost some of its flavor with the ashy taste of impatience in her mouth.

Gabriel wrapped up half of his burrito and stuck it back in the bag. He wiped his hands on his pants and his mouth on his sleeve, the napkins long since disintegrated. Glancing around the street, he said, "Keep an eye out, I have to get into the money bag."

He opened the back door before she could react. Adrienne tried to look in every direction at once without moving her head; her pleasantly-full-of-burrito belly suddenly felt full of cement. Gabriel rustled around inside the gym bag and furtively slid something in the gap between the front seats. Adrienne looked down and her cement stomach filled with lead. Gabriel slid back into the driver seat, locked the doors and showed her a slim stack of hundreds in a paper band.

"Ten thousand. We'll exchange this at a few places along the way so we have plenty of pesos, but I want you to hide some of these bills in different places on your body, in your clothes, your backpack. In case we're robbed or get separated."

Adrienne took the cash, stared fiercely into his eyes and pointed at the space between the front seats. "A gun, Gabriel? You brought a gun across the Mexican border?"

"If they found the money, we were already in trouble. I had to take the chance. It's better to be armed where we're going." He pointedly ignored her glare and tucked his share of the bills away before merging into traffic. On the freeway, he set the cruise control for seventy.

"What else are you hiding from me?" she demanded.

"Nothing, I'm an open book now." Gabriel patted her knee, flashing a grin. "What do you want to know? I'll spill my guts, okay? I grew up in Berkeley. My dad had a propane business, my mom was a first-grade teacher. When I was eight, she left us. After high school I went to San Francisco State to get a degree so when I enlisted in the Navy, I could join as an officer. I once thought flying was all I needed to be happy."

She stared at his profile as he reeled off facts in a dry monotone. "Did you see combat?"

He hesitated before replying, eyes on the road. "I saw some things." Gabriel flicked a quick glance her way. "I don't like to talk about it."

She watched his face for a long moment before turning her gaze to the side window. "Understood," she said. "We all have things we don't like to talk about."

"I thought I could put in my twenty years and get a pension, but I hated it. I left after eight years, took my savings and backpacked for three years."

"Three years? Backpacked to where, the moon?"

"All different places. The Appalachian trail first because I heard it was best for beginners, then the Pacific Crest. My last big trip was the Camino de Santiago, over five hundred miles on foot. I made that trip last for six months."

"No girlfriends through all these years besides Cindy?" Adrienne couldn't keep the sneer from her voice when she said that woman's name.

"Nothing serious. Cindy wasn't supposed to be serious. I was trying to figure out what to do with my life and starting a family wasn't on my radar. Since high school, my future was pinned to a military career I no longer wanted. I spent a lot of time wondering why my mom left, why my dad wouldn't talk about her. She's the big mystery of my life. I envy people with close family."

"You're not close to your dad?"

"We're in touch but I wouldn't call us close. I'm angry with him for not talking to me about my mom, for not trying harder to find her and make her come home. I know it's pointless to hold that anger for all these years but it lives inside me."

After a long silence, she said in a low voice, "Was your father mean? Did he hit you?"

"No more than any other dad."

There were moments in Adrienne's life when she thought maybe she was lucky to not to have a dad. "Did he hit your mom?"

Gabriel didn't speak for several miles. "I saw him hit her a couple of times," he spoke in broken syllables, painfully pulling the words from his chest. "There were times she had bruises. But she could have made him go to counseling." A muscle in his jaw jumped. "She could have taken me with her. She left without saying goodbye."

"Did you ever think that she didn't leave of her own free will?"

He glanced at her, confused. "What do you mean? Like she was kidnapped?"

"No..." Adrienne said, hesitating. "Like she was killed?"

"You're suggesting my father murdered my mother?"

"Did he report her missing?"

"I don't know. I was eight, heartbroken and fucking furious. I don't remember police at the house or anything like that."

"I'm sorry, that's the way my mind works. I watch too many murder shows."

He gave her a flippant wave and kept his gaze on the road, the muscle flexing in his jaw. She turned back to the view. The passing countryside was nothing to look at—flat, dry and brown with occasional humps of small rocky hills and a row of power lines stretching for miles like a stark-naked forest. She looked away from the desolate landscape to his granite face.

"If it makes you feel better," Adrienne said. "My mother was a crack whore and my father died in prison before I was born. Your childhood sounds like a dream to me."

He turned his head to search her face.

"Eyes on the road, cuz. I'm not telling you this so you'll feel sorry for me. I'm giving you perspective on the different varieties of crappy parents. I would appreciate it if you didn't tell Cindy. This isn't something I normally share."

"I won't tell her." Gabriel's voice was gruff. "But if you ever want to talk, I'm here to listen."

She reached for the radio. "I'm tired of talking."

CHAPTER THIRTEEN
CHEESEBURGER IN PARADISE

Dustin and Jarrett showed the photo of Cindy to every employee in Walmart and every customer who would stop long enough to look, until management chased them out. They accosted people in the parking lot with Cindy's photo for a few minutes, but it was blazing hot and steamy, and the Bay Area boys wilted in the oppressive humidity. They snuck back inside Walmart and bought two mandarin Jarritos and a bag of chicharonnes before taking a break under a tree.

"What next?" Dustin said, glum-faced. "If we lose her trail here, what's our next step?"

Jarrett ran his salty fingers through his hair, sticky with perspiration, red curls inching towards clownish. "I don't know, but I'm sick of Vallarta. I'm sick of being sweaty all the time."

"Cindy took the bus to Walmart because she wanted to buy something, right? And after she buys the thing, where does she go? She gets on another bus." Dustin felt like a cartoon character with a light bulb over his head. "She was probably tired of being sweaty, too. Let's go back to the bus stop and show her picture to the drivers."

"I need to be standing in the ocean with a beer in my hand," Jarrett whined, using the sleeve of his shirt to wipe his brow.

Across hectares of sweltering asphalt parking lot, they made their way to the covered bus stop, only marginally cooler under the shade. Dustin and Jarrett took turns showing Cindy's picture to the drivers. They showed it to people waiting to get on the buses and people who got off the buses. The comments were repeated with boring regularity: She looks familiar. Is she famous? She's a movie star? Most people would glance at the photo, shake their head and walk by.

A bus pulled up and Jarrett poked Dustin's leg. "Your turn."

Dustin waited for the passengers to get off and on before he stepped on the bus, handing the driver the photo of Cindy. "Pardon me, sir, have you seen this woman?"

This driver took the photo, his dour face cracked a smile. "She's very tall?" His gesture was eerily reminiscent of the driver who dropped them at Walmart. "I remember her. When she got on the bus, she gave me a piece of candy. Her smile, wow!" The driver shook his hand like his fingers were on fire. "She gave everyone candy, all down the rows."

"Do you remember where she got off the bus?"

"Where all the tourists get off the bus. Sayulita."

"Is that a beach?" Jarrett said.

"Si, a beautiful beach. Seventy pesos."

"Sweet, that's like seven bucks US," Dustin said. He hauled his wallet from his front pocket and paid the driver.

They were lucky to get seats. In the ninety unairconditioned minutes it took for them to arrive in Sayulita, the bus filled with sweaty people like sardines in a sticky, smelly can. 'Standing room only' didn't begin to describe it. Jarrett stuck his head towards the window that only rolled down halfway. Dustin in the aisle seat shrank against Jarrett's side, the standing people nearly landing in his lap with every bounce, jounce and bumpy stop-and-go movement of the bus. Getting off the bus was as irritating as getting off a plane.

"What is going on up there?" Jarrett rose halfway and craned his neck down the crowded aisle. "Just get up and walk out, it's easy. Go, people, go."

His face eye-level with every slowly passing crotch, Dustin sat with his head averted until he could slide out of the seat. They followed signs to the town square plaza, five blocks from the beach. Breezy and at least ten degrees cooler than Vallarta, Sayulita smelled of the salty ocean, fried food, and a medley of booze, as if the tourists wore their alcoholic beverages as body spray. The narrow, cobbled streets were lined with vendors, some offering remnant souvenirs of the long past Cinco de Mayo. They stopped at the first bar that advertised air conditioning and cold beer. The a/c claim was dubious, but the Corona was ice cold.

"We need to find a room for the night." Jarrett rolled the wet bottle across his sweaty face.

"Rooms will be expensive here, and we're running out of money fast." Dustin waggled his fingers at the bartender who brought them two more dripping Coronas. "Muchas gracias, amigo," Dustin butchered the Spanish language. "Can you recommend a cheap room for the night?"

"My brother's house might have a bed," replied the bartender. He wiped his hands on a grimy towel hanging from his pocket.

"Oh! Your brother rents rooms? Interesting."

"No, it's a hostel. It's called My Brother's House. Men only hostel."

"You mean sleep in a room with a bunch of strangers?" Jarrett's face twisted in revulsion. "What's the next cheapest option?"

"Try Expedia, man, I'm not a travel agent," the bartender grumbled and walked away.

"Fuck you," Jarrett mumbled very low under his breath. He pulled out his smartphone and found an apartment that came with a queen bed and a futon for less than forty bucks a night. Without consulting Dustin, he booked three nights. "Let's pay this guy and head to the beach."

"We're here to find Adrienne and Cindy, not party."

"Let's go to the beach and cool off." Jarrett was already standing. "We can show her picture around later."

With a generous tip, the bartender agreed to mix them a triple margarita on the rocks and put it in a big paper cup with a straw to go. Strolling down cobblestone streets, sipping their cocktails, Dustin and Jarrett passed row after row of colorful concrete buildings that housed restaurants, bars, and shops selling everything from gourmet snack food to jewelry to snorkel gear and tacky t-shirts. The pathways to the beach were crammed with vendors wanting your money, and shoppers eager to part with their money. The two men slipped under a shady palm-frond palapa and settled on the hard wooden bench with identical gusty sighs.

Jarrett reached under the table and slipped off his Nikes and sweaty socks. "My feet are shouting thank you right now."

Dustin closed his eyes and moaned in pleasure, wiggling his own aching feet in the coarse sand. "My toes are having multiple orgasms."

"Excuse me, gentlemen."

Dustin opened his eyes to see a young woman in a tropical print tank top and tight white shorts, holding an order pad. Her name tag said Dena.

"Do you need to see a menu?" Dena asked.

"Nah, we're good." Jarrett raised his extra-large paper cup.

"You can't sit here unless you buy something, sir. This is a restaurant."

Dustin blurted, "A bucket of Coronas and two cheeseburgers, please."

Jarrett waited until Dena had sashayed off before lifting his cup and hissing, "We have a half pint of tequila in here, why do we need six Coronas?"

"I don't plan on leaving this spot," said Dustin, scrubbing his bare feet in the warm sand. He tapped the envelope containing the photos. "We can't leave this lying around, so we go to the water one at a time and camp out here until we're ready to go to the room or they kick us out."

"A cheeseburger sounds pretty good." Jarrett grudgingly added, "I guess you have a good idea now and then."

"All of my ideas are better than you telling Gabriel we stole Fife's money," Dustin said around the straw. He sucked in a deep gulp of the tequila-heavy concoction and coughed. "Where is this place you rented?"

"The app says it's a ten-minute walk."

* * *

When Dena asked them to leave three hours later, they were sloshing drunk, soaking wet, sandy and sunburned. Jarrett mapped directions to the apartment. Maybe it was a ten-minute walk in the daylight and sober. Maybe. Straight up Gringo Hill in the dark they stumbled, sweating, falling, and cursing creatively on the path that switched randomly from dirt to gravel to cobblestones to brick. Jarrett consulting his map app again and again until they found the place.

"This is it." He tapped a code into an electronic lock on the ornate steel gate.

"Twenty-five and a half? Is this a door to Hogwarts?" Dustin giggled. The last Corona was warm, flat foam on the bottom of his soggy paper cup. He sucked up the dregs loudly.

"Shhh...no, it's a basement apartment." Jarrett shined his flashlight down the tiled walkway and tapped another code at the front door. He flipped a switch on the wall and a dim, yellowish overhead light revealed a low-ceilinged cinderblock room painted ancient aqua. A queen size bed and a musty futon comprised the furniture.

Dustin checked the settings on the mini-split and cranked the thermostat down to sixty-five, holding his hand in the thin trickle of air. "I don't think this works." He wrinkled his nose at the predominant scent in the room of damp and rot, with low notes of fish, dirty feet, and ass. "I'm rinsing off before bed."

The bathroom was a fully tiled shower/toilet combo. Dustin hunkered under the lukewarm dribble and tried to clean his crusty body and clothes, using the provided miniature bar of soap stamped 'Best Western' and an unmarked plastic bottle of shampoo in Pert green. He shut off the water, opened a plastic storage tub, pulled out a thin towel and wrapped it around his waist.

Jarrett lolled on the bed. "How was the shower?"

"Better than nothing." Dustin unfolded the futon and shook out the sheets, checking for bugs. He brushed off some sand. "At least it's only one night."

"It's for three nights," Jarrett said casually. "I like it here and we deserve a break."

"We're supposed to be looking for Cindy and Adrienne," Dustin barked. "And we're on a tight budget."

"We can spend a little money. Tomorrow we'll pick up a few things and show her picture around. She probably shopped while she was here."

"Yeah, her and a million other tall blondes from California. This is a tourist town." Dustin squeezed his sopping clothes and hung them over the edge of a curtain rod. The curtain covered cinderblock instead of a window, a trick to make you forget you're in a basement.

"This is where Cindy's trail brought us, and I think we should see this as a sign. The universe wants us to relax." Jarrett hoisted his bulky frame upright, stripped and opened the door to shake the sand off his clothes before he padded naked to the bathroom.

Dustin covered his face with both hands. "Why am I friends with you?"

*   *   *

Walking back to town the next morning in wet clothes was a fuggy, chafing experience. The men found a shop selling cheap t-shirts and board shorts and gave up another fifty bucks to buy dry clothes. They stuffed their wet clothes in the plastic shopping bag and stopped at a fancy coffee shop, a place a spoiled rich girl might visit. A lanky, dark-skinned woman with curly black hair, heavily outlined eyes and the nametag Estelle took their order for two extra-large lattes. When she came back, Dustin slipped Cindy's photo from the envelope.

"Have you seen this woman?"

Estelle glanced at the photo sideways, not taking it from his hand. With a skeptical frown, she said, "Who is she?"

"My sister," Dustin said. It seemed the easiest lie and most inclined to generate a sympathetic response.

"Which one of you is adopted?" Estelle snickered. "Sure, I remember her. Sexy girl. Tall. Sweet, too. She seemed well-traveled, you know? Like, she knew things the typical tourist wouldn't."

"Such as?" Jarrett leaned forward on his elbows.

"She asked if we served Cafe Altura. It's a local coffee, only grown in one place."

"Where?" Jarrett prodded.

"San Sebastian del Oeste."

"How do you spell that?" Dustin asked.

Estelle gave him some hard side-eye and waggled her fingers for Jarrett's phone, tapped the screen and handed it back. "Can I get you anything else? Or will you be leaving soon?" She gave more side-eye to their plastic bags.

"We're leaving," said Dustin. On the sidewalk he said to Jarrett, "We need to find a cheaper place to eat. French toast was like eighteen bucks in there."

After a quick breakfast at McDonald's, they began showing Cindy's photo down one side of the street, up the other side and on to the next block. The shops were close together and there were a lot of them, the process was tedious and the lack of response dispiriting.

"The only lead we have is this San Sebastian place." Jarrett stared at his phone as they ping-ponged down the crowded sidewalk.

"That's not a lead," Dustin scoffed. "She likes their coffee."

"Got any other ideas?"

"No, but we have a lot of places to check."

At happy hour, they called it a day and rushed back to the palapa to lounge at the beach drinking Coronas and scarfing cheeseburgers until they stumbled back up Gringo Hill to their smelly basement apartment.

CHAPTER FOURTEEN
SORRY NOT SORRY

On a deserted stretch of Highway 2 South between Sonoyta and Caborca, where the road rises and the steepening terrain offers more hills and less civilization, the left rear tire on the Honda blew. Gabriel wrestled the car to a wide, flat spot in the sand, behind a low screen of whatever scrubby bushes and trees survive in this heartless place.

"Fuck." He unlocked his seat belt. "You'll need to get out and stand guard."

"Stand guard?" Adrienne narrowed her eyes. "You mean, watch you change a tire with a gun in my hand?"

"Absolutely, yes. Do you know how to shoot this?" He handed her the flat, black pistol.

"Nine-millimeter, thirteen round magazine." She eyeballed the gun before reluctantly accepting it. "I know how to use it."

Gabriel gave her a long, appraising look and threw open the car door. "Stand on the passenger side, keep your eyes moving. Yell if you see anything strange, cars slowing down, people staring, stopping." He unloaded the spare, jack, and tire iron from the trunk as he spoke.

She paced along the passenger side of the car. The low, scruffy trees and bushes around them made good camouflage and the speeding cars on the highway didn't slow. The Honda rose high in one corner, like a dog hiking its leg. Gabriel grunted and swore, metal clanked, the car trembled and shook. Lightning fast, the jack was released, and the car lowered to all four tires, one smaller than the others.

"Impressive," Adrienne said. "I'm fast but not that fast."

The words were no sooner out of her mouth when a giant blue Ford pickup, lifted on tires of ludicrous size, swooped in behind the car, kicking up a fan of sand. From the other side of the Honda, Gabriel said something in Spanish and straightened. Adrienne went on high alert; moving to the far side of the open passenger door, she thumbed off the safety and racked a bullet into the chamber. Two men wearing plaid shirts and predatory grins jumped out of the truck.

"Hola, amigos," said the driver in a thick accent. He walked towards Gabriel with his hands behind his back. "Car trouble? You need some help?"

"Nope. Just changing a flat tire." Gabriel's jaw flexed.

The passenger shifted his eyes from Adrienne to Gabriel to his buddy, shuffling his feet nervously. His hands dangled at his sides, fingers flexing.

The driver bared his teeth in a crocodile smile. "You don't need no help? Good, good." He took another step closer, and Gabriel raised the tire iron level with his waist. The driver's smile disappeared. "Good thing you don't need no help, hombre, but I do. I need some help." The driver whipped his hand from behind his back and pointed a silver revolver at Gabriel's head.

Adrienne didn't hesitate. The moment she saw the sun glint and spark off metal, she straight-armed the nine-millimeter over the top of the Honda, sighted it in the middle of the driver's chest and pulled the trigger. The report echoed as Gabriel clocked the guy upside the head with the tire iron. The passenger turned to run, and this time Adrienne hesitated. She heard Gabriel shout, "Shoot him!" She shot the man in the back, and he crumpled to the ground, unmoving. She shot a man in the back, a man who tried to rob them and tried to run away. A man who had a mom and maybe a girlfriend or sister who might miss him. A man who would have let his friend rob them and possibly kill them. She stood frozen, every nerve numb. *I had to do it. I had no choice.*

Gabriel wiped the bloody tire iron on the driver's shirt and tightened the last lug nuts while muttering, "Let's go, let's go, let's go."

Like a machine that had been activated, Adrienne sprang into action. She knocked the driver's door closed with her shoulder and dragged the dead man to the far side of the truck, grunting and straining with effort, blocking the image of his crushed head and bloody chest. Relieved that the other man was already lying outside the view of passing traffic, she slammed the truck's passenger door before returning to the Honda, breathing heavily and shaking from head to toe like a skinny tree in a high wind.

Gabriel dropped the jack and tire iron in the trunk and barked, "Let's go, let's go, before someone stops."

The car was moving but Gabriel continued to mutter, "let's go let's go" until they reached highway speed. It was only then, after a long, long look out the back window, did Adrienne allow herself to unclench her stiff muscles.

"Are you sure they're dead?" She hugged herself, sweat freezing in the arctic blast of air pouring from the dash.

"They looked dead to me," Gabriel said.

"I killed two people." Teeth chattering and struggling not to vomit, she roughly cranked the a/c down a few notches and cracked the window to bring in the warm outside air. Her heart thudded hard enough to bruise her insides, and every muscle trembled tautly, like cables of high-tension wire in a storm. "I killed two people," she repeated in a monotone.

"I think the first guy was alive when I bashed his brains in," Gabriel said in the same dull voice.

Acid in her stomach clawed its way up her throat. She gulped from a lukewarm plastic bottle of water. After ten or so miles of silence, she said, "Now what?"

"Nothing changes. The spare tire will last until Hermosillo. We spend the night, buy a new tire, and drive more tomorrow. The plan is to get our asses to San Sebastian in one piece."

*　*　*

Adrienne's thoughts circled like a skip on a vinyl record. *I killed two people. I killed two people.* They drove in tense silence for miles, eyes in constant motion, checking the rearview mirrors, peering up and down cross streets. She felt like there should be a squadron of screaming police cars behind them, or a helicopter. The bandit's truck was screened from passing traffic and people were not inclined to stop on that road, but it seemed impossible that two men died back there and no one was chasing them.

Highway 2 doglegged east at Caborca, putting the setting sun at their backs. Gabriel finally broke the silence. "Where did you learn about guns?"

She flicked her eyes at the space where the pistol waited. "One of Mom's boyfriends. One of many, but this one guy, Dennis, he stuck around for a couple of years. Dennis was certified nuts about guns and an angry drunk, the exact type of man who shouldn't own guns. He liked to show off his arsenal and I caught on quick. Knowing how to use guns has come in handy for me in past situations." She didn't look his way. "It came in handy today."

"No shit," Gabriel breathed. He rested a hand on her fidgeting knee for a quick squeeze. "You did the right thing, Adrienne. You saved my life and your own. If those guys knew you were a woman..."

He didn't have to finish. She was painfully aware of her gender's vulnerability.

"What other desperate criminal skills do you have?" He squeezed her knee again and left his hand there.

She leaned in, touching his forearm. The crackle of his skin on hers made goosebumps return. "Standard stuff. I can change a tire and drive a stick-shift, ride a motorcycle, and craft a delicious meal from other people's garbage. All handy skills for desperadoes."

He scanned her face, turned his eyes back to the road. "What's your mother's name?"

"Celeste."

"And where is Celeste these days?"

"She died ten years ago. Hep C and alcohol destroyed her liver. She wouldn't let anyone put her on a donor list, said she deserved what she did to herself." Adrienne rolled her head in a circle, rubbing her stiff neck. "One of the few times I agreed with her."

"Sounds like you didn't get to be a kid."

She glanced at him; he kept his eyes straight ahead. Turning back to the passenger window, she said, "I was never a kid. I had to fend for myself, and sometimes for her. I worried they would put me back in foster care, and I worried when they let her keep me."

"How did you meet Dustin?"

"I scraped together enough money to get a real estate license, but I couldn't find an agency to take me on, so I got a job with a staging company, decorating the listed properties so the house looks like HGTV. Dustin was a client. I had met him at two or maybe three jobs before he asked me out. We've been together since. Well, until you kidnapped me."

"Sounds like you didn't know him long before you got married."

"I move fast when I need to." She saw no point in lying. "I tried to make myself love him, but I married him because I needed a safe place to live. He had money, and I knew he would make more." Running a finger across the knuckles of Gabriel's hand, she said, "I married him because he was soft. He seemed like a man who wouldn't hurt me."

Gabriel shot her a look. "I'll never be able to tell you how sorry I am that I hurt you."

"Yeah, I know." She patted his hand, still resting on her knee. "You told me that already. And Dustin found his own way of hurting me so I wasn't as smart as I thought I was."

They drove in silence for several minutes before he spoke. "No siblings, grandparents?"

"Nobody but you, cuz. You're all the family I have left."

"Cindy will be your family. I think you'll like her."

Adrienne turned on the radio and shifted in her seat, shaking his hand off her knee. They didn't speak again until they passed a sign that said **Hermosillo 17 km.**

"Keep your eye out for a dumpy motel, single story, with parking by the door."

"Do you want me to turn on the phone and do a search?"

"The kind of place I want won't be on the internet."

A few meters before the first stoplight on the northern edge of town, Adrienne jerked her thumb, signaling him to turn right. A dirt-colored adobe motel with a faded red tile roof was partially hidden by a Pemex. Gabriel pulled into the gas station and scoped out the area while the attendant pumped gas. The motel was close enough to the gas station to benefit from the glow of industrial lighting but situated where the station's cameras didn't reach the interior courtyard. With an easy hop back on the highway, the motel was positioned for a quick getaway.

Gabriel checked them into a room with two double beds and the office was happy to take his cash, no credit card required. He backed the car into the space marked **8**.

"Eight is my lucky number," Adrienne said. She pointed at the gun. "You getting that?"

"I need to carry the money. Can you get the backpacks and gun so we can do this in one trip?"

Double-checking the safety on the pistol, Adrienne tucked the gun in her waistband and bloused her shirt to cover it. She twisted in the seat and hooked the straps of both backpacks on her left arm and motioned for the key. "I'll have the door open by the time you get the bag out."

If they had practiced it a dozen times, transferring their belongings to the motel room could not have been quicker or smoother. They saw no one. Gabriel shoved the bag of money under the bed farthest from the door and collapsed on top of the bed, arms and legs stretched wide.

"What a fucking day," he groaned.

Adrienne dropped the backpacks on the floor between the two beds and went to check out the bathroom. It was cleaner than she expected, considering the gritty exterior, and she decided a shower was the next thing on her agenda. She felt crusted in dirt and sweat. And blood, even though she had no visible stains on her murderous hands. *Out, damned spot.* "I'm taking a shower," she said, digging in the backpack for toiletries.

The water was just the way she liked it, scalding, and she took her time, scrubbing her skin nearly raw. She stepped out of the shower and wrapped herself in the hotel's flimsy excuse for a towel, skin glowing pink. When she opened the bathroom door, steam wafted into the room and she had a misty view of Gabriel stripped down to his boxer briefs, splayed across the bed, one arm curled over his eyes.

"Your turn," Adrienne said in a whisper. Her eyes traveled across his body; he looked vulnerable and trusting and possibly asleep since he didn't reply. She dropped the towel, walked to the bed naked and straddled him.

He jerked his arm away from his face. "Adrienne..."

Her bare butt resting low on his belly, she leaned forward to cup his hairy, pronounced pecs, pinched his nipples playfully and laughed when he grabbed her hands.

"Adrienne, you know I'm with Cindy."

"Not today." She collapsed, crushing him the best she could with her small self, and kissed his whiskery jawline. "Today you're with me. I want you. I've wanted you for a long time. I killed for you. I saved your life. The least you can do is fuck me." She pressed her face into his neck, biting not-too-gently on his salty, rough skin. "Fuck me, goddammit. You owe me."

Gabriel cupped her face in his hands and gazed into her eyes. Chest to chest, their hearts thudding a primitive beat in rhythm. He kissed her gently, then fervently, hot and wet, exploring tongue and lips. His hands skimmed across her naked back, light as feathers. When he came up for air, he said in a low voice, "Tonight, I am yours."

CHAPTER FIFTEEN
YOU KNOW I'M NO GOOD

"I've wanted you since the moment I saw you," Gabriel mumbled against her throat between kisses. His hands caressed her damp naked skin, inch-by-inch, his mouth everywhere he could reach while holding her tightly to his chest. His mouth descended wetly on one nipple, then the other, clutching her body close while she moved sinuously against him. "I'll never hurt you again." He worked his mouth down her body, kissing and licking. "Let me make love to you, Adrienne." He didn't wait for permission before burying his face between her legs.

Twisting her fingers into his hair, she forced herself to focus on sensations, not emotions or thoughts or worries or regrets. *I am an animal receiving pleasure from a fellow beast.* She pulled a pillow over her face to muffle animal noises while he tortured her with lips and teeth and tongue and fingers. The first orgasm pulled her inside out, the second turned her upside down. "Stop," she moaned. "It's too much, it's not enough, I need you inside me." She yanked on his hair, grinding herself against the hard bones of his face.

He crawled slowly up her body, kissing her quivering flesh all the way up to her mouth. "I don't have any condoms, beautiful lady."

She gripped him through his underwear. "I don't care. I can't get pregnant. Do you have any dirty dick diseases? No? Then get these shorts off."

Tortuously slow, excruciatingly deep, he gave her everything she asked for and more. The sheets of one bed twisted into knots, wet with sweat. They showered together, lingering touches and kisses, rubbing slick, soapy bodies together, and climbed into the other bed to sleep, limbs twined together. He took his hands off her body long enough to set the alarm on the cell phone before pulling her back into his arms.

The alarm woke them at five. Without speaking, they leaped out of bed and hurried to get on the road. Gear by the door, Gabriel peered outside, motioned to Adrienne, and she dashed to the passenger side to drop the backpacks inside while he stowed the bag of money under the back seat. By five-fifteen, they were cruising at sixty-nine miles per hour headed due south on Highway 15.

Gabriel rested a heavy hand on her thigh. "Can you look at the map, reinita, and tell me how many more miles to San Sebastian?"

"What is reinita?" Adrienne eyeballed him quizzically as she unfolded the map.

He took his eyes off the road to send a sexy smile her direction. "Little queen."

"I hate to be called little." She suppressed a smile. *But little queen isn't so bad.* Amusement faded as she calculated the discouraging distance. "Almost thirteen hundred kilometers. We can't do that before dark."

He chewed the inside of his cheek. "How far to Mazatlán?"

She ran her finger down Highway 15. "Almost nine hundred kilometers."

"We'll stop this side of Mazatlán tonight, that will put us in San Sebastian tomorrow afternoon." He ran his hand down her thigh, a quick caress before returning his hands and eyes to driving. "One more night together, reinita. Tomorrow we start our new life."

She didn't turn her gaze from the passenger window. "I got what I wanted. We can go back to being friends now." Staring at the glass, she shifted her focus from near—her blank expression and still-startling short hair reflected in the window—to far: the hot, dry, desolate landscape, as forbidding as the surface of Mars. *I knew it was a lie when he said he would never hurt me again.* Tomorrow she would stand aside while Cindy and Gabriel had their reunion. Waiting and watching for a better opportunity, the way she had always lived her life.

*   *   *

They left Hermosilla too early to buy a new tire; using the smartphone, Adrienne found a shop in Guaymas. After the tire was changed, they chanced possible cameras and splurged on a drive-through meal at Burger King. With their disguise of sunglasses and baseball caps, they were two typical American tourists in a mid-size city that saw plenty of the same. Adrienne scrolled through news stories but found no fresh details, just the same bare facts: people missing, cash missing. They were a mere blip on the social media radar; the masses had moved on to mass shootings, reality television and politics. She powered down the phone.

"It seems no one is looking very hard for us." She twisted in her seat to face him. "Or the police are keeping secrets from the media."

"The police probably try to keep secrets. They would assume we're watching the news. People are looking, I promise you. Dustin wants to know where you are, and he wants the money. Law enforcement wants to know. Fife wants to know. Random opportunists could recognize us. People will kill for three mill."

"I know." She glared with icy blue eyes. "I killed for it. And I'll be fucking pissed if I went through all of this to be disappointed at the end. I would rather go to jail or die than find out your stories of San Sebastian are lies. That this magical family we're supposed to be creating is just another fucked up bunch of liars and criminals. This better be worth all we've done."

"Tomorrow, reinita, the city will take your breath away. It's like walking into the past. You and Cindy will be friends, good friends, like sisters. We'll grow vegetables, have chickens, and be part of a community so tight that even if someone tracked us to San Sebastian, no one would admit to knowing us."

Adrienne yearned to believe him, because what choice did she have? Go back to San Rafael and maybe jail? Divorce Dustin? Get a job, commute, pay bills, go shopping, have her nails done, have her hair done, drink wine and eat restaurant food because she is too tired and stressed to cook a meal? Inconceivable when compared to the sweetly simple life she fantasized living in a remote Mexican village. A magical town, according to the people who make such things official. *All those people wouldn't lie, would they?*

"How do you feel about church?" Gabriel asked.

She recoiled instinctively but paused before speaking to put church in context with her little fantasy village. "Church is fine. It's religion I have a problem with."

"To me, church is family and community, being good and kind to each other," Gabriel said. "No one needs more religion than that. I think it would be smart to attend church, so the locals will see us as part of the community and not just American expats."

"But I won't have to be a boy?"

"You can be whoever you want to be. But you should try to make yourself look as different from Adrienne as you can in case someone from your old life wanders into town. It's a popular day trip from Vallarta."

"Is that how you and Cindy knew about it?"

"Yes, but we went at different times with different people. When I flew her family to Disneyland she wanted to sit in the cockpit. We started talking about traveling and San Sebastian came up. Something clicked between us, but she asked *me* out. I would never ask a client for a date. When Cindy told me she was pregnant, my first reaction was no, no, not her. Not now. We had been so careful. She told me she was on the pill, and I used condoms. Then we realized, this child was supposed to happen." He flashed a crooked half-smile. "I know how that sounds, arrogant and more than a little crazy. But that's how we feel. This baby was meant to be."

"What a lucky baby." Adrienne leaned against the headrest and turned her stinging eyes to the land rushing by. *Imagine being born into so much love.* She added an infant to her fantasy village life, a toddler, a teenager. Sunday mornings with light streaming through stained glass windows. Cindy as a sister, not competition, not someone to hate or resent. Co-parents. *Maybe I'll meet a nice man in church.* She rolled her head to look at Gabriel's profile from the corner of her eye. *Let him go. Let him go?* Her gaze traveled to his broad-fingered hands, hands cruel and tender, and she shivered. *I have to let him go.*

* * *

After a long, uneventful day, Adrienne scouted a seedy motel near a Pemex, just north of the bustling resort city of Mazatlán. After settling their bags, Gabriel turned on the television.

"I'll find some news, then I'll go get some food. There's a taqueria across the street."

"I can walk over there," she offered.

"It's best if you stay hidden. I blend in better," Gabriel said, distracted. He paused on a local news channel showing a weather report. "Here, reinita, watch this while I get us some tacos. If there is any news about those bandits it should be on this channel."

Adrienne plopped on the bed in front of the television and stared at the screen, unfocused, unseeing, the babble of Spanish words filtered through her ears without revealing a particle of information. The temperatures were Celsius so even the weather report was useless. She stood to pace, paused at the window to peek through the curtains, went back to the bed and sat down. Several commercials later, the news was back with two serious-looking reporters seated at a desk with a big screen behind them. A photo appeared on the screen and Adrienne jumped to her feet, moving closer to the television, knees shaking. It was the bandit's truck, the bodies lying where she left them. Straining to pick out any words of Spanish she might know, she heard muerto. Dead.

The door opened and she choked on a scream. "Jesus, knock or something. You scared the hell out of me."

"Sorry, reinita," Gabriel said as he emptied the greasy brown bag. "We have carnitas street tacos with beans and rice, salad…"

"Looks good, thanks, but stop what you're doing and listen to this." She pushed him towards the television.

He crossed his arms and rocked back on his heels. After a moment, he said over his shoulder, "No witnesses and no leads." He listened more. "They estimate the men were dead four to five hours. A woman saw the truck when she drove to Sonoyta, and it was still there several hours later when she drove back." Gabriel returned to the food and pulled two Coronas from the bag.

"We were hundreds of miles away by the time they found the bodies. The gun is unregistered. There is nothing to tie them to us."

"What about tire tracks? The Honda had a skinny spare on it when we pulled out."

"After five hours in this wind? There are no tracks."

"Now we know for sure they're dead."

"Better them than us." Gabriel ate a street taco in two quick, snapping bites.

Adrienne dug into her food, too hungry to argue. She was alive because of her decision to kill, and those men were dead because of their decision to be armed robbers. They were dead because of her. Because of Gabriel. Because of Dustin. Because of Cindy. Choices and decisions, lives tangled together to weave a story where those men died. *Better them than us.*

Gabriel watched the rest of the newscast before flipping restlessly through channels between bites and sips of beer. After an hour or so, he dropped the remote, stood and stretched. "Do you want another beer?"

"No, I'm taking a quick shower and going to bed." Adrienne shoved the remains of her dinner back in the bag. When she turned around, Gabriel was there. She steeled herself not to flinch when he raised his hand to stroke her shorn head of hair.

"You said you took all you need from me?" His hand cupped the back of her skull, he bent to press a firm kiss on her mouth, spicy lips and darting tongue. "I have more to give, reinita. It would be a shame to waste this time together."

He bent for another kiss, this one warmer and wetter. When she responded, he lifted her in his arms, she wrapped her legs around his waist and kissed him savagely, releasing harsh moans of pent-up frustration. Her pulse thrummed, her heart galloped, her skin tingled. Sore nether regions throbbed. Tender nipples hardened. *Let him go? No. He's not Cindy's yet.*

CHAPTER SIXTEEN
HAD A BAD DAY

Detective Lyle Cooper of the Marin Police Department leaned across the glossy cherrywood desk and shot Lawrence Fife a level gaze. "We've tracked Austin and Berg to Sayulita, Mexico. Austin used a credit card to rent a room and the transaction triggered a call to law enforcement."

"They're a couple of buffoons." Fife swallowed his anger, along with the last dim hope that Berg and Austin would find Cindy before the police. In his perfect world, Cindy and Adrienne and Gabriel would simply disappear, taking the paltry three million and the stupendously stupid Berg and Austin with them. Fife wanted life to go back to the way it was before Gabriel stole his plane. Next best option: Cindy comes home on her own. Bridget and Barbara stop nagging. The police and press leave him alone. A man can dream.

"Now what?" Fife asked. "Are you sending someone to pick them up?"

"I've contacted the local police. They said someone would go to the address but frankly, the locals won't waste their time with our criminals. Sayulita is a busy town and they have more than their share of work."

"I appreciate you keeping me posted, Detective. I had a private investigator researching Navarro, but the man is slippery. The PI couldn't find anyone willing to share a thing about Gabriel's personal life."

"Let me ask you something, Fife. In your opinion, is Adrienne Berg hostage or accomplice?"

"I'm telling you what Berg told me, there appeared to have been a struggle. He didn't elaborate and he seemed upset. When you find him, you can ask him."

"I'm asking for an opinion. Based on what you know about her, do you feel Mrs. Berg could have assisted in this crime?"

Fife leaned back in his chair and linked his fingers behind his head, making elbow wings. He looked to the ceiling, face scrunched, chewing his bottom lip. "People are capable of doing something out of character for the right amount of money. Was she so miserable she gave up her comfortable life to run off with Gabriel, another woman's boyfriend? It doesn't make sense. In my opinion, Adrienne is a hostage."

"I agree," said Cooper. "Our team will be focusing their efforts on her. We're looking for the others, of course, but Adrienne is the person considered most at risk. I'm going back to their house with a search warrant and a forensic team."

Fife stood, an unsubtle hint. "Please keep me in the loop, Detective. I hope you find them all safe and sound." He didn't offer to shake hands.

"I'm assuming you'd like to have your money returned as well." Cooper made a noise in his throat that could have been a chuckle, or it could have been a cough. "Even when you're rich, three million is a lot of money."

"I've already replaced the shareholder's money from my personal account. The other missing funds have been seized and the account frozen. The money is the furthest thing from my mind. Bring Cindy home, bring Adrienne home if that's what she wants, the rest of them can stay lost. In fact, I'm withdrawing the embezzlement charges. Don't even waste your time with Austin and Berg." Fife stared at Cooper until he turned away.

"Enjoy your afternoon, Mr. Fife," Cooper called over his shoulder on the way out.

When the door shut, Fife muttered, "Fat chance," and called Jarrett Austin with stabbing jabs on his cell phone.

* * *

They were sleeping when Jarrett's phone rang; the theme from 'Jaws' indicated it was Fife calling. Both men sat straight up in bed, as if their buttholes had simultaneously puckered. Jarrett held the phone to his ear, grimaced and turned sheepish eyes to Dustin. "I fucked up," he said, holding the phone away from his ear as they listened to Fife's expletive-filled opinion of them.

"Maybe you can wiggle your way out of town, but I'm not warning you again," Fife barked. "And don't call me to bail you out after you're arrested. You dipshits are on your own."

"We have a lead on Cindy," Jarrett hurried to say. "She asked a barista here about a rare type of coffee that's only grown in one place on earth." The server hadn't used those exact words, but they were close enough and sounded impressive. "We're headed there now."

"You'll probably lead the police straight to her." Fife said. "And that's fine with me. They can scoop up the whole lot of you at once."

Jarrett stared at his phone. "He hung up on me." He cocked his head at Dustin's bemused expression. "What's so funny?"

"You're full of shit. You are a full of shit person. We hadn't discussed going to San Sebastian and just because Cindy knows her coffee doesn't mean that's where she's going."

"Got a better idea? We can't stay here. I guess we could try showing her picture at the bus stop and see how long it takes for the cops to notice us."

"I say we get the next bus out of town. I don't care where it's going." Dustin gripped his aching head with both hands. "Goddammit, Jare, what were you thinking using your credit card to book an Airbnb? You know the cops are looking for us."

"How did you think I paid for it?" Jarrett murmured sullenly.

"Well, now the cops know exactly where we are. We gotta get out of this room." Dustin glanced around wildly, as if uniformed police were about to burst from the walls.

* * *

They grabbed their shopping bags and hurried down Gringo Hill, buttholes indeed puckered now with the very real possibility of running into the police along the way. They stopped to get coffee and a doughnut at the far edge of town, casting furtive glances around the crowded square.

Jarrett shook his crumpled plastic bag that smelled of mildewy clothes with a sneer of distaste. "So tacky. I should buy a backpack."

"Sure, just put it on your credit card. Maybe I can mark 'spending time in a Mexican prison' off my bucket list while I'm here."

"Sarcasm, nice, very helpful."

Jarrett and Dustin tromped barefoot to the firmer sand at the water's edge. Heads down and perspiring, they turned west towards the curling arm of the cove, passing the last of the sunbathers to stop in a rocky area shunned by the beach folk. They hunkered in the shade, scanning the beach for police while sipping coffee and discussing their next step.

"I say we go to San Sebastian," Jarrett said. "At least cross it off the list."

Dustin squeezed his eyes shut and shook his head. "You act like we're on a grand tour."

"It's literally on our list." Jarrett shook his plastic bag. "The list of places Cindy has visited in Mexico. I know you don't have a better idea."

* * *

Thirty minutes later, they were in the bus station, asking at the ticket counter for the best way to get to San Sebastian. The woman gave them an amused but sympathetic glance, rattled off some words they didn't understand, handed them two tickets and pointed. The bus had empty seats and was ready to leave.

Dustin handed the ticket to the driver. "How far to San Sebastian?" The bus driver laughed and said more words in Spanish. "Gracias," Dustin said and slumped to the empty seat next to Jarrett. "I don't know what anyone is saying. Look it up on your phone."

"Look it up on *your* phone," Jarrett said, wrestling the plastic bag in his lap.

"The battery is dead." It wasn't, but Dustin was in no mood to discuss the issue.

Jarrett pulled out his phone with a theatrical sigh and opened the map app. The bus had merged into traffic when he reached an unhappy conclusion. "This bus doesn't go to San Sebastian." He looked at Dustin. "No buses go to San Sebastian. After the last stop, it's another forty kilometers by car."

"We don't have a car."

"Thanks, Captain Obvious. I guess that means we're walking to this coffee wonderland or we find a new plan."

"How long would it take to walk forty kilometers?"

"According to this app, over eight hours."

"Oh, hell, no." Dustin grabbed the phone. "Look, the bus stops in Puerto Vallarta. Let's go back to our room and think about this before planning an eight-hour hike."

*   *   *

The bus stopped a few times, filling up fast, and soon it was stuffed with sweating passengers. Two rough-looking men hung at Dustin's side, laughing raucously every time the bus hit a bump and Dustin got beaned with an elbow or hip. The bus slowed and pulled up to a sign that said Las Cinco Cruces. One of the rough men poked Dustin's shoulder.

"Hey, what you got in the bags?"

"Dirty clothes." Dustin made himself smaller, shrinking around his sparse possessions.

"This is your stop." The man bared his teeth, sharklike. "Get up, we want your seats."

"This isn't our stop. We're going to Puerto Vallarta."

"Get your shit and get off the bus or we keep your shit and throw you off," the man snarled into Dustin's face.

Dustin and Jarrett exited with their bags and watched the bus roar away without them, spitting sand from their teeth.

"Rude! I would have given them our seats." Jarrett rubbed his mouth and whined, "I just want to go back to my room. Is that too much to ask?" He raised his arms imploringly to the sky.

As if in answer to his prayer, a rusty green Ford Fiesta pulled over and rolled to a stop next to them. "You guys need a ride?" said a surfer dude in California English.

Dustin started to wag like a golden retriever, but Jarrett had lost all semblance of trust. "Why would you give us a ride?"

"I'm an Uber driver. I pick people up here all the time."

"He has an Uber sticker on his window," said Dustin. "How much to take us to Vallarta?"

"Fifty bucks."

"Fifty bucks! The bus was like seven."

The surfer shrugged. "So, wait for the bus. There should be one in about an hour. Or you could be in Vallarta in forty-five minutes. You pick."

While Dustin and Jarrett discussed this in low whispers, a wreck of a yellow taxi skidded to a stop behind the Uber. The taxi driver jumped out screaming, "Scab! Filthy gringo scab!" Surfer dude skedaddled, spraying them with sand and gravel. The taxi driver brushed off his clothes, turned to Jarrett and said in polite, carefully pronounced English, "Do you need a ride?"

They paid the driver fifty dollars and rode in grumpy silence to Vallarta. Jarrett waited across the street as Dustin crept to the window of their motel room; he had left the curtains pulled apart about an inch, an alert in case someone went in the room while they were gone. He peered inside before motioning to Jarrett and unlocking the door. They collapsed on their beds.

"What a fucking day," Jarrett groaned. "Let's go find some booze."

"Seriously?" Dustin sat up to give Jarrett a dirty look. "I've just had one of the worst days of my life. I'm not going back out there."

"If I don't get drunk right now," Jarrett glared back, "this will officially qualify as my very worst day of all time. Stop being a little bitch and walk with me to the OXXO."

* * *

Within hours of his meeting with Fife, Detective Cooper and his team broke into the Berg's home with a search warrant. They started downstairs and worked their way up. The warrant was fairly broad; they were looking for evidence that would tell them if Adrienne Berg was abducted or part of the scheme to steal three million dollars. Scanning Dustin's bedroom with a black light, the technician alerted Cooper they found blood stains, and focused their search efforts on the bedroom. An officer opened the bedside table and found the recorder. Curious, the officer pressed Play and Adrienne's shrieks filled the room.

Cooper lunged from the walk-in closet, his hand on his gun. "What the hell? Let me see that." He turned down the volume before tapping Play. Adrienne's screams caused his arms to break out in gooseflesh. "I think we can rule out accomplice." He swallowed hard and played it again. "Berg never told anyone about this," he said, with a note of steel in his voice. "How could the man not report this?" To the officer, Cooper said, "Keep looking around. I'll check with the neighbors to see if they noticed anything unusual. They didn't take her car and they sure didn't fly away. Someone saw something."

CHAPTER SEVENTEEN
YOU BELONG WITH ME

Adrienne jolted awake when the alarm went off, captured by Gabriel's heavy leg flung across her like a beefy anchor. He pulled her into his arms, rolling to his back and hoisting her body on top of his in a smooth motion. He nuzzled her neck and stroked her bare skin. "We have time. Let me love you again before we leave."

Even as her body responded, her heart cracked in a fragile place and filled with anguish, knowing he would be touching another woman soon, and wanting him still. *I will never be able to tell him no.* "A quickie." She bit his bottom lip and smiled when he yelped. "We need to get on the road."

They did not have a quickie. By the time they finished hot, sweaty sex they were over an hour behind schedule. Adrienne turned on the phone to check the news as Gabriel steered them into a Pemex, volume off while the station attendant stood by the open driver's window.

Scrolling through search results for local news, an image appeared, and her finger jittered to a stop. Her heart thumped like a frightened rabbit was in her chest. The link was a video, and the thumbnail showed an enlarged photo from the bandit's murder scene—the big truck with the two dead bodies that were blurred but unmistakable. Two uniformed Mexican police officers flanked a man in a business suit. She tapped Gabriel's leg, and he leaned closer.

"Are we almost done here?" Her wide eyes shot a glance from him to the phone.

"Almost," he said with questions in his voice. After forever, the thirsty tank was full, the attendant paid and tipped, and Gabriel rolled slowly away from the pump. "Can you tell me what you found while we drive or should I park?"

"We should watch this together."

He pulled up to a supermercado and parked, engine running. Adrienne started the video and the man in the suit began to speak. In Spanish, of course. Gabriel translated, "Thank you for coming, blah, blah, the man in the suit is a detective. This press conference is to give the media and the public new information regarding the murder of these two men. Three witnesses told police they saw a man changing a tire on this stretch of highway the day of the murders. Two witnesses said the car's plates were from California. Oh, shit," Gabriel interjected and continued his translating, "Another witness told police he sold a tire to someone in a car like this with California license plates." The detective in the video held up a stock photo of a black four door Civic. "The driver is a big man with a beard and a young boy was with him. Both wore baseball caps and sunglasses." The detective held up crude sketches that could be anyone. "These people are wanted for questioning in connection with the murders." The video ended.

"At least we know your boy disguise works." Gabriel rubbed his temples. "This is not good."

"We have to get rid of the car," Adrienne said.

"The only way to reach San Sebastian is by car. We could take a taxi or a tour bus, but our big bag of money would attract curiosity." He glanced around the parking lot. "We need a Mexican plate. Not from here, we've already been here too long. See if there is a neighborhood near the highway."

She consulted the map app. "Turn right after Little Cesar's, there's a bunch of houses behind there."

Following her directions, they found an area that vaguely resembled a neighborhood you might see in the States, but the grid of streets was made of brick and stone instead of blacktop. The front doors of the colorful stucco houses lined up even with the sidewalk. Very few homes had a front yard and courtyards were tile, not grass. Every window and door were caged in metal bars, some plain, some ornate; it seemed more a style choice than any indication it was a dangerous community.

The car clattered down the street. Even at idling speed, the tires were noisy on the bricks and noisier on the stones, a cacophony seemingly designed to attract attention. An old man, his face hard and weathered as a fence board, stopped his shuffle down the narrow sidewalk to watch them pass.

"Not many cars here to choose from," Adrienne said.

"I only need one." Gabriel glanced over his shoulder. "None of these, he's watching us."

They cruised slowly, noisily, around the corner. A dismal playground took up one block with empty, orderly rows of metal slides, swings, and teeter-totters baking in the direct sun. The grass was patchy and parched without a speck of shade in sight. To Adrienne's American eyes, it looked like an exercise yard for small prisoners.

"This one will work." Gabriel parked in front of a dark gray Civic more battered than theirs. "Hang tight, I'll be right back."

Adrienne twisted in the seat to watch him, right hand resting on the gun; the sun glinted off his knife as he bent to unscrew the back plate of the gray car. He hurried back, switched the plate and darted to the front to remove the other one. After one last glance up and down the deserted street, he opened the back seat a crack and slid the California plates on top of the money bag. They were back on the main road in minutes.

Using the sideview mirror, she watched the road behind them for miles before asking, "How long before that person notices their plate missing?"

"Probably not long but it buys us a little time." Gabriel gripped the steering wheel, his eyes moving from the windshield to the rearview mirror to the side and back, a constant loop of vigilance. "Keep searching for breaking news, reinita. We don't want to lead anyone to San Sebastian."

"There's no mention of anything that connects the dead bandits to the missing money or us," she said, tapping at the phone. "No one we know would ever recognize us from those sketches. I told you I look like a twelve-year-old boy." She tapped the screen. "That's new. A San Francisco journalist made a timeline." She skimmed through the article and paraphrased, "Dustin and Jarrett stole the money from Fife, funneled it through an account in the Caymans and cashed out three million. They're missing and wanted, with felony warrants for embezzlement. Then you stole the money and the wife. It says the cops found the bloody pillows. Dustin is such a pig. He's in trouble for not reporting me missing." She scanned the last few lines. "I'm considered abducted and at-risk. You are armed and dangerous, holding me hostage and presumably meeting up with your lady love, Cindy, also reported missing. A quote from Cindy's mom, 'I just want Cindy to let me know she's alive. All is forgiven.' There you go," Adrienne chirped. "You and Cindy can go back to San Rafael and live with her mom." She laughed at his sour expression. "The police are asking for your help in locating any of these people. The search is focused on Mexico." She lifted her eyes from the tiny screen to gaze at the vast empty land out the window. It looked like a good place to hide, a place to get lost. People go missing every day.

"I wonder why it took so long for Dustin and Jarrett to get busted?" she mused. "Gabriel, do you honestly think we're going to get away with this? At first it was like no one was looking for us and now it feels like everyone is looking."

"We'll give it our best shot, reinita. I brought you into this mess and I won't rest until I see you safe and happy. More and more I think about how stupid I was to take the money. And you. If I had just left town, Cindy's mom would be my only problem."

"But then I might not know you." Adrienne returned her unfocused gaze to the window. "If you knew how often I step outside myself, and watch myself thinking what a terrible actress I am. I'm not fooling anyone. Those Bay Area women look at me like I have toilet paper stuck to my shoe. No matter how I dress or behave, I'm a street kid and it shows." She ran her fingers through her cropped hair. "This is who I really am. Willing to take risks to get what I want. And I finally know what I want. What I need. A life of peace in a magical town. That's it, that's all. The rest of the world can fuck off."

Six hours later—many of those hours with magnificent views of the Pacific Ocean to their right—Gabriel and Adrienne were near Puerto Vallarta, winding their way east on Highway 544, the last leg of their journey. The decrepit asphalt road was two narrow lanes with a faint yellow stripe down the middle now and then. Roadside stands made of tarps and pallets and bald tires populated the dirt shoulder, selling everything from fresh produce to agave candy to live chickens. The speed limit was merely a suggestion; Gabriel drove fast when he could but most of the time they were stuck behind a slow-moving vehicle of some kind, and once a herd of sheep.

"Do we have cell signal here?" Gabriel rolled his tight shoulders. "La Encinera is the last stop for gas, can you see how far we are?"

"Less than ten miles," she said and did another calculation. "We're twenty miles from San Sebastian. Are we going straight to our house after this pit stop?" Adrienne's nerves, already frayed over the past two weeks, were raw. Apprehensive, agitated, nervous, scared, the dark feelings simmered in her stomach like anxiety soup. "Where are we meeting Cindy? Is she even called Cindy these days?"

"Her passport is in her real name but in town she calls herself Rachel Green, like Jennifer Aniston?"

"Okay, good to know. Andy, Laz and Rachel, the new cast of Friends. Where are we meeting Rachel?"

"Our plan was for her to take a couple of daily walks around the plaza so the locals get used to seeing her. Her last walk will be just before sundown, and we'll be waiting for her."

"You don't know where she lives?"

"We haven't spoken in over three weeks. She was supposed to find someone willing to sell us some property without paperwork."

"You can do that?"

"In some places you can. I pray she found something." Gabriel pulled into the Pemex and the conversation was put on hold until the transaction was complete.

The moment they pulled away, Adrienne blurted, "Wait, you don't even know if Cin...Rachel has a house? We could be camping?"

"I'm sure she found us a decent place to live. A hundred years ago, twenty thousand people lived in San Sebastian, and they made houses of brick and stone. The houses survived even as the town dwindled to a thousand people. We could squat somewhere and most locals would turn a blind eye. But anything that brings dollars to the town makes us more welcome."

*   *   *

They climbed in altitude, the air grew cooler and the desolate landscape turned lush. Mountains in the distance were cloaked in mossy clumps of green and the jagged peaks were shrouded in clouds. A crush of green surrounded them, a twisted tangle of trees, vines, bushes, and wildflowers crowded the dusty road that ran alongside geometrical fields of feathery corn and spiky blue agave, with thousands of hectares of coffee beans like wild berry bushes. The rutted ochre dirt and ancient cobblestone road twisted, switchbacked, and cut roughly through the mountains. At first, they laughed about the car bouncing and jolting down the road, clicking their teeth together, but the jostling got old fast. The rare appearance of random asphalt, even patched and cracked, was a relief to the body like a drink of water on a hot day.

Adrienne gripped her seat on the hairpin turns. "I didn't realize we would be in the mountains."

"It's almost five thousand feet."

"Oh, no, that means snow." She clutched her hands to her chest. "You didn't tell me there would be snow."

"You have Wikipedia in your hand." His salty grin stayed in profile, unable to take his eyes off the challenging road for a second. He pulled over at a wide spot on the dirt shoulder so a tailgating tour bus could pass; the driver offered a brief salute with the arrogant confidence of one who had driven this road many times.

Putting the car in park, Gabriel reached for her hand. "You'll see all the seasons here. This place is not like the Bay Area where every day is spring.

Imagine our magical town in winter, snow for Christmas." He kissed her knuckle. "You will love the snow, reinita."

"Do you plan to kiss my hand in front of your girlfriend? And I don't think she's going to like my nickname." The anxiety stew was a rumbling boil in her guts. *Let him go.* In a very short time, she would have no choice, and accepting what you cannot change is easier said than done.

Gabriel dropped her hand and leaned back in the seat, his eyes checking the mirrors and avoiding hers. "You're right about me, Adrienne. I'm an asshole. No, I'm worse than that." The words poured out in a rush. "I'm a bad man. I broke the law and hurt people with this crazy idea, this selfish plan to give my perfect magical child a perfect magical life and I can't even think of her as my girlfriend. I only think of her as the mother of my child." He turned his eyes to Adrienne. "I'm not in love. We hardly know each other. Maybe she feels differently about me but what I experienced was a few fun dates. She got pregnant, Barbara flipped out and Cin...Rachel wanted to be far from her mother. We talked about what kind of future we saw for our baby and agreed that we feel the same way about raising this child, with his feet on the earth and surrounded by kind people and clean air. Rachel and I agree about things that matter and we'll find a way to fall in love. Our kids will have parents who love them and love each other."

"Kids?" A bitter bubble rose in her throat. "You plan to have more?"

"I hope he or she won't be an only child, but who knows what the future will bring?" Gabriel slipped his hand under hers. "I'm an asshole for hurting you, for taking you, for making love with you." Kissing her knuckle, his lips moved against her skin as he spoke. "I'm an asshole for saying I love you when I know we can't be together this way. I hope you love me a little, enough to be part of my family."

"You're such an asshole." Adrienne clenched her jaw, turning her head just enough to look at him sideways. "I hate you." She looked away. "I don't know why I don't hate you. I think it's because we're both nuts. Rachel, too. What a completely insane thing for people to do." She gazed at the road ahead: steep, twisting, rocky, and surrounded by a lush tunnel of green. "What we're doing is stupid and scary, but I feel alive. I'm not just filling hours until I die." Adrienne gripped Gabriel's hand in both of hers, grinding the bones of his knuckles with all her strength, wanting to hurt him. "The night we met, I felt something powerful. Something inevitable. And when I saw you in my garden, I thought you came to seduce me. Not kidnap me." She blew a harsh puff of air, incredulous at the memory. "I thought you came to fuck me, and I would have let you. I couldn't have told you no."

"And then I terrorized you."

"How *does* a rational person get past that? I'm clearly out of my mind." She blinked her eyes rapidly against a sudden sting and flapped her hand impatiently. "Let's go home."

CHAPTER EIGHTEEN
DO YOU BELIEVE IN MAGIC

They bumped down the long and winding road at a noisy, teeth-rattling five miles per hour. Rounding a curve, civilization appeared at last: an arch on the left advertising a fancy restaurant, Via Nogal. On the right, a massive brick structure styled like a medieval gateway and topped in red roof tiles with steel letters spelling out **Bienvenidos San Sebastian del Oestre** and **Pueblo Magico**. A delicate metal swirl, a spiky asterisk in rainbow colors, added to the sense of entering a charmed place filled with art and warmth and whimsy.

"Welcome to San Sebastian of the west, a magic town," Gabriel read with awe in his voice. "We're here, reinita, a few more meters and we can rest."

Maybe it was the spell of Gabriel's words, but to Adrienne, the world became a different place as they passed the welcome sign, the air fresher and cooler, the light clear and golden. On their left, past the fence marking the property of Via Nogal, was a row of boxy, two-story stucco buildings all painted the same snowy white with a wide stripe at the bottom in rusty red. To their right, a white pipe railing led pedestrians to a wide sidewalk shaded with gnarled oaks and bordered by a centuries-old rock wall. Victorian-inspired black iron streetlamps and benches of scrolled metal and weathered wood lined the sidewalk, modern touches that contrasted but also blended with the ancient mossy stacked stones.

They passed an elementary school with a stunning mountain backdrop, and one white-over-rust building after another, each topped with a red tile roof, arched doorways neatly framed in red and white brick. Every color in nature was riotously represented in rows of pots overflowing with vibrant flowers, and trees studded in jewels of avocados, mangos, lemons, limes, oranges. Masses of bright butterflies flurried about on butterfly missions. Crossing a stone bridge, Gabriel pointed to a large building. "The cultural center. See the stage there in the ravine? They have plays and art classes. It's the second most important place in town. The church is number one."

Rows of buildings blocked the late afternoon sun, and the narrow street was dark as a canyon until it abruptly opened to the town square. Two-story white and red stucco buildings ringed the cobblestoned plaza, dominated by the church steeple with a pale aqua dome that contrasted with the cobalt of the sky. The walkways in front of the buildings were deeply shaded, the cover supported in arches and columns. In the center of the plaza was an extravagant green space alive with roses of all colors, and a graceful white iron bandstand with fanciful creatures holding globe lights in the corners. Mariachi music drifted from speakers. Ancient benches beckoned under twisted, squat shade trees.

Gabriel drove in a slow circle around the plaza before backing into a parking spot in front of the restaurant Los Arcos de Sol. After one more careful look around, he turned off the engine and leaned back with a sigh. "What do you think? Isn't it beautiful?"

Adrienne gazed at the sleepy, tidy town, and a gossamer peace settled over her, although not enough to quell the jitter of nerves. "It's nothing I imagined, and everything I hoped for."

Less than a dozen cars were parked around the square. Tourists in shorts and tank tops meandered down the covered arcades alongside wrinkled abuelas in faded cotton dresses and shawls, peeking into windows and strolling into shops. A man rode past them on a burro. Two old men chatted on a bench, weathered hands gripping canes. She felt a sense of straddling time, a plane of existence where right-now and long-ago blurred and crossed. No one was in a hurry. No one gave them more than a passing glance.

"Sundown is not for another couple of hours. What do we do now?"

"Let's grab a snack from the market over there." Gabriel tipped his chin. "It will look strange if we wait in the car, but no one will pay attention if we sit in the square for hours."

* * *

They took their time inspecting the myriad of offerings inside the little shop named Artes y Dulces—Arts and Sweets. Clothing, jewelry, soaps, chocolates, breads, jams, tequila, every shelf held different treasures and almost every item was locally produced. Unable to decide and having plenty of cash, Adrienne and Gabriel picked out too many things and carried heavy paper sacks to a bench facing the plaza and the car.

All day, fog had shrouded the nearby peaks and chilly, cotton-candy wisps were now drifting into the village. Once the site of a prosperous silver mine, the four-hundred-year-old town nestled in a bowl, a caldera created by the violent eruption of a volcano eons ago. The sun sank behind the Sierra Madre mountains and the temperature dropped. Adrienne and Gabriel grazed on snacks and added warmer layers from their musty backpacks. Long silences were punctuated with short bursts of giddy laughter about nothing. The town felt safe, insulated, and the unrelenting stress of driving, hurrying, hiding, and worrying already seemed distant; this new quality of time—San Sebastian time—was slow and sweet as cold honey. Shadows grew longer, six-foot men cast twelve-foot giants of themselves across the glimmering cobbled square. One shadow-giant, slimmer than all the others, made Gabriel straighten on the bench.

"There she is," he said, rising to his feet.

Adrienne-now-Andy followed his gaze and saw Cindy-now-Rachel for the first time. Rachel managed to look stunning in a long, faded cotton dress, stretched cardigan and dirty Keds. At least six feet tall, long-limbed and willowy, she gracefully crossed the square, dress whirling around her calves. Tendrils of blond hair escaped from under her straw hat to flutter in the breeze. She smiled and nodded to each person she passed, only faltering slightly when she caught sight of Gabriel-now-Laz. Her face broke into a sunny smile and her stride lengthened, gliding effortlessly across the uneven surface of the square. Andy stayed seated, straight-backed, clenching the paper sack in both fists, and watched Laz and Rachel meet halfway. Their two shadow-giants became one, tangled on cobblestones that shimmered gold in the fading light. They embraced, a tight hug that went on and on. Rachel kissed Laz on one cheek, then the other before leaning back to smile into his eyes.

Their heads came together in a guarded conference that lasted several minutes. Laz nodded towards Andy; she stood and stiffened her spine. Rachel stared for a long beat before taking Laz's hand, she walked towards Andy on impossibly long legs, smiling like a model in a minty gum commercial. Keeping a tight hold on Laz, Rachel gripped Andy's right hand with her left. Her fingers were cold, her icy blue eyes skipped across Andy's gaze. She bent at the knees and kissed Andy on each cheek, her touch fleeting as air. Briskly, Rachel said, "Welcome to San Sebastian." Turning to Laz, she said, "Where's the car? That's it? Let's go home. I'll drive."

*   *   *

Andy took the back seat before Laz could say a word. From a glance, the interior looked normal, but the springs were gone, and the back seat was hard, unyielding. Andy caught Rachel staring at her in the rearview mirror and looked away, hiding her eyes behind dark glasses. The car rumbled slowly across the square, heading out the direction they came in, and they were past the cultural center before Rachel broke the heavy silence.

"We live near the panteon antiguo." She rolled her Spanish words perfectly, catching Andy's eye in the mirror. "The old cemetery. How much do you know about the area?"

"Not much." Andy looked away from the mirror and back again to see Rachel's eyes on her. *Watch the road, bitch.*

"The news said you were missing. I didn't know what to think," Rachel said, poking Laz's leg hard with one finger. "But the news didn't say that Adrienne-the-hostage is now Andy-the-accomplice."

"We watch the same news." Andy shoved the sack of goodies between the front seats and glanced down to see the gun still in its place. "Anyone want snacks? Laz? Rachel?"

Laz twisted around to face her; his eyes were also hidden with dark glasses even though most of the light had left the sky. "No, thank you, Andy." He opened his mouth as if to say more, turned back and settled in the seat.

"No thanks, Andy." Rachel's enormous blue eyes pinned her in the mirror. "I heard the guys who stole the money from Uncle Lawrence are on the run. That would be your husband and his buddy, right? They're somewhere out there?"

"Somewhere out here," Andy echoed. She turned her gaze to the window, determined not to look at that mirror again.

"While you two were camping in the redwoods all cozy, I was busting my butt cleaning up our place." Rachel's voice was falsely perky and brittle with sarcasm. "I took pictures so, yeah, you can thank me later that I did all the hard work." She squeezed Laz's thigh and gave him a playful shake. "I can't wait to hear all about how the sexy kidnapper convinced his terrified hostage to switch teams." Her words dropped like stones, one by one, hard and heavy.

Laz made a noise as if to respond but Andy interrupted. "It wasn't like that." She lowered her sunglasses to laser-beam Rachel with her own baby blues. "I went with him willingly. I wanted to be gone. I wanted adventure, a different life. I would have fucked him in my rose garden when he came to take me. Laz never tried to convince me of anything."

"So did you?" Rachel's eyes blazed in the mirror; the car's crawl slowed to a stop. "Fuck him?"

Andy flipped her hand and snorted. "Laz is committed to you. He told me that from the start. I'm not here to fuck up your relationship, Rachel. Even if I wanted to, which I don't, Laz wouldn't allow it. How about you thank your lucky stars that you have a loyal partner. Look at all he's done for you. And maybe pull that stick out of your butt so we can try to be friends."

Rachel twisted around for a face-to-face. They stared unblinking at each other for a long beat before she smiled. "I think we're going to be friends,

Andy." She turned back to her driving, picking up the clickety-clackety pace with her eyes on the road ahead.

Studying the passing scenery, Andy mulled this over. Rachel's voice sounded sincere, her expression, her smile, almost seemed genuine. But a wall was in her eyes, and ice in her words. *She doesn't trust me.* Andy was smugly pleased that Laz didn't say a word. Any information he wanted to keep from Rachel was just fine. *We share something she never can.*

*   *   *

They rattled down a road more narrow, bouncy and overgrown than the one leading into town. Around a sweeping corner, the road steepened and forked. Almost invisible, a corrugated tin roof glinted from a tangle of green in the last red light of the setting sun. Rachel turned sharply right at the tin roof and the road slanted downhill. A narrow, rutted trail ran through a green gauntlet of brush and trees that scraped the side of the car. The leafy tunnel opened to a large sandy clearing; the broad space was encircled by a jungle of greenery and towering trees that framed the first stars glittering in a sky of deep purple velvet.

"Home sweet home," said Rachel.

Left of the clearing and against a low rise was a long, low house constructed of bricks in the same orange-brown as the dirt. The corners of the bricks were chipped and worn; the sharp edges softened. Signs of age marked the red tile roof with cracks and moss in colors from black to bright green. The tin roof that indicated their driveway covered a lean-to carport addition built between the back of the house and the side of the hill.

After wandering around alone for a few minutes, Andy crossed the clearing to the forested edge where Laz and Rachel were standing. Together, but not close. It was nearly full dark and the growth beyond the clearing was a dense, smothering green that was somehow comforting instead of scary— another secluded stage, but now the play had three actors.

"I hear chickens." Her first real smile of the evening crossed her face. "I hoped for chickens." Andy reluctantly allowed Rachel to take her hand.

"I'm so glad to hear that. You can help me name them." Rachel motioned for Laz to come closer and twined her fingers in his. "I waited so we can pick names together. But I plan to eat some of those chickens so only the egg chickens are allowed to have names." She giggled, her voice earnest, her expression unreadable. "We can take care of the chickens together. And the garden." Rachel dropped their hands to fling her arms wide. "It's going to be paradise!" She cradled the suggestion of a curve at her belly. "We'll raise this baby together in paradise."

CHAPTER NINETEEN
TRUST ISSUES

According to public records, Lorenzo Navarro purchased his modest 1960s Berkeley bungalow for just under two hundred thousand dollars in 1994. Today, the house was worth more than a million. Lyle Cooper noted the home's pristine condition, drought-tolerant landscape, and fresh peach paint. One of the smallest houses in this gracious old neighborhood, the pride of ownership was as obvious as any of the mansions. Gabriel Navarro lived the first twenty years of his life in this house and Cooper was certain someone on this block had an idea where Gabriel might be, but no one was giving up any information. There had been no activity on Gabriel's phone, bank accounts or passport but people did not just disappear. Someone knew something.

Cooper walked up concrete steps through the arch of the porch, rang the doorbell and stepped back. Footsteps thudded, a curtain twitched, and a man opened the front door, leaving a decorative screen between them. He was tall, wide, his face brown and lined as a walnut, with a black and gray buzzcut and a blooming five o'clock shadow. Silent, he raised his eyebrows.

"Excuse my interruption, sir, are you Lorenzo Navarro? Gabriel's father?"

"I told the police twice, I don't know where he is," Lorenzo said from behind the screen, arms folded.

"You wouldn't tell me if you did know." Cooper flashed a phony grin. "But I have some questions and I thought it would be pleasant if we talked at your kitchen table with a cup of coffee. More pleasant than answering questions at the police station."

"Do I need a lawyer?"

"You have that right, of course. But you're not in trouble. Yet. If I find out later that you know something, you'll be charged with obstruction. There is a woman missing, and I believe she was taken by force. I believe she's in danger and there is evidence Gabriel is involved. It's my job to find her and your duty as a human being to help me. With respect. Sir."

Lorenzo studied him a moment longer before he uncrossed his arms and opened the screen. "What's your name, officer?"

He pulled out his badge. "Detective Lyle Cooper, you can call me Lyle."

"Detective Cooper, Gabriel would never hurt a woman."

He stomped away, leaving Cooper to shut the door. The inside of the house was as immaculate as the outside, with wool rugs flung over gleaming dark wood floors. He followed the man to a dining nook with a square wooden table and four chairs. Cooper sat at the table, pulled out his notebook and pen. Lorenzo continued into the galley kitchen and opened the refrigerator.

"I can't have coffee this late, I won't be able to sleep."

"I'll have what you're having," Cooper said agreeably. He sat up straight in the wooden chair and looked around. The dining nook opened to the living room, furnished with a couch, a recliner and a table between them. Built-in bookshelves surrounded a small fireplace, tasteful paintings graced the other walls. No personal photos or clutter except a book and a pair of reading glasses by the recliner. A bottle of Corona clunked on the table in front of him.

"You want lime?" Lorenzo held out a small white bowl.

Cooper took a wedge. "Thanks. I don't usually start drinking this early, but it's been one of those days. You're probably retired now but you remember having those days."

"Don't start off with bullshit. You know I have a propane delivery business. I don't drive the truck myself very often but I'm still a businessman. I work, I'm not retired."

"But you could retire. You served twenty in the Marines, you're getting a nice pension and the guys that drive for you wouldn't mind more hours."

"Damn, you're a nosy fucker. You questioned my employees?"

"Gabriel doesn't seem to have many friends. In fact, only one name has ever come up as a friend. Billy Jones. What can you tell me about Billy Jones?"

Lorenzo tilted his head back to take a long swallow of his beer. He thumped the bottle on the table and leaned forward to stare Cooper in the eye. "Billy was not a good person to be friends with. I went out of my way to help those boys be friends and by the time I knew enough to regret it, I had lost control of him."

"Does Billy live around here?"

"He used to live in Canyon. Have you heard of Canyon, detective?"

"Not until I talked to your employees. That's the only route you still drive, why is that?"

The man's face turned a darker shade of angry. "The narrow roads can be dangerous. I don't trust anyone else to drive that route."

"Is that the only reason?"

Lorenzo pinched the bridge of his nose, squeezing his eyes tightly shut. "I hate sounding like a sentimental pussy, but I love that route. Canyon is a place that gets under your skin."

"Does Billy still live there?"

"I haven't seen him in at least five years."

"Does he have family in Canyon?"

"Not at the house where he grew up. It's rare that property changes hands but Billy's parents sold their family home to some dotcom millionaire as a weekend getaway. They made a fortune."

"What was Billy's address in Canyon?" Cooper wrote in his notebook. "And you don't know where they moved?"

"I have no reason to keep track of them."

"But Billy grew up there, went to school there? And people don't leave Canyon, that's your impression?"

"It's a unique place. Imagine a pristine redwood forest populated by third and fourth generation hippies. That's Canyon. The original settlers were a bureaucrat's decision away from being tossed out as squatters. The houses weren't built to code, there are no public utilities. People left their cabins to their kids and each generation made it better. Canyon borders the most expensive zip codes in the Bay Area and their school has a waiting list a mile long."

"Who else does Gabriel know there?"

"No one he's ever talked about. He was not a sociable boy, but Gabriel and Billy hit it off and I felt sorry for them both. Billy with half his face covered in a birthmark and my son with half his heart missing because his mother left. I used to drop off Gabriel at Billy's house and let them hang out while I drove my route and pick him up on my way out. Sometimes Billy would come home with us, sometimes Gabriel would stay at his house. I found out later Billy was breaking into cabins, and not just the empty ones. He was caught stealing mail and I heard he did time for identity theft. I don't know why a young man from a good family feels the need to steal. It's not like he needed the money."

Cooper wrinkled his brow. "We could say the same about Gabriel."

Lorenzo gave him a heavy-lidded glare, nostrils flaring. "I guess I'm a bad parent. Maybe I could have done better but what's done is done and my son needs to accept responsibility for his choices. I haven't made choices for him in a long time."

"When was the last time you spoke with your son?"

"May fourteenth. He called on my birthday."

"Over a month ago, is that typical?"

"We're not close, we talk maybe a dozen times a year. I saw him last Christmas but that was our first Christmas together in years. He has his own life."

"Tell me about his mother. When was the last time you or Gabriel talked to her?"

"I was a worse husband than a father, detective. Laura left over twenty-five years ago." Lorenzo's jaw muscles jumped. "She threatened to leave many times, but I never thought she would leave her son behind. Gabriel has never forgiven me." He drained his beer and rose to grab another. "I guess your next stop will be Canyon?"

Cooper tapped his notepad. "Starting with this address." He stood and pulled a business card from his pocket. "If you hear from your son or think of anything else that might be helpful, I would appreciate a call, Mr. Navarro. There's a missing woman whose family is very worried."

"Gabriel didn't hurt a woman." Lorenzo tilted his chin. "I know him, he couldn't."

"People do strange things when they're pushed in a corner." Cooper gave him a nod. "I'll see myself out." He paused on the porch and tapped Billy's last known address into his phone. Canyon was only ten miles away—half that as the crow flies—but the road was so twisty it would take over forty minutes to reach his destination, and that's not counting traffic. It was really turning out to be one of those days.

*　　*　　*

Dustin whined and dragged his feet, trying to convince Jarrett to go to the OXXO without him but Jarrett insisted they not be separated. Dustin changed his rumpled Sayulita clothes for a fresh t-shirt and shorts, changed his tired sneakers for flip flops, stuck his phone in one front pocket, his wallet in the other and fastened his money belt around his hips, tucking it inside his shorts.

"We're just going down the block." Jarrett was dancing with impatience in the same wrinkled, sandy, salty clothes he had been wearing for most of three days.

"I'm not going anywhere without my money and my passport, and you shouldn't either."

"I have everything right here." Jarrett held up the plastic shopping bag they used as luggage on their beach vacation.

"Don't come crying to me if someone yanks that out of your hand," Dustin sniffed.

Which is precisely what happened as they left the convenience store.

* * *

The OXXO was seven sweltering blocks away. They argued about what alcohol to buy: Dustin wanted cold beer and Jarrett wanted hard stuff. "More bang for the buck," is how he phrased it. Dustin didn't want to get drunk, he wanted something refreshing. They settled on two icy Coronas and a half pint of Wild Turkey. Jarrett pulled his wallet from the plastic bag, paid the cashier, dropped the booze, wallet and change in the bag. They stepped outside and a scruffy kid on a skateboard zoomed past them, yanking the bag from Jarrett's hand without slowing. Jarrett looked from his empty hand to Dustin's face, turned and ran down the street shouting. A few blocks away, the skateboarder dropped the plastic bag with a crash and veered around a corner.

Chest heaving, face dripping with sweat, Jarrett picked up the bag. It tinkled with broken glass, beer and whiskey dribbled in a reeking mess from puncture wounds in the plastic. He carried the bag to the nearest trash can and spread a newspaper across the top before dumping the bag upside down. He snatched at his dripping wallet, first with a cry of joy, then a hiss of pain as a sliver of glass pierced his palm.

"The kid took the cash but left the rest," Jarrett said, picking through shards of glass. "He even left my passport."

"Wasn't that kind of him," Dustin snarked. "What did he get? About two thousand dollars?"

"Sixteen-hundred and thirty-two-dollars US, another couple hundred in pesos." Jarrett wrinkled his nose at the mess from his bag: t-shirt, shorts, toothbrush, comb, all covered in glass and alcohol. He found a dry piece of newspaper and pressed it against the seeping cut on his hand. "I'm throwing the rest of this away and I still need a drink."

"Fuck that, we're going back to the room." Dustin stomped away, muttering as he pounded down the pavement, "Everything you touch turns to shit. You have fucked this up from the first day. I told you we didn't need to take Fife's money so fast. We should have never breathed a word to anyone, especially not the damn pilot. What was I thinking? You're as big an idiot as I am."

"Hey, I'm not an idiot. I came up with the code."

"I wish we had never done this. Adrienne is somewhere hurt and we're going to jail. We're both idiots. Stupid, greedy, selfish, idiots." He skidded to a stop, grabbing Jarrett's arm. "Someone's in our room." Light spilled from the open door of the motel and a police car idled at the curb.

"Let me guess, you paid for the room with a credit card?" Dustin hissed, cowering behind a palm tree.

"You paid for the room with cash, dummy, remember?" Jarrett scuffed his foot across loose gravel. "I used a credit card when I had that pizza delivered but that was days ago."

"Way to go, genius. They have all our stuff."

"Hey, if we hadn't gone for booze we would have been caught," Jarrett protested. "In fact, if I hadn't forced you to walk to the OXXO, you would have been asleep when they raided our room. You should be thanking me."

"Thanks for nothing." Dustin rubbed his hands across his face. "I need to get drunk. Let's get some more Wild Turkey and go to the beach. Somewhere dark so I don't have to look at you."

CHAPTER TWENTY
ALL THE STARS

The sandy clearing shimmered gold and silver in the light of a nearly full moon and countless stars. Andy turned in a circle, arms held away from her sides as if poised for takeoff. The night sky was unlike any she had seen before, a pure, clear black that made every star pop with cold brilliance. "We don't have skies like this in the Bay Area," she said. "Too much pollution." Pollution of every kind: light, noise, smog, people, cars, and the joy-stealing weight of things no one needs, but everyone wastes their lives chasing. *I'll never go back to that other world.*

Rachel walked closer, holding hands with Laz. "You must be tired." She draped her arm around Andy's shoulder for a swift squeeze before dropping Laz's hand and striding away. "Let's put the car away and go inside. I'll move the four-wheeler. Laz baby, you back the car in."

"She's a bossy thing, isn't she?" Laz said from the corner of his mouth. He cut his eyes to Andy. "How are you feeling?"

"Good. I feel good." She flashed a smile, brief as a spark. Rachel rolled the four-wheeler out of the carport, tires crunching on the gritty soil. "Better move the car, Laz baby." Andy caught his death stare before she turned away to study the starry sky.

Laz backed the Civic into the small carport until the rear end touched the hillside, squeezed himself out the driver's door and locked the car. Rachel rolled the four-wheeler into the carport and dropped a black tarp over the opening.

"Okay, kids, let's go inside." Rachel waved them towards the front door. "I hear a beer calling my name."

Laz gave her a sharp look. "Should you be drinking?"

"The doctor said I can have one beer a day." Rachel grabbed his hand and kissed his cheek. "But the baby and I appreciate your concern."

Andy was curious to see the inside of the house but damn, Rachel was bossy. And handsy. She was constantly touching Laz, and touched Andy often enough to be annoying. Rachel flipped on a light switch and Andy forgot to be annoyed. "We have electricity." She took in the large living space, her mouth open in amazement. "This is beautiful, Rachel."

"Aww, thank you." She touched Andy's forearm. "The furniture came with the house and the money I spent buying the decorations from the shops in town made me very popular." Rachel slipped an arm around Laz's waist and patted him on the chest. "Like we planned, baby. Everyone loves Rachel Green. Anyone who comes to San Sebastian looking for Cindy Moore is going to be disappointed. There's one lady who calls out 'Jennifer Aniston' when I walk in her shop," she said. "Makes me giggle every time. And the pillow lady calls me Verde." She touched Andy's arm again. "That's green in Spanish."

"Thanks. I'm picking up a few words here and there."

"I'll be teaching both of you Spanish, starting tomorrow. You can't live here and not know the language." It was the most alpha phrase Laz had uttered since Rachel took over.

The living area was rustic, the rough wooden floors strewn with sturdy rugs and thick blankets hung on the brick walls. A blackened fireplace dominated one corner. No sign of electronics except a speaker cube near the hearth with an iPod propped on a charger. The heavy furniture looked as if it had been chiseled from the native trees: four chunky chairs with rough edges, topped with a profusion of pillows in various shapes, sizes and colors. Two larger pieces of log furniture looked less like couches than storage for the blankets that were folded, layered and pooled in puffy piles. The light came from a single LED bulb on a large table lamp, the base made of hand-thrown clay, the shade a pastel striped rough cotton. The large space opened to arched doorways at either end.

"Obviously this is the living room." Rachel sketched a Vanna White pose. "Come this way, Andy baby, I know you want to see your bedroom." She headed to the right-hand hallway.

Andy couldn't stop herself; she caught Laz's eye and mouthed, "Andy baby?" She had to pinch her nose to stop a snort at his expression.

Rachel stopped at the first door in the hall. "Here's the toilet." She flipped on a switch to light a room covered in mismatched tiles—floor, walls and ceiling. The throne looked like something from an RV. The world's smallest sink was attached to the far wall. "It's a composting toilet. We'll go over the details later but it's very efficient. There's also a backup outhouse."

"Let me guess, the shower is outside?" Andy made a face.

Rachel gave a careless wave. "Don't worry, the shower is nice, you'll love it." At the next doorway, she paused. "This is where Laz and I will sleep." She ran her hand down his back and gave him a wolfish smile as they continued down the hall.

Andy stopped in the doorway to survey their room. The moon glowing through the small window offered enough light to make out a double bed with a small, rough table on each side. A thick wooden dowel was bolted to the wall and laden with clothes on hangers. She turned at the sound of Rachel's not-subtle throat clearing.

"This will be *your* room, Andy," she said with a flourish of her long arm.

This bedroom was a near twin of the other room, with a neatly made double bed and two side tables built of old pallets. Another beautiful clay lamp sat on one bedside table. Andy flipped the switch, and the cold glow of an LED bulb lit the room. A packet of chocolates and droopy flowers in a terra-cotta pot brightened the other small table. Andy turned off the lamp to see how her room looked with only the light from the window. The milky glow made her breath catch in a sigh. "It's wonderful, Rachel. But how did you know I was coming?" She glanced over Rachel's shoulder to catch a look at Laz. His face was in deep shadow, his eyes hooded.

"This is the guest room. I've been keeping it nice, just for fun." Rachel smiled sweetly. "Of course I didn't know Laz was bringing his hostage with him!" She tinkled a laugh, clutching Andy's arm with both hands. "But you are welcome in our home. I like you so much already."

"I feel at home, thank you." Andy picked up the sack of chocolates to read the label so she wouldn't have to look at either of them. "Let's have candy with that beer you mentioned."

"Sounds awesome!" Rachel gave Andy a quick one-shoulder hug. "Let's go see the kitchen."

She led them across the living room to the other doorway which opened to a room roughly the size of the two bedrooms put together. A high table and four tall stools made of reclaimed pallets took up one side of the room. A white porcelain sink and a smooth wooden countertop lined a wall, along with a small four-burner stove/oven combo and a dorm-room-size refrigerator. Above the sink, a large window offered a view of the clearing and the bottom of the driveway.

Rachel opened the fridge and pulled out three cans of Modelo. "Our electricity is only fifteen amps, so we have a small fridge." She loosened three beers from a case on the floor. "Take out a beer, put one back or else you'll have warm beer."

Laz raised his can in a toast. "Let's drink to us." He splayed the fingers of one hand across Rachel's tummy. "The four of us." He smiled, his gaze moving from Rachel to Andy. "To us."

Andy raised her beer and looked him in the eye. "To us." She tore her gaze away to look at Rachel and tapped her beer.

"To us," Rachel echoed, her lips in a thin line. She took a long gulp and stifled a burp. "Do you like to cook, Andy? The stove runs on propane and works great." Without waiting for a reply, she moved on to the sink. "Our well is in good shape, and the pump. I had the water tested and they claim the contaminants are at safe levels, whatever that means. I'm not drinking it." She opened a cupboard at the end of the counter. "We have bottled water here and I keep a some in the fridge, too." She leaned her back against the counter and wrapped one long arm around herself. "I'll show you pictures tomorrow. You have no idea how hard I worked to get this place in shape."

"It looks fantastic," Andy said.

"Is this ours, Rachel?" Laz said, gazing out the window. "Do we own this place?"

"Not technically." She took a sip before continuing, "I met a man a couple days after I arrived, a British expat named Trevor Clarke. We were talking over coffee in the square and I mentioned I was looking for a place. He owns a big hacienda. If we had continued straight instead of turning down our driveway you would have seen his place. Back in the day, the hacienda servants lived here. That's why we have electricity and a well."

"He's charging us rent?" Laz tugged on his beard, frowning.

"No, baby. Trevor said we can live here for free, just pitch in for electricity. And we're planning to switch to solar anyway. He has no use for this house, and he didn't want it to go to waste. Trevor is so cool, you'll meet him soon, maybe even tomorrow."

Laz fiddled with the taps, ran his fingers across the dials on the stove, opened the refrigerator and cupboards before turning to gaze out the window. "Yes, I need to meet this man. This kind and generous man who helps strangers for no reason."

"People are kind here, Laz. That's why we chose this town." Rachel pulled him into her arms. "Neighbors help each other. Someone may need your help someday, then you can repay the generosity." She twined her fingers in his hair and kissed his mouth.

Andy turned away. "What's this door?" She opened it without hearing Rachel's muffled answer and stepped gratefully into the darkness. A chill in the air cooled her burning cheeks. Just outside the back door was a brick and wood enclosure with a familiar black plastic bag dangling above it. The outdoor shower. It was larger and sturdier than the shower she used at the Canyon cabin, but the mechanics were the same. Andy opened the door and peeked inside. Three bowls of stone sat on a brick ledge, each holding several chunky bars of soap. Written on the bowls in thick, black marker: body soap, shampoo, conditioner. She sat on a built-in brick bench and tipped her head back to sip her beer, caught sight of the Milky Way, and dropped her hand without drinking. She gazed at the painterly sky with her lips parted, eyes wide with wonder.

"There you are," Rachel's voice interrupted as she flung the door open. "I told you the shower was nice."

Andy stood and forced a smile. "Is it okay if I shower now?"

"Do you need me to show you how this works?"

"No, I've used one like this before."

Rachel hooked her arm in the crook of Andy's elbow and escorted her through the back door. Laz sat at the high table, giving Andy a curious look as they sailed by him to Rachel's bedroom.

"I know you've been living out of a backpack and probably don't have a clean nightie or robe to wear, am I right?"

"Rachel, I can't wear your clothes. You're a foot taller than me."

"I have a robe and a t-shirt you can wear to bed." Rachel pulled her inside the bedroom and flipped on the lamp. She turned to look Andy in the eye. "I'm sure Laz has seen you in less."

"Laz has been very respectful of my privacy," Andy said evenly. "He's a gentleman."

Rachel searched Andy's face. "He's still a man, and you were his prisoner. It's an unusual situation." Her eyes narrowed. "I'm aware of his effect on women, and so is he. Very aware."

"I never felt like a prisoner." Andy stared back solemnly. "He's a good man, Rachel, you can trust him."

"I do trust him." Rachel added emphasis on 'him' and flashed a quick smile. "Kidding! I'm kidding, sorry. I've just missed him so much. We haven't spoken in three weeks, and I've been imagining all kinds of things. When he said he was taking a hostage I told him I didn't want to know any details." She gripped Andy by both hands and pulled her down to sit next to her on the bed. "I should have told him not to do it. I let him do this terrible thing to you." Rachel's eyes glistened. "I had to get away from my mother and I didn't want to think about how Gab...Laz was going to make that happen." A single perfect tear trickled down Rachel's cheek. "My mother was going to put abortion drugs in my food. She laughed, like she was joking, but I know my mother and that's something she would really do." Rachel jumped to her feet and tried to pace but she could only take shallow steps in the small room. She plopped back on the bed. "Did Laz tell you how we met? How we connected over San Sebastian?" At Andy's slight nod, Rachel firmed her mouth. "That's right, you've had time enough with Laz to hear all about us."

Rachel stood again to pace, twirling her long hair into knots around her finger. "I wasn't supposed to get pregnant. I don't want you to think I planned this or tricked him. But it happened and we made choices and decisions and I'm truly sorry that you were pulled into our mess. But Andy, I have to believe this happened for a reason. I have to believe the Universe has some purpose for making you part of our journey."

She knelt on the floor beside her and Andy cringed. *I must reek of him.* Laz had been inside her body only a few hours ago. While his girlfriend sat at her feet, Andy flashed back to the torrid sex she and Laz had this morning. It seemed like a million years ago.

"It's hard for me not to feel jealous, but I'm trying," Rachel said. "I want you to be part of our family for as long as you want to be."

"Thank you. I would like that very much." Andy stood and rubbed her temples. "Sorry, it's been a long day. I appreciate the offer of clean clothes. I am so ready for bed."

Rachel clambered to her feet. "Of course you're tired." She walked to the hanging clothes, long dresses and skirts, blouses arranged by sleeve length, all colorful, all natural fibers. She pulled out a yellow t-shirt and a hot pink cotton robe. "Will this work? Oh, take this dress for tomorrow and we'll go shopping for new clothes."

"This is very generous, thank you." Andy turned for the door.

"You're more than welcome." Rachel followed her to the kitchen where Laz sat nursing a beer. "Be sure to leave some hot water. I haven't touched my man in weeks. I'm gonna wash him up, then tear him up." She gave Laz a sizzling look, pushing his legs apart and sliding between them. "We can shower together."

Andy hurried outside where the dark could hide her tears. Her chest felt like Rachel had opened her up with sharp, shiny red talons and yanked her beating heart out by its roots. *This hurts even more than I imagined.* She turned on the shower and after rinsing herself thoroughly, she soaped her body and hair with the water off, crying silently, her face drawn in a wordless howl of misery. *Every time I go to my room, I have to walk past theirs. I might even hear them through the wall.* She opened the nozzle to rinse the soap, and quickly shut the water off when a wave of dizziness made her stomach flip. Leaning over, soapy hands braced on slippery knees, she clenched her jaws against the surge of nausea. *I don't think I can do this. I can't watch Laz love someone else.* Under the shush of falling water, she cried. "You said you would never hurt me again." A Canyon whisper, hoarse and nearly inaudible. "I was right to not believe you."

CHAPTER TWENTY-ONE
YOU OUGHTA KNOW

The murmur of voices from the other side of the wall could be her imagination, or the rush of blood in her ears, but Andy put a pillow over her head anyway. The pillow smelled of lavender. She lay on her side in a fetal curl, staring out the window, curtains open so she could see the moon and stars and the forested jungle and remind herself why she was here. Laz had seduced her with whispered stories of a magical town. Andy ran a finger along the ridge of her jawbone, tracing the still-red scar. Laz will keep their secrets. He won't tell Rachel about the murdered bandits. He won't mention the sex, or that he said 'I love you' to Andy and cut her more deeply than the knife. *We share something she never will.* Now he shares something with Rachel, something different but just as exclusive and inevitable.

*   *   *

She woke in the morning to the smell of baking bread, and pale light streaming through the window, gray with fog; Andy briefly considered sleeping more but the smell of food and the pressure of her bladder forced her out of bed. She slipped on the cheery floral print dress Rachel loaned her and was surprised to see that it fit; the stretchy fabric hugged her slight curves and Andy felt feminine for the first time in weeks. Instead of a comb, she ran her fingers through her cropped hair and opened the door a crack to peer down the hall. Rachel's bedroom door was closed. Andy hurried to the bathroom and answered her bladder's demands before crossing the living room to the kitchen where the aroma of coffee greeted her. Bracing herself for Rachel's morning chatter, she hesitated when she saw Laz alone in the kitchen, pulling a cookie sheet of biscuits out of the oven.

"Hey you." Laz smiled, eyes crinkling. He shook off the oven mitts and gently laid his hands on her shoulders. "Good morning, Andy." He pressed a soft kiss on her cheek. "I'll make you some coffee." He turned to the stove and grabbed a steaming teakettle. "Just instant for now. We'll go to town later and have a proper coffee." He spoke without looking at her, busying himself with scooping Folgers Crystals and stirring the brown water. "I'm surprised Rachel doesn't have a fancy coffee maker, but she's been busy. She's done so much, she worked so hard, and there's still so much to do." He set the cup of coffee in front of her, cream no sugar because of course he knows how she likes it. "How about a warm biscuit? I noticed last night we had butter and honey in the cupboard and went to sleep thinking about biscuits."

He's babbling. Nervous? Embarrassed? Andy considered some sex/biscuit jokes but thinking about Laz fucking Rachel wasn't funny. "A biscuit sounds good, thanks." She started to rise.

He pressed on her shoulder. "Drink your coffee, let me serve you," Laz said with a warm smile and sparkling eyes.

Andy had to say it, but she waited until his back was turned. "You're in a good mood. Guess you got serviced last night."

"Don't," Laz said over his shoulder. His eyes caught hers and narrowed to slits. "Don't," he repeated and turned back to the food. Silence weighed heavy between them, a smothering blanket of unsaid words. He thunked breakfast on the table. They faced each other across orange ceramic plates, each plate cradling two huge biscuits, steaming and dripping with the molten gold of hot butter and honey.

"Thank you, Laz," Andy said in a quiet voice, eyeing her food. She dragged a finger across the pool of gold and stuck her finger in her mouth. Her eyes closed and she hummed in pleasure. This was not grocery store butter or mass-produced honey; if you could put sunshine in your mouth it would taste like this, rich and fresh and pure. Andy opened her eyes and caught Laz staring at her from under lowered lashes. She pulled her finger out of her mouth with a pop and looked down at her plate to break off a piece of the biscuit. "So good," she said around a mouthful. "You should make Rachel get up before these get cold."

"She likes to sleep late." Laz watched every move she made. "How did you sleep?"

"Fine. You know, first night in a strange bed is never easy." Andy dipped a corner of the biscuit in a pool of sweet-salty sunshine and examined it closely. "Better than an air mattress in a van." She popped the perfect bite in her mouth and chewed with her eyes downcast.

"Are you mad at me?" Laz rumbled. "Do you hate me now?"

Andy mopped up another savory bite, avoiding his eyes. "I'm not mad at you." She shoveled the biscuit in her mouth to end the conversation.

Rachel sauntered in and broke the silence. "Oh, my god, that smells good." She wore a baggy blue button-down shirt, her blonde hair a wild tangle halfway down her back. She rubbed her eyes with both fists like a child. "Did you make biscuits?" She yawned, patting Andy's shoulder.

"Laz made them."

"They smell heavenly, Laz baby." Rachel planted a kiss on top of his head and picked up the kettle, pouring hot water in a mug. "How long have you two been up?"

Andy held up her empty plate. "I've been awake for two biscuits."

"I've been up since that bird woke me at dawn, the bird that sounds like a car alarm." Laz rubbed the bridge of his nose. "Does he start that early every day?"

"I don't know, sweetie, I sleep with earplugs." Rachel stirred her coffee, broke a biscuit in half and sat at the table before taking a bite. "Cold," she pouted.

Laz jumped up. "I know a camping trick to warm them."

While he fiddled at the stove, Rachel gave Andy a smug-cat smile and winked. "He's so sweet, isn't he? He tries so hard to please me."

"Yes, he's very devoted." Andy mirrored Rachel's confidential tone as her eyes drifted to Laz. He wore shorts and her gaze lingered on his bare hairy thighs and muscular calves. She dropped her eyes and adjusted the hemline of her dress. "Thank you for letting me borrow this. I feel like a girl today."

"Anyone paying attention would never believe you were a boy." Rachel's smile was bright but didn't quite reach her eyes. "The hair works for you, are you going to keep it short?"

Andy rubbed the top of her head. "Yes, I think I will."

Laz delivered a plate with a halved biscuit drizzled with gold. "Here you go, nice and hot."

"Oh, you steamed it, you're so clever." Rachel pulled off a tiny edge. "Yum, so rich. I'll need to keep an eye on you, mister. You're going to make me fat." She took another tiny bite. "Are you ready to meet the chickens, Andy?"

"Ready when you are."

Rachel rose from the table, leaving her almost untouched breakfast behind. "Get some shoes on and I'll meet you outside."

Laz kept his eyes on Rachel as she crossed the living room in long, unhurried strides; he didn't move until she closed her bedroom door. He turned to find Andy staring at him with a smirk.

"What?" He frowned. "What's this face you're making?"

"She's got you dancing like a puppet," Andy said, mocking, "Oh, Laz, warm my biscuits. Oh, Laz baby, you're so clever."

"Go meet the chickens, Andy. She's waiting for you." Opening the back door, he turned with a grim smile. "She's playing you, too, can't you see?" he said, and shut the door behind him with a firm click.

We'll see about that. Instead of rushing to meet Rachel outside, Andy washed, dried and put away the dishes, wiped down the stove, counter, table and chairs. She was sweeping when Rachel flounced in.

Hands on hips, she said, "I thought you were meeting me outside? Where's Laz?"

"Laz left and I cleaned the kitchen," Andy said placidly, bending to use the dustpan. "I'm ready to meet the chickens now." She flashed a cheery smile. "I wonder where Laz ran off to?"

"He's probably looking for places to hide the money. I thought he would never stop asking questions last night, ugh." Rachel rolled her head on her stem of a neck. "I didn't really fall asleep until he got up. That bed is too small."

We've slept on smaller. "I'll get my shoes and meet you outside for real, I promise." Andy headed out of the kitchen.

Rachel followed. "We'll walk outside together. And you don't need to clean so much, I have a girl who comes almost every day."

Andy grabbed her flip-flops and focused on keeping a pleasant face and a closed mouth. Words were clawing to come out, words about wasting money on hired help when three unemployed adults lived in the house, and the potential danger of strangers invading their privacy. Laz would have to say something. *Not my job to school her.*

They made their way to the chicken coop. "Tell me about yourself, Andy," Rachel said, as if they were at a cocktail party. "Where did you grow up?"

Andy halted and turned to face her. "I know how this sounds," she said. "But I don't talk about my past." Rachel stared, unblinking. Andy continued, "If you want to tell me about yourself, be my guest. I'm a good listener and I'm sure you're an interesting person. But please don't ask questions about my past." Andy resumed walking to the chickens, one calculated step at a time so it didn't look like she was running away.

"I don't really like to talk about myself either," Rachel declared. "Let's talk about chickens."

*   *   *

They spent the morning naming, feeding, and talking about chickens. From chickens they had known in the past (very few) to chicken recipes. Andy knew they would never be best friends or sisters, but she also knew there were worse ways to spend the day, and worse people to spend the day with. She was determined to make this new life work and, like it or not, this life included Rachel. They needed to get along or this new life would be hell on earth.

"Do you like to read?" she asked Rachel when chicken talk had reached a lull. Andy was pleasantly surprised to find they liked the same authors, another deep well of conversation, another shared interest. They made lunch, sat at the high table in the kitchen and talked about books, as relaxed as two strangers could be, until Laz walked in.

"Laz baby!" Rachel slipped off the chair to hug him like she hadn't seen him in years. "I missed you. You should have left a note. Ooh, you're all sweaty. Where were you?"

Extricating himself, Laz opened the fridge, pulled out a cold beer and replaced it with a warm one. He popped the top and took a hefty drink. "I met our landlord, Trevor."

"Landlord? Psshh, Trevor's a friend, baby."

Laz gave her a long look and took another sip. "A good friend, I hear. He likes you a lot."

"Well, sure, who doesn't like me?" Rachel poked him and giggled. "You're acting jealous."

"Am I?" Laz rolled the beer across his forehead. "I apologize. Our plan was to make friends here and that's what you did. Trevor mentioned he would miss your frequent dinners now that your boyfriend is home. He wasn't surprised to see me. How did he know I was here?"

"I texted him when we got home last night. I thought he might hear the car and be curious or worried about me, so I let him know you were here."

"You're very thoughtful." Laz set his beer on the counter and rested his hands on her waist; Rachel took that as an invitation to entwine herself around him. "He showed me around his property. It's a nice place, as you know. He invited us back for drinks. I told him yes for all of us, but you don't have to go." He said this close to Rachel's ear, while looking into Andy's eyes.

"I want to go," said Andy. "I need to get out there and meet the neighbors, too. We spent all day here talking about chickens and books."

"We had a great day, babe. Andy is really fun to hang out with." Rachel patted his chest. "But you already know that don't you? From spending two weeks together in the cabin. How was the cabin, Andy?"

None of your fucking business. "Basic, nothing like this. Outhouse, no electricity."

"So...what did you do to pass the time?"

"Played cards, cribbage, mostly read books."

Rachel turned to Laz. "Sounds boring. What did you do for fun?"

"We weren't there to have fun. We were there to wait for Billy." Laz drained his beer and reached for another. "We're grownups, Rachel, we don't need constant entertainment. Some people are content with their own thoughts."

"Are you saying I talk too much?" Rachel's eyes snapped flinty blue sparks.

"I didn't say a word about you," Laz said, his voice soothing. He cupped her cheek. "Let's not talk about the cabin or anything that happened before. We're here now, together and safe. That's all that matters." He wrapped his arms around her from behind and put both of his big hands on her belly. "Have you felt him move yet?"

"Not yet, but soon." Rachel melted into his arms. "The doctor said it happens around four or five months."

Andy stuck her head in the fridge to cool her flushed face and grabbed a beer. "When are we expected at Trevor's?" she said without looking their way.

"I came home to get you two, we can go whenever you're ready. Do you want to change clothes or put on makeup?"

Rachel laughed and tossed her hair. "Put on makeup for Trevor? Not a chance."

"I don't own any makeup." Andy shrugged.

"You're lucky to have such thick, dark eyelashes. Look at me, I have the eyelashes of a rabbit."

Andy didn't bother to comment on Rachel's obvious beauty. "Should we head on over? Drink a beer on the way? Or is that tacky?"

"Not tacky, efficient." Rachel opened the fridge and felt the beers, her lower lip poked out. "I think all the cold ones are gone."

"Take mine," Laz said. "I'll take a warm one."

"So sweet." Rachel cupped his jaw, and they shared a lingering kiss.

Andy fled the kitchen to wait for them outside.

Trevor's hacienda was stunning. Decadently renovated and modernized, the sprawling adobe estate included central air conditioning and a pool area that would look at home in Hollywood. Trevor was warmly gracious, relaxed and tanned with shaggy blond curls—a Jimmy Buffett version of Pierce Brosnan with his elegant British accent and the look of a man who had enjoyed a bare-knuckle brawl in his younger days.

They lounged poolside as Trevor's live-in staff brought trays of nibbles and bottles of wine, with sparkling water for Rachel. The sun set behind the mountains; Trevor left the outdoor lights off and they searched the sky for constellations. Citronella candles flickered and sparked, the scent mingling with the steamy green perfume of the jungle that surrounded them. Classical guitar drifted from hidden speakers.

At first, Andy was skeptical of Trevor's over-the-top British affectations and outlandish flirting; she thought he was 'taking the piss' as the Brits say, having a laugh at her expense. Afternoon became evening, and she adjusted her impression of him to amusement. Moonstruck Trevor seemed determined to charm her panties off. Andy became intrigued, then captivated by his cheeky banter and roguish smiles, his seemingly genuine fascination. She encouraged him, flattered to be so effusively admired, and devilishly pleased to see Laz and Rachel looking uncomfortable with Trevor's extravagant compliments.

"I know I'm being impolite, darling, but I cannot take my eyes off you," Trevor said in his posh voice, blue eyes twinkling with mischief. "You are simply gorgeous. And you're related to this big hairy mutt exactly how?" He roared at Laz's expression and reached across the table to grip his forearm. "Forgive me, Laz, you're a handsome man but you two look nothing alike."

"We're cousins on his father's side," Andy drawled. "And I'm adopted."

"Well, that explains it." Trevor lifted his glass. "Here's to family." After they toasted, he leaned closer to Andy. "How would you feel if I asked you out on a date?"

"I don't know. Ask me and we'll both find out." She bit her lower lip, suppressing a smile.

"Andy, beautiful, ravishing Andy. May I have the pleasure of your company for an evening of fine dining at Los Arcos Friday night, followed by the elementary school rendition of Peter Pan at the cultural center?" He lifted her hand to his lips. "Say you will, or my heart will be broken."

"I would love to go out with you on Friday," Andy said, then frowned. "When is Friday?"

"This lifestyle will make one lose track of the days." Trevor glanced at his watch, something mechanical and luxurious. "Today is Wednesday, dear heart. I'll pick you up in two days, say five o'clock? Time for a cocktail before dinner."

"Two days, five o'clock. It's a date." Andy lifted her wine glass. *I have a date with a sweet, sexy man who thinks I'm beautiful. Rachel and Laz look unhappy. Life is good.*

It was nearly dawn when they said goodnight and began the walk home, Laz and Andy buzzed and stumbling a little, Rachel soberly fuming.

"Trevor was not himself tonight," Rachel said. "He was sort of rude, don't you think?"

"Because he only flirted with Andy and not you?"

Rachel blew a raspberry. "It's rude to ignore your guests."

"I apologize again for acting jealous earlier. Obviously Trevor flirts with everyone," Laz said.

Andy smacked him. "You're saying he flirts with everyone including skinny little ugly Andy?"

Laz rubbed his arm. "That's not what I meant. I'm just saying he's a player. Be careful."

Andy gave a short bark of laughter. "Funny words coming from my kidnapper."

CHAPTER TWENTY-TWO
ONE WAY OR ANOTHER

Dustin woke to a swift kick in the butt and a harsh voice with a thick Spanish accent saying, "Get up, pendejo, you can't sleep here." He opened his eyes and snapped them shut again with the sun emblazoned across both retinas. Another kick and Dustin sat up, brushing imbedded sand off his cheek. Blood thumped a pulse in his head like a nine-piece mariachi band. The empty fifth of Wild Turkey lay within his sightline and beyond that, what could only be a puddle of puke. He slowly turned his pounding head, neck creaking, to see who kicked him. The thin crack in his eyelids widened when he saw a man in uniform.

Scrambling to his feet, Dustin said, "Buenos dias, officer." From the corner of his eye he saw Jarrett talking to a bigger man in uniform.

"Buenos dias my ass," said Dustin's smaller policeman. "Why are you sleeping on the beach? Don't you see the signs? Can't you read English?"

"We fell asleep by accident, sir." The words slurred. Dustin's tongue was thick, furry, and he was still a little drunk.

"Let me see your passport." The officer held out his hand and waggled his fingers impatiently.

Dustin clutched his stomach and felt the hard ridge of his money belt tucked in his shorts. Acid rose in his throat, he swallowed, choking and coughing. "I left my passport in the hotel room."

"It is the law for you to have your passport with you at all times."

"Yes, sir, I know, but like I said, we didn't intend to sleep here. We had a bad day and came to the beach to have a drink and next thing I know you're kicking me."

"You passed out drunk on a public beach. Not only shameful and disrespectful, it is illegal. And you don't have your passport. How do I know you're not a wanted man?"

Dustin stifled a moan. "I swear, nobody wants me. We're really, really sorry. I can take you to our hotel and show you my passport." And be arrested anyway but at least he could use the bathroom first.

The cop's face hardened, and he pointed a stern finger. "I make you a deal. You pay a fine now, and we skip the paperwork. But you are banned from the beach."

Struggling to respond with his dry mouth and clouded brain, Dustin croaked, "How much?" He licked ashy lips with a sandpaper tongue. "How much is the fine?"

The officer took a step back, looked Dustin up and down, glanced at Jarrett who was deep in negotiations with much arm waving and muffled angry voices. "One hundred US dollars. Each. Your friend says he has nothing so you pay his fine, too."

"What if I don't want to pay his fine?" Dustin reached into his front pocket with a sigh of thankful relief when he found his wallet there.

"We arrest him for vagrancy," said the officer mildly.

The idea was tempting. "I have one seventy US and two fifty in pesos." Dustin opened his wallet wide to show the truth. "That's it, sir, that's all we have."

The officer motioned with his fingers, folded the cash in a thick bundle and shoved it in his pocket. "Pick up your trash and go. I don't want to see your face again." He clumped across the sand to his partner, speaking sharply in Spanish.

Dustin staggered and nearly fell while kicking sand over the puke. Bending to pick up the whiskey bottle, he held his hand against his forehead and groaned in agony. He got lucky with his wallet and money belt, but his phone was gone. Both phones were gone. Dustin and Jarrett sifted frantically through the sand until the officers shouted for them to leave.

* * *

They stumbled to the nearest shade. Dustin pulled out his wallet, slid a folded twenty-dollar bill from between two useless credit cards, and handed it to Jarrett. "My emergency stash. Walk to that store and buy water."

"Why do I have to walk?" Jarrett whined.

"Because I'm paying. Go." Dustin pushed at him. He was dying of thirst and the sight of the endless ocean was torture. He rubbed his hand across his face and hissed at the hot sting of gritty sand across his sunburned cheek.

Jarrett came back swinging the handles of two two-liter bottles of water. Dustin grabbed one and gulped frantically; cold spiked his forehead, his eyes filled, and tears spilled to mix with the water dribbling down his chin.

"I want to go home," he sputtered. "I don't care if I go to jail. I'm tired and I want to go home. Let's turn ourselves in at the embassy."

"No way, Jose, I'm not giving up. You do what you want but I won't go to jail." Jarrett sipped his water, staring at the ocean.

"Okay, then what's your next move? You have no money and I'm not giving you mine. Speaking of my money, I'll take the change from that twenty." Dustin held out his hand and Jarrett grudgingly pulled bills from his pocket. "You own the clothes you're wearing, that's all you have in the world. How are you going to live?"

"I'll figure it out." Jarrett waved his hand flippantly. "I'd rather give blowjobs in the airport bathroom for money than do it for free in prison."

Dustin shuddered. "That's an unhealthy way to make a living."

"Whatever. I'll figure out something. I've stolen before."

"And look where that got you."

"Let's go back to the room." Jarrett stood and stretched his arms straight up, his dirty, rumpled shorts sliding down to expose his pale freckled beer belly. "The cops can't still be there, right? Maybe they left some of our stuff."

* * *

After careful surveillance, Dustin scuttled to the door of their motel room. If it had been a modern place with electronic locks, he wouldn't bother to try but the metal key in his hand still worked. He walked in, hands up in surrender, cringing at his impending arrest but the room was empty except for their two suitcases, packed and waiting on the floor. He grabbed the suitcases and trundled down the noisy road to where Jarrett was waiting on a bench in the shade.

"Our bags were packed," Dustin said, breathless. "I wonder if they were planning to come back later and take them?"

"I bet they planted tracking devices in them," Jarrett said, running his hands over the hard shell of the suitcase. "We need to find someplace to unpack these."

"Just when I think you could not be a bigger idiot, you say something intelligent." Dustin rubbed his throbbing temples. "I don't know why else they would take the time to pack our stuff."

Jarrett slapped Dustin's thigh. "Here's a plan. We buy backpacks and leave these suitcases in a dumpster so it looks like we're still in Vallarta. Then take a bus to San Sebastian and find Cindy. Maybe Fife will tell the cops to leave us alone."

"We're going to San Sebastian because Cindy likes the coffee? That's a damn feeble lead."

"It's a better plan than walking into the embassy to be arrested."

*   *   *

Dustin spent some of his money belt stash to buy tickets on a tour bus to San Sebastian. They couldn't just buy a seat, they had to pay for the tour, and the bus didn't leave until eight o'clock in the morning. They discussed a taxi but decided on the more anonymous transportation; the idea of a stranger staring at them in the rearview mirror through miles of wilderness was not appealing.

"One hundred and forty dollars," Dustin grumbled. "Cindy better be there. We're running out of money and ideas."

"What do we do until tomorrow?"

"We get a room," Dustin said. "What choice do we have? We sure as hell can't sleep on the beach again."

"No, but we can go back and look for our phones."

"You really do want to see the inside of a Mexican prison." Dustin started down the sidewalk, dragging the noisy suitcase. "Let's go Waldo's for backpacks and then get the cheapest room we can find." He stopped to let Jarrett catch up. "Nothing stronger than Corona tonight, got it?"

"You're not the boss of me," Jarrett said in a snotty schoolboy tone.

Dustin stomped away. "Fine, buy your own alcohol. Oh, but you don't have any money." He stopped abruptly and pointed the opposite direction. "The airport bathroom is that way."

"Nothing stronger than Corona," Jarrett said in a childish singsong. He hurried to catch up. "Okay, Corona it is, boss."

* * *

Lyle Cooper didn't expect anyone to be at Billy's last known address in Canyon but out of protocol, he tried. After no one answered, he got back in his car and drove to the nearest neighbor; in this part of Canyon, the nearest neighbor was a good bit away. Mr. van der Zee was very helpful, inviting Detective Cooper inside for coffee and holding forth with great detail on the subject of Canyon in general and Billy Jones in particular. Both had legendary reputations.

"Next time you go looking for Billy, save yourself a drive and check with the local jail. He spends as much time there as he does in the woods."

"He sleeps in the woods?" Cooper sipped his coffee, eyebrows raised.

"The woods, people's couches when he can find one. He probably stays with his folks, too, but don't go asking me where to find them."

Cooper spent an interesting hour with Mr. van der Zee before leaving the forest in search of cell signal; he called his office and waited while they checked the system for Billy Jones who was indeed in jail: Contra Costa County jail in Martinez to be exact. Hikers had come upon Billy dismantling a florist's van in the Canyon forest and called 911; he was tearing out the catalytic converter when the police arrived. The battered

Dakota that was Billy's personal vehicle held a smelly jumble of fast-food wrappers, dirty clothes, and a grocery bag containing over fifty thousand dollars in one-hundred-dollar bills. Cooper arranged to interview Billy in jail.

"Where did you get the money, Billy?" Cooper asked again, leaning close to the mesh screen between them. "I know the money came from Gabriel Navarro and you better start talking. He kidnapped a woman and I believe she's in danger."

"Kidnapped? Ha!" Billy clamped both hands over his mouth as if to stuff the words back down his throat. His eyes were as wide as they could go.

Cooper sat up straight. "What do you know about Adrienne Berg? No more lies, Billy, kidnapping is federal. Start talking."

Billy laid his head on the table and covered it with his arms, ostrich-like. "Fuckety-fuck-fuck-fuck," he said. "Fucking Gabriel." He lifted his head. "I need a lawyer."

An attorney was presented, and Billy spilled his guts; he wasn't taking the rap for kidnapping. The public defender seemed to be nodding off during questioning.

"Gabriel told me he needed a passport, then later he called and said make two. That's all I know about the girl."

"Woman," Cooper corrected automatically. "You met her. Tell me why you said she wasn't kidnapped."

"I could see the way they moved around each other, the way they looked at each other. Those two were having a grand time together." Billy added a leer and a wink.

"What are the names on the passports?" He wrote them in his notebook and called his office to start a trace. "Adrienne was traveling as a male?"

"Yeah, her hair was real short, like a flattop. And she wore clothes like a teenage boy would wear. I didn't think she looked like a boy." Billy gave an exaggerated shrug. "She looked like a pretty girl with short hair and baggy clothes."

"When was the last time you spoke to Gabriel?"

"That day, when I gave them the passports."

"What day? What was the date?"

"Fuck, I don't remember, man. I don't keep track of days."

"How did you know what day to meet Gabriel?"

"Oh, shit, that's right. June twenty-third, my grandma's birthday. That's the only reason I remember the date," Billy said proudly. "He wanted me to come sooner, but I was...held up longer than expected."

Cooper called his office again and added the date. He pointed at Billy. "Where were they going? I know he told you."

"He said Mexico, that's it, I swear. He wouldn't say the name of the town, he said it was better I didn't know. In fact, I heard the girl...I mean, the woman say she didn't know where they were going. He didn't even tell her."

"And she seemed to be going willingly?"

"Very."

Cooper pointed a finger at Billy. "Tell me where they were hiding."

"It doesn't have an address, sir." Billy leaned back in the chair and crossed his arms. "It's an unmarked trail through the forest. I can take you there, but I can't explain how to get there."

"The forest? They were hiding in Canyon?"

"Lots of places to hide in Canyon."

"I'll get a pass tomorrow." Cooper paused in the doorway. "Forensics is working on the van. If it was used in the abduction of Adrienne Berg, that makes you an accomplice." He turned to the sleepy-eyed public defender. "Explain to Mr. Jones why it's in his best interest to cooperate."

CHAPTER TWENTY-THREE
NEVER BE THE SAME

Andy woke early and tiptoed past Rachel's bedroom door; it was propped open with a brick, and she paused, stealthy-like, to listen for Laz's breathing. After a stop at the bathroom, she went to the kitchen, put on the kettle, and gazed blankly out the window until the whistle threatened to blow. She mixed a cup of instant coffee and took it outside to say good morning to the chickens. They gurgled back in sleepy-chicken voices.

Footsteps on the gritty soil made her stupid heart lurch. "Jerk," she grumbled to herself as Laz headed towards her. He wore a snug white t-shirt and navy board shorts, his beard just this side of unruly. Carrying a steaming mug, his face pleasantly neutral, he stopped several feet away.

"Good morning, Andy."

"Morning, Laz. Are you awake enough to talk about something serious?" she said, businesslike, conscious of the shift in their relationship with Rachel on high alert for any interaction that looked or sounded too friendly. The rules had changed with the addition of a new player.

He cocked an eyebrow. "How serious?"

"I don't think having a maid is a good idea."

Laz absently stroked his beard. "I don't know if Rachel will give up her maid." He caught Andy's eye. "I understand your concern but it's not a bad thing to help the local economy by giving someone a job. It builds loyalty. You know, like your friend Trevor. He employs a couple dozen locals and they love him."

"*My* friend? I just met him."

"You just met him yet you're going on a date."

"Sure, to know him better. That's what grownups do. Besides, we're supposed to blend in with the locals." Andy kept her attention on the chickens, fascinated with chicken society routines, their posturing and busy-body ways. The chickens gave her something to look at besides Laz's biceps bulging from the sleeves of his tight shirt. "I'm going to town with Rachel today."

"Yes, she told me. I slid some pesos under your door." He touched her arm, a feather stroke, and dropped his hand.

"I need access to cash. I don't like to ask you for money," Andy said, sidling a step away. She added a soft, "Thank you."

"No. Thank you." Laz moved a step closer. "I wouldn't be here if not for you. Rachel would be here alone, wondering. I owe you my life."

Andy took a big step backward so she could look in his eyes without her neck creaking. "You would have done the same."

"I put you in danger. I can never forget the debt I owe you."

"Forget," she snapped. "Stop talking about it. I want to *be* Andy. I want to forget my life before San Sebastian. Got it? Stop talking about the past." An echo from her life before, speaking a similar sentence to Dustin. *Forget the past.* You cannot change it, you can only learn from it.

They were scowling fiercely at each other when Rachel walked out the front door, and they moved apart, so smoothly it seemed choreographed. "Why do you look so grumpy?" Rachel said, yawning. She twined an arm around Laz's waist and leaned her head on his chest. "Good morning, hot stuff," she purred.

Laz planted a light kiss on her temple. "I was about to start breakfast," he said, slipping from her grip. "Fresh tortillas and scrambled eggs, coming right up. Don't stay out here too long or your food will be cold." He took long strides back to the house.

Rachel watched him, chewing on her bottom lip. "He's so perky in the morning, how do you stand it?"

"I never noticed him being perky before. Must be something you're doing for him." Andy tossed a handful of feed at the chickens and smiled at their antics.

"I'm not doing as much for him as I would like," Rachel mumbled around her coffee cup.

Andy tossed the last of the chicken feed and wiped her hands on her shorts. "Let's go have breakfast," she said, and walked away without waiting to see if Rachel would follow. *I do not want to hear about your sex life, lady.*

* * *

Rachel and Andy rode the four-wheeler to town, wearing pants and long sleeves to avoid being scratched by the overgrown bushes on the way. The retail shops were open, and Rachel took Andy to each one, introducing her to the shopkeepers. It was hard to believe Rachel had only been here a few weeks; she was greeted at each shop with shouts and cheek kisses. After introductions, Andy got her cheeks kissed, too. Everyone knew Trevor, and knew Rachel lived in his guest house. The entire village would soon know that Rachel's boyfriend and his cousin had also come to make San Sebastian their home.

The women bought something at each store and soon the basket on the four-wheeler was crammed: a new dress for Andy's date, candies and pastries to take home, a drip coffee pot to use on the stove. They added some of the local organic coffee and a grinder to their pile of loot. Andy made a lot of new friends, because of her generous spending, and because she was friends with Senor Trevor.

Andy was relieved that the pharmacist, Senor Aguilar, spoke fluent English. They discussed her thyroid medicine while Rachel browsed the shelves. Senor Aguilar told Andy that levothyroxine could be purchased over the counter, no need to see a doctor or get a prescription. He did not stock the pills, but he would add some to his next order that would come in three weeks. Andy did a mental calculation. It would be close but even if she had to cut her dose in half for a few days, she would be fine. For a few days. More concerning was the possibility that ordering this medication would somehow alert the people searching for her. Levothyroxine is common and worthless on the black market, so this mildly troublesome worry Andy kept to herself. Laz had enough on his mind.

Most people Andy met that day spoke at least some English and she made a point of asking them to name things for her in Spanish. Her clumsy accent had them roaring and she laughed at herself freely, wholeheartedly. More than anything she wanted to assimilate, immerse, and become part of the village, wishing she could already be five years in the future, knew every name and spoke fluent Spanish. Twenty years from now she wanted folks to say they didn't remember a time before Andy and Rachel and Laz.

Ending their day with cocktails under the white and rust arches of the shady Los Arcos patio, Rachel toyed with a glass of iced white wine and Andy sipped a margarita made from local tequila and mangoes. They sat in long silences between idle chatter, people watching—and being watched. Andy was disconcerted at how often Rachel was greeted and how many people went out of their way to speak to her; it would be impossible to keep a low profile in this small town. *If someone from my past walked by, would they recognize Adrienne Berg?* Maybe today, even with short hair. But by the end of summer, she would be tanned and rounder. Curvy. Andy planned to eat everything she wanted since she no longer cared about looking slim for designer clothes and phony people.

"I'm making myself a promise, Rachel." Andy tipped her sunglasses down.

Rachel mimicked her gesture. "Yes?"

"From now on, all my waistbands will be stretchy. I plan to be plump as a peach."

"I'm on board with comfy clothes, but I refuse to get fat. I'm not gaining one pound more than I have to." Rachel cupped her left breast, wincing, and plunked her hand back in her lap. "Oops, I shouldn't be groping myself in public. But my boobs hurt and they're getting bigger. It will be stretch mark central in there." She pursed her lips. "Do you have kids?"

Andy shot her a glare. "I wouldn't be here if I had kids." She took in Rachel's look of wide-eyed curiosity. "I can't have kids. On purpose."

"I'm pretty positive this will be my only kid," Rachel said lightly and tasted the tiniest sip of wine. "Laz might not like it but it's my body, my choice."

Since Laz had already told her he hoped to have more than one child, Andy knew he wouldn't be happy with this news. It was Rachel's decision to make but Andy's heart broke a little for Laz. She swirled her drink, watching the ice spin and blinking back the sting in her eyes, feeling sorrow for his loss, but also feeling a rush of hot glee that this news would cause him pain.

*   *   *

They headed home on the fully loaded four-wheeler with long-legged Rachel driving and tipsy Andy clinging to her back like a monkey, gripping Rachel's waist with one hand and a paper sack full of smoked ribs in the other. They rode home screaming and laughing over bumps and they were still laughing as they rolled down the green gauntlet, ducking and dodging low branches.

"I see Laz by the chicken coop." Rachel gunned the engine, jerking them forward.

Andy shrieked and clutched at her shirt. "Don't make me drop the ribs!"

Bare-chested, shorts riding low on his hips, Laz plucked his shirt from a nearby branch and used it to wipe his face.

"Don't put on your shirt for us, you sexy, dirty man." Rachel leaned forward to kiss him without touching him. "I like you topless."

He tugged the shirt over his sweaty head. "Did I hear the word ribs? I smell ribs." Andy shook the bag. "Aha! I see ribs, and I'm starving. But before we go inside let me show you what I did here." Laz led them to a long, deep, wooden storage bin attached to the back of the chicken coop, raised two feet from the dirt on bricks and undetectable from the other side. He lifted the lid. "Their food, medicine, all the chicken shit goes in here. Straight down, under the bricks, is all but a hundred thousand of our cash. If we're in a hurry to get it out, the three of us can yank the whole thing off. Otherwise, we undo these screws, this comes off. Move the bricks and dig. It's buried about three feet down, wrapped up tight in a tarp."

"Aren't you smart! You worked real hard today, Laz baby." Rachel blew him a kiss and started the four-wheeler. "Wash up, sweet cheeks, and let's eat."

Laz winced visibly at 'sweet cheeks' and Andy's lips curved in a wry smile. *She doesn't know him at all.* Taking another look at Laz's work, she was struck by the irony, to think of all they went through for this money, to live in a place where they hoped to not need money. Pain, fear, dirt, sweat, tears, and blood for a pile of paper buried under chicken shit. Andy had to believe all this happened for a reason, otherwise they were a clusterfuck of fools.

* * *

The three of them pressed close together and scarfed down sloppy ribs standing over the kitchen sink, talking about their day. Rachel made a point of standing between them, but Laz was close enough for Andy to inhale his familiar spicy, sweaty man-smell. She wanted to rub barbecue sauce on his throat and bite, she could taste his earthy skin in her mouth. But she couldn't touch him. She couldn't even catch his eye in a hot glance of longing, a secret communication sure to be intercepted by Rachel. It was something she had to accept; they would never taste each other again. A thing she cannot change.

* * *

They had a sort of cozy, friends-at-home evening, and Andy expected this would become their routine. They settled in the living room and put on music, lounging on the furniture and repositioning piles of pillows and blankets that were fast becoming their favorite thing to joke about. Rachel found a deck of cards and they flopped on the floor to play three-handed spades. Creating a safe space for the baby was the main topic, and they discussed improvements for the property like an indoor shower and tub.

They talked about what to plant in their first summer garden and how much to plant; they wanted to grow enough produce to share, sell or barter—anything to deepen their roots in San Sebastian.

The evening was pleasant enough, but the undercurrent of tension was like a bad smell or a faint but persistent high-pitched whine. Rachel would drape a long arm or leg across Laz, and he would find an excuse to move. He avoided any reason to touch or look at Andy, to the point of absurdity. Rachel watched Laz's hands with a hawk-like intensity, only shifting her gaze to watch his eyes. The strain was wearying.

Andy yawned. "I'm going to bed," she said, scrambling to her feet. "We have a big day of playing in the dirt tomorrow, kids. Best get some rest."

"Good night, Andy," Rachel said, sliding into Laz's lap. "Speaking of playing..."

Blocking out the sound of Rachel's throaty purr, Andy closed her bedroom door and left the lamp off to move about the room by the light of the moon. She undressed and stood naked at the window, indulging in a fantasy of Laz walking into the clearing and seeing her. He would hold his finger to his lips...shhh...and motion for her to meet him in the forest. She would climb out the window, follow him naked into the deep green to grope and grapple and howl like animals. *That can never happen.* A small noise escaped her. *That can never happen.*

She replaced Laz with Trevor, rolling around on the forest floor, and it was still exciting, but the feelings were superficial lust. *I may fuck Trevor, but I made love with Laz. We both know that, and we will never be the same.* Laz's promise to Rachel was frustrating but Andy respected him for his loyalty, twisted as it was, and loved him in a strange way because of his commitment to his baby. She acknowledged this was an irrational sort of love and respect, springing from the bond of their secrets. A bond so secret it felt sacred. Their church of two. *Rachel could leave him someday.*

Andy lifted her shoulders in an infinitesimal shrug and crawled into bed, sun-dried sheets crisp on her bare skin. She dreamed of a garden with the tallest, ripest corn, silk waving golden in the sun, row after row of meaty heirloom tomatoes in reds and greens and purples—a vast, fecund garden studded with all colors of peppers and giant sunflowers with happy faces.

The garden was obscenely lush, steamy, squishy underfoot. Andy was filled to bursting with pride and a bright joy to see all the food they had grown to share. Feeling secure, safe, with a sense of belonging. And breathless anticipation, knowing that Laz was waiting for her beyond the rows, in the forest. Waiting for her with his welcoming body.

CHAPTER TWENTY-FOUR
SOMEBODY THAT I USED TO
KNOW

Andy woke with vivid memories of her dream-garden. After breakfast, she used a sharp branch to draw long straight lines in the clearing while Rachel and Laz stood by with matching bemused smiles. Andy scratched in big letters: corn, tomatoes, peppers, sunflowers, chattering all the while about her dream—leaving out the Laz part—and how they had grown enough food to feed the entire town. She tossed down her stick and turned to face them.

"Well?" Andy waved her arm in a wide swoop. "What do you think? Is this too much?"

"It seems like a lot for three of us." Laz laid a hand on the small of Rachel's back. "And how long can you help in the garden before your belly is too big? Then you'll have a baby to care for. We'll help as much as we can, but you'll be feeding him."

All eyes went to Rachel's boobs, she covered them with both hands. "Yes, I know I have to breast feed. I mentioned getting formula at the market and you would have thought I planned to give the child dog food."

"What if we hire people to help in the garden?" Andy meandered barefoot down her dirt-marked rows. "Just to break up the dirt, that's the hard part. Then we plant, water, weed and eat."

"I like that idea," Laz said. "Rachel? Do you want to delegate some labor?"

"Hmm, let me think." Rachel struck a dramatic thinking pose. "I was *so* looking forward to hoeing this hard packed dirt."

"We'll ask the helpers to leave you some." Laz squinted at the sky. "Let's drive into town and post something in the cultural center for help wanted."

Andy blurted, "Should we be using the car?"

"What's wrong with the car?" Rachel said.

"I was being extra cautious and ditched the California plates." Laz picked at a callous on his thumb. "The plate on there now was stolen in Mazatlán." He leveled a look at Andy. "I don't think anyone in San Sebastian is checking plates."

"I'm walking to town." Andy held up her hand at his protest. "I'm doing this. You two can have some alone time." She needed some alone time of her own; the pain of seeing Laz with Rachel was constant, ranging from a sharp stab to a dull ache, sometimes faint but always present.

*   *   *

Andy grabbed her sunhat and a bottle of water; town was a ten-minute walk on a rarely traveled dirt and cobblestone road. Ten minutes alone in the sights, sounds and smells of her new home. Ten minutes to think of nothing but cloud shapes and birdsong, to think of anything but Rachel and Laz touching each other and trying their damnedest to fall in love. Andy didn't see another person until she reached the main road into town, and that road was busy. She waited for a tour bus to pass and darted across the square to the candy shop.

"Hola, Andy." Natalia, owner and candymaker, greeted her from a tall chair by the cash register, her perch from dawn to dusk. "Where's Jennifer Aniston?"

"She stayed home this time. I had to have more of your delicious coconut candy."

"Andy is here for candy?" Natalia cackled at her rhyme. "My nickname for you now is Dulce."

Andy smirked. "You should pick a different nickname. I'm not very sweet."

Natalia cackled again. "Keep eating that coconut candy and sugar will run through your veins."

"This candy is amazing. You have a gift." Andy paid her as she ate out of the bag. "I need a favor, Tia Natalia." Bold, calling her Auntie after only one meeting, but that's what Rachel called her. "Can you write a notice for me to post in the cultural center? In Spanish. We want to hire some people to help start our garden." Laz would have done this for her, but after saying she would do this alone, Andy didn't want to ask him for help.

"I don't know of anyone looking for work. Senor Trevor hires everyone."

"You mean I have to headhunt gardeners from my landlord?"

"Headhunt!" Natalia chortled. "Don't take any heads, Dulce. Trevor pays his people well and I sell a lot more candy since he came to town."

"Everyone knows him."

"He's been here I think two or maybe three years. A kind and generous man." Natalia nodded sagely. "Y muy guapo, very good looking."

"Si, muy guapo," Andy laughed at Natalia's horrified expression. "My accent is bad, I know. Laz is trying to teach me Spanish."

"I heard Jennifer Aniston's boyfriend is your cousin? I heard he is also muy guapo."

"Muy, muy guapo," Andy agreed and added a crooked smile. "For a cousin." She watched through the window as the tour bus emptied, the passengers flooding the square in small bunches. The bobbing sunhats made her think of quail. "Thank you for the candy and advice, tia. I see more candy lovers headed your way." Andy slipped around the corner as a covey of tourists verged on the store. She gave the square one last glance, and from the corner of her eye she spotted a big man with bushy red hair. Taller than average, he stuck out above the crowd. Andy's brain had time to think...*huh, he reminds me of Jarrett*...but when she turned back for another look, the redhead was gone.

With no other business in town, Andy headed home, hurrying to reach her turn and get off the narrow and busy main road. After the turnoff, she slowed her pace and her mind called up the sultry, fertile garden of her dream and the heavy, hot feeling of knowing Laz waited for her in the forest.

A low moan escaped her throat. Startled, she looked around to make sure she was alone. Nothing to see but the birds and the trees. "I know I have to let him go," she said to the crows. "I can't help it if I dream about him."

* * *

At the turn to the driveway, Andy paused. Laz and Rachel probably expected her to be gone longer, and she had practically insisted they have sex. *If I walked in on them fucking in the kitchen or living room I would claw out my eyes.* She continued down the road, skulking in the shadows as she passed Trevor's driveway and made her way to the ancient cemetery where the road ended. The cemetery was small, with only five grave markers, and looked older than its mid-nineteenth century beginnings. The humid jungle encouraged moss to grow on the old brick and stone monuments; this mark of nature was left to flourish but the tall grasses were mown, the vines and low branches trimmed and pruned. Andy walked slowly from one marker to the next, admiring the handiwork, although her nearly non-existent vocabulary was not helpful in reading the chiseled Spanish words. She heard a noise and turned to see Trevor standing at the entrance.

"Tell me you want to be alone and I'll go," he said.

Andy waved him closer, smiling. "No, it's fine. Isn't this an interesting place? It reminds me of Mayan ruins. Not that I've been to any Mayan ruins, but I've seen pictures."

"I come here often. It's quiet and one feels the weight of history." Trevor stood a respectful six feet away with a wistful smile curving his lips. "If ever you would like to see Mayan ruins in person, simply ask and I will make it happen."

"Are you magical?" Andy teased.

His blue eyes sparkled. "Yes, darling, I thought you had realized that by now."

"Can you magically produce a few people to help us prep our garden?"

"That doesn't require magic, beautiful Andy. I know just the team to help." His smile turned to a frown as his phone rang. "Excuse me one moment." He stepped away and spoke briefly in Spanish before turning back to her. "I apologize for the intrusion and the subsequent interruption but duty calls." He brought her hand to his lips for a warm lingering kiss. "I'm looking forward to our date tonight."

She kept hold of his hand. "I'll walk you home."

"I may faint from happiness."

Trevor's boyish grin made her heart do a flippy thing, even as Andy laughed at his hyperbole. He kissed her hand again as she left him at the top of his driveway, and she walked the last few meters home thinking how much she liked Trevor. He was silly and sweet and funny and kind and generous, and damn easy on the eyes, too. *I wonder what he's hiding.* Because San Sebastian was that kind of place—you're born here, or you're hiding.

At the back door, she paused to listen for noises in the kitchen and opened the door to an empty room. She crossed the living room to the hall. Rachel's door was closed. Andy froze hearing Rachel's high-pitched giggle, and her skin turned to ice at Laz's answering deep-throated chuckle. *Where to go?* Not her room, they shared a wall. She thought about having a beer at the kitchen table and pictured the moment Laz and Rachel walked past her on their way to shower off the sweat of afternoon delight. Andy tiptoed to her room for a robe, now on a mission to use all the hot water.

She came back inside to see Rachel draped across Laz's lap in one of the big chairs, Laz stroked Rachel's hair with a tender smile curving his lips. Andy's ever-present heartache delivered an icy-hot stab that took her breath away. Toweling her hair, she walked, nonchalant, past them, muttering, "Hey..." over her shoulder. She made it to her bedroom without incident, without Rachel trying to touch her or Laz connecting with a furtive glance.

Andy focused her thoughts on Trevor and prepared for her date early, staring unfocused out the window and massaging every inch of her damp skin with lotion she bought in town. It smelled like passionfruit. She bought the lotion because it smelled good enough to eat, and the artisan swore it would inflame the senses of any man. Not that Trevor needed help inflaming his senses. She slipped on her new dress, a turquoise and coral gauzy slip that left her shoulders bare and whirled around her knees. No need for a bra, plain white cotton panties (all she could find in town) and clean sandals—ready for her date in minutes instead of hours. No Spanx, no makeup to paint on, no hair to blow dry or curl. Holding a hand mirror, Andy ruffled her damp hair: boy-short, and two-toned with her natural light brown showing at the roots of her dark dye job. She checked her eyebrows and tweezed a couple of strays, flossed and brushed her teeth. When she had run out of things to do in her bedroom, she walked down the hall to hang out with her roommates until Trevor arrived.

She found them at the kitchen table and struggled to keep her envious thoughts from showing on her face. *Look at those two sexy beasts.* Rachel was radiant, glowing as only a freshly fucked mother-to-be can glow. Laz smiled lazily at Andy. "Looking good, cuz," he drawled. His golden eyes caught her gaze for a microsecond before sliding away.

"Aren't you pretty." Rachel purred, as if holding a canary in her mouth. "Trevor is going to lose his mind."

"Thank you, thank you." Andy twirled her dress for them. Her twirl was punctuated by the chirp of Rachel's phone.

"It's Trevor. He's asking if you're ready?"

"Hmm, he's early," said Andy. "Should I make him wait?" She screwed up her face as if thinking. "Tell him to come on down. I'll be at the end of the driveway."

"A gentleman would come to the door," Laz said, his face solemn.

"I've no use for a gentleman," Andy tossed over her shoulder.

She picked her way through the green gauntlet, stepping carefully to avoid getting her sandals dusty and reached the top of the driveway as a filthy, maybe-white Volkswagen Bug rumbled down the road. The paint was badly scratched in long lines, the scars of driving these narrow, overgrown backroads. The windshield was dirty, and the sun glare prevented her from identifying the driver, but Andy took a chance and struck a sexy hitchhiker's pose. The car stopped a few feet from her, the engine sputtered off and Trevor stepped out.

"All the gods have smiled on me today." He walked towards her, his smile making deep crinkles at the corners of his eyes. "You look divine, darling," he said, kissing her knuckles, "and you smell delicious."

Andy felt a blush warm her already steamy cheeks. "Thank you, kind sir. Would you give me a ride?" She stuck out her thumb, fluttered her eyelashes and bit her lip.

Trevor chuckled. "Would I give you a ride..." He crooked his arm, led her to the passenger side and opened the door, waiting until she was settled before he clunked it closed. He ran around to his side, climbed in and started the engine. "What do you think of my jungle chariot?"

"It's perfect." Andy glanced around the interior. "Cleaner than I expected."

"I spent the afternoon preparing the inside for our date, darling. I considered washing the outside but I'm afraid the dirt is all that holds this jalopy together."

*   *   *

The evening began on the patio at El Fortin with raicilla cocktails, made from a potent roasted agave concoction that had Andy's head spinning. They crossed the square to Don Mata for a lighter drink, the local's favorite michelada. The center of town was crawling with bus tourists; from the patio at Don Mata, they laughed as the harried driver tried to round up his passengers like a mama duck herding ducklings.

Trevor was attentive, charming, flirtatious, never missing a chance for suggestive wordplay, always ready with a preposterous compliment. He seemed happy to carry the conversation, regaling Andy with stories about his travels. She was content to watch his remarkable crystal blue eyes— deeply lined at the corners as if he spent a lot of time laughing—and the fascinating pronounced bow of his top lip. After a fantastic tale about hunting elephants in India with a raja, Andy shook her head, laughing. "Why do I feel like most of what you're telling me is not true?"

He leaned forward to murmur, "You're wise to be cynical. I'm a bit of a scoundrel."

She lifted her glass. "All of my favorite people are scoundrels."

The tour bus driver pulled out a bullhorn, shouting loudly and unintelligibly. Trevor frowned. "Well, that certainly ruins the mood. Shall we go to Los Arcos for dinner?"

"Can we try La Lupita instead? I haven't been yet and I hear it's very good."

"Your wish is my command, darling. It's a bit of a trek, shall we walk or drive?"

"Let's walk." Andy smiled into his eyes. "The evening is just right for a stroll."

"The evening will be perfect the moment I no longer hear that madman screeching." Trevor dropped some bills on the table and settled a firm hand at the curve of her lower back.

* * *

The square emptied as the passengers loaded on the bus. The driver bellowed through his scratchy bullhorn; it was impossible to make out the words, but he got his point across—the bus was leaving, and they were counting heads. Andy and Trevor made their way down the narrow main road to Comedor La Lupita, one of the oldest restaurants in town and a five-minute stroll from the plaza.

Trevor greeted the waitress with a kiss on the cheek. "Hola, Maria, como esta?"

Maria, a woman in her seventies, blushed. "I'm very well, Senor Trevor. Please, take this seat by the window. And who is your new friend?"

"This is Andy, she lives in my guest house with Rachel."

"Mucho gusto, senorita Andy. You are friends with Jennifer Aniston?" Maria's face split in a grin and she held her hand high above her head. "Muy alta."

Andy smiled. "Yes, she's very tall."

"Miss Maria, would you be so kind as to bring us your famous passionfruit raicilla cocktail? Andy is passionate about passionfruit."

Maria walked away giggling.

Andy eyed him warily. "You're trying to get me drunk."

"I would never." Trevor's expression was a caricature of wounded innocence.

She laughed. "Do you ever tell the truth?"

"Ask me anything. I promise to tell you the best truth I can think of." Trevor's smile slipped and he turned to look out the door, which was wide open and facing the main street. "What the devil is going on in the square today?"

Maria set the drinks in front of them, an icy concoction in a thick clay mug. "My cousin called me from El Fortin. He says the bus is leaving and they're missing two people. Everyone is looking for them."

"Very inconsiderate. They're causing an unwelcome fuss in my quiet square." Trevor looked personally affronted. "I apologize, dearest, my plan was for a quiet dinner."

"I'm having a great time. And how often do you get excitement like this in San Sebastian?" Andy sipped her drink and coughed. "Too strong," she croaked.

Trevor smiled sympathetically. "A little goes a long way when one is so tiny." He tsked. "Quite breathtaking in your fragile loveliness, but it comes with a price."

"I'm tougher than I look." Andy took another sip, even though the drink made her eyes water.

"I would not dream of underestimating you." He tipped back his head and contemplated her from behind thick honey-gold eyelashes. "You remind me of a kitten. Soft and pretty but mind the teeth and claws." He reached for her hand on the table, turned it palm up and made one long, slow stroke from the pulse on her wrist down her middle finger. "Ferociously adorable."

Andy grabbed his finger and brought it to her mouth for a gentle bite. "You think you have me figured out?"

"Why would I want to figure you out?" Trevor's voice was husky, his bright blue eyes half closed. "Be whomever you like, lie to me, be a mystery to me."

"I can do that," she said with a Mona Lisa smile.

When the last tour bus from the square clattered past, Maria was refilling their ice water. "They are very late. Never have I seen a bus leave town this late." She nonchalantly set the pitcher on their table and pulled out her ringing cell phone.

"I wonder if they found their missing passengers?" Trevor asked. He didn't seem very interested and concentrated on getting the right amount of pico de gallo on his tortilla chip.

Andy caught a glimpse of two rumpled men wearing backpacks running full speed past the window—one tall man with bushy red hair, one shorter man, pudgy and balding. Her heart climbed into her throat, choking her. More men ran down the street after them, yelling.

"Yiii! There they go." Maria cackled. "My niece at Los Arcos called me just now. Those men are the missing passengers. They tried to check into the hotel and the mayor caught them. Now they are chasing down the tour bus."

"How odd for someone to take a tour bus here to stay the night." Trevor touched her hand. "Darling, are you alright? You look as if you've seen a ghost."

Andy gulped water, hands trembling. "Do you mind if we call it a night?"

Trevor was already rising to his feet. "Maria, can you add this to my tab, please?" He held out his arm for Andy and watched her face as they walked to the door, concern in his eyes. "You look quite pale, sweetheart. Do you want to wait here? I'll bring the chariot around."

The tour bus had stopped but as she watched, it started again and tottered down the cobblestones, unfurling a faint dust cloud. The men who chased the bus were making their way back to the square at a leisurely pace. *Did I really see Dustin and Jarrett? Impossible. What do they put in these drinks?* She rubbed her throbbing temples. "I'm fine, we can walk to the car." Disappointment shimmered behind her anxiety; she had hoped to spend a few hours getting to know naked Trevor but now all she wanted was to talk to Laz. "I'm sorry to spoil our evening, but can you take me home?"

CHAPTER TWENTY-FIVE
NOT GUILTY

The driver had scowled at Dustin and Jarrett when they boarded the tour bus that morning with their bulging backpacks. "It's an eight-hour day and you look like you packed for a week."

"We like to be prepared for anything," Dustin had said without meeting his eyes.

Now, ten hours later, the driver was scowling at an entirely different level; his face fire red and dripping sweat, with bloodshot eyes and spittle at the corners of his mouth. He pointed at the two empty seats directly behind him and waited for Dustin and Jarrett to sit before he rose to stand over them, hands on hips.

"I could strangle you in front of all these people," the driver shouted and waved an arm at the grumbling passengers. "And I would get nothing but applause." Every passenger clapped their hands, some whistled and cheered. "Never in all my years of service have I lost a passenger or been more than a few minutes late. My wife is upset, my boss is upset, and all these people are upset. What were you thinking?"

"We thought it would be nice to stay longer," Jarrett said, cowering. The woman sitting behind him whacked him on the head with a shopping bag.

"That's not how this works." The driver started the bus and let forth an unmuted stream of Spanish that Dustin couldn't translate but it was clear the ass-chewing continued.

"I knew this was a stupid idea," Dustin said through clenched teeth.

Arriving in Puerto Vallarta a miserable and bumpy two-hour drive later, two police officers were waiting for the first two passengers off the bus. "Dustin Berg and Jarrett Austin. You are under arrest for an outstanding warrant in California." The smaller policeman cuffed Dustin and said with a grin, "I thought you said nobody wanted you, amigo?"

They were given one phone call, neither of them had a single phone number memorized and Dustin had to beg the officer to let him look in his wallet. He dug out his business card and called the office.

"Hello, Joan, it's Dustin Berg. I need to speak with Mr. Fife right away. It's urgent, life or death urgent."

"I'm sorry," Joan replied in a frosty voice, unlike the warm, grandmotherly tone she had used with Dustin for the past several years. "Mr. Fife is out of the country and not accepting phone calls. Would you like to leave a message?"

"No! No, Joan, listen. Me and Jarrett are in a Mexican prison." Jarrett poked him and mouthed 'jail'. Dustin poked him back harder and added a death stare. "We're in a Mexican *jail* but they're flying us back to Marin and we need a lawyer. Can you help?"

"Help? Help you?" Joan barked, so unlike her. "You stole from the company and got your wife kidnapped? Possibly murdered? And you want me to help you get out of jail? I hope you rot. Have a good rest of your day."

"No...don't hang up," Dustin pleaded to the dial tone.

They had pissed off the wrong person when they pissed off that bus driver, he had pulled some big strings to convince the local authorities to cooperate and they were tucked away in a cell to await a speedy extradition. Dustin had pictured something from 'Midnight Express' and he wasn't far off. The cell was dirty, smelly, and crowded with eight sets of bunk beds, mostly full. He had never felt softer or whiter.

"Fuck, I wish we had never done this stupid shit." Dustin took one look at the thin, grossly stained mattress on the bottom bunk and climbed to the top without comparing. Impossible for the top mattress to be worse, right? Wrong. He found a semi-comfortable position among the mystery splotches and tried not to touch anything. "Why did I ever think this was a good idea? Why did I let you talk me into this?"

"Quit whining, you fucking baby." Jarrett, lying on the bottom bunk, poked Dustin through the slats. "Don't try to pin this all on me. You helped me carry that bag on the plane."

"You shouldn't have made that joke about it being full of money," Dustin grumbled.

"You shouldn't have made a joke about hiding it in your closet. Gabriel didn't even have to look for it."

"Stupid, stupid, stupid." Dustin rubbed his eyes. "I just want someone to tell me that Adrienne is okay. I can live with my punishment if she's okay." He looked up to see the biggest, smelliest and dirtiest of their cellmates standing in front of him.

"Hey pendejo, give me your shoes."

Dustin was glad that was all he had to give up; Jarrett had to give the man his shirt. They were told Detective Cooper was waiting for them in Marin and he wanted them badly enough to charter a jet and lock them in a jail closer to home. Dustin was eager to relocate to an American jail cell while he still had clothes and a scrap of dignity left.

*   *   *

"Welcome home, boys." Detective Cooper did not look welcoming as he sat across the table from Jarrett and Dustin at the Marin County jail. "I am not interested in the money. Fife is doing his best to have the embezzlement charges dropped which I think is complete bullshit but not my business. My business is Adrienne Berg. We found her blood in your bedroom, Mr. Berg. And a very scary recording of your wife screaming that someone is cutting her. Your wife was abducted and you said nothing? You just took off for a Mexican vacation?"

"Fife sent us to look for Cindy Moore before he knew about the money," Jarrett said. He kept his gaze on the scarred table and his cuffed hands clasped.

"Cindy Moore is Gabriel's girlfriend," Dustin said.

"Yes, we know. Cindy is pregnant and ran off because her mother disapproves of the relationship. If Gabriel hadn't made the dumbass decision to steal the money and take your wife as a hostage, I would be done with Cindy Moore and her mother. Gabriel made this a big fucking deal when he kidnapped your wife. And you made it worse by not reporting it. Even if Fife doesn't care about the money, I need to know that Adrienne is alive and well."

Dustin blinked back tears. "That's all I care about. Do you have any idea where she is?"

"Somewhere in Mexico, but I have bad news, Berg. It doesn't seem as though your wife is trying very hard to get away."

"How hard can she try? Have you seen Gabriel? He's three times her size."

"I've seen video of them crossing the border together. She's traveling as a boy. Or a man, I guess. The passport says twenty-two but in the video she looked like a twelve-year-old boy."

"Where are they going?"

"We don't have any sightings of them since they passed through customs, but a description of the vehicle and the license plate has been sent to every Mexican police station that has internet. Miracles of modern technology. Another miracle would be for those underpaid, overworked Mexican police officers to give a shit about our problems."

"Why wouldn't they care? She's a kidnap victim. Gabriel took her by force, you heard the recording." Dustin slammed his hand on the table, chains rattled. "I'm her husband and she loves me. Adrienne didn't know about the money. No way she left willingly. Gabriel has some kind of power over her."

Cooper stared at Dustin, unblinking. "I *will* find your wife and she can tell me herself." He cut his eyes from one public defender to the other. "Until I hear otherwise, we're charging both of you as accessories to kidnapping."

"Wait, so even though we're not in trouble for stealing the money, we have to stay in jail?" Jarrett tried to stand but the chains yanked him back in his seat.

"Until I talk to Adrienne and she convinces me she was part of the scheme to steal the money, she is a kidnap victim. The money is no longer the point." Cooper stood and stretched exuberantly, as if to mock them for their chained wrists. "When Fife gets back in the country, the DA will have a chat with him. We'll see how quickly he changes his mind about cooperating with the embezzlement investigation." Cooper slammed the door on his way out.

Assuming their jail cell was bugged, Jarrett and Dustin whispered frantically behind cupped hands. It was completely unfair—and probably unconstitutional—to charge them with Adrienne's kidnapping.

"Why didn't you tell Cooper about that woman I saw in San Sebastian that looked like Adrienne?" Jarrett had only caught a glimpse. When he grabbed Dustin to look at the woman, she was gone.

"Fuck that guy!" Dustin said loudly because he didn't care who heard it. He lowered his voice to whisper, "He can do his own searching. I didn't see anyone in San Sebastian who looked like Adrienne and if Cindy Moore was there, the locals would remember her. She's memorable."

"I thought that one lady recognized Cindy's picture, the lady in the candy store?"

"I know!" Dustin cried, then lowered his voice. "She said she recognized her and I got excited."

"Yeah, then she said it was Jennifer Aniston." Jarrett shook his head. "I mean, they're both gorgeous blondes but they look nothing alike."

*　*　*

Billy Jones led Cooper to the hideout in Canyon. The cabin had been well cleaned but they found traces of blond hair caught in the tall weeds that they would test against Adrienne's DNA. Cooper eyeballed every inch of the tiny cabin, touched every utensil and dish, shook out every sheet and blanket, opened pillows, pulled apart the games and rifled through every book. If Adrienne stayed here for two weeks, she could have left something behind. A note that would tell him she was a hostage, or not. While standing at the window, checking each playing card against the light, Cooper saw scratches on the floor. Hash marks were dug into the wood, two neat groups of four straight and one slash, with three singles. Thirteen. Next to the hash marks was scratched 'Andy'. He called over his shoulder for a technician who took photos and lifted a section of a thumbprint.

"Andy," Cooper mused. He knew the names on the phony passports, Adrienne was traveling as Andrew Cardenas. Was she calling herself Andy because of Gabriel's demands? Or did she pick her own nickname? The more he dug into this case, the more questions Cooper had. Typical when unraveling a crime with as many moving parts as this one but what was not typical was how each 'crime' was not what it appeared. Fife refused to press charges. Adrienne might not be a hostage. Could she have faked those screams? Cut herself to leave bloody evidence? Cooper had looked for any indication that Adrienne and Gabriel knew each other before the abduction and found nothing. She had never been in the company plane or any of the vehicles that Gabriel drove for Fife. What they had in common was no close friends or family. Other than Billy Jones, Cooper couldn't find another person who called themselves Gabriel's friend. Which meant Gabriel had one friend more than Adrienne. How does a woman live thirty-two years in the same area and not have a friend? She was married to Dustin, who had plenty of friends, but none of the wives or girlfriends claimed to know Adrienne beyond casual cocktail party conversation. Cooper was left with a shadowy outline of a quiet, socially anxious introvert who preferred books over people. Who seemed to prefer anything over people. Was she so unhappy she plotted this with Gabriel? The need to hear answers in Adrienne's voice kept Cooper awake at night.

CHAPTER TWENTY-SIX
SHE WILL BE LOVED

"Are you sure you're alright, Andy?" Trevor asked again as they began their drive home.

She attempted an expression of embarrassment while in her guts, fear was churning. "I'm fine, I just drank too much." Andy trilled a silly-old-me laugh, her attention on the passing fields. "Isn't this a funny place? So strange to see coffee beans growing wild." Trevor didn't reply so she turned to look at him. "Hey, shouldn't you be watching the road?"

"The face I saw in the restaurant was not the look of a lady who had too much to drink." Trevor flicked a glance at the road, and returned his sharply curious gaze to her. "It was the look of a lady who's had too much drink and sees the lights of a policeman behind her. I saw a lady afraid."

"That's the face I make when I think I might throw up." Andy grimaced a smile. "Like, oh shit, I hope I don't barf in front of my date. That kind of fear."

"I promise not to pry further, kitten." Trevor gave her a sweetly stern expression. "But if you ever feel afraid, you can tell me. I swear on my life you can trust me and I am eager to be at your service in any small way." He patted her knee once and put his hand back on the steering wheel. "Any service at all."

"Actually, there are some services I'll require in the near future." Andy put her hand on his knee and let it linger. "I'll keep your generous offer in mind." She took her hand back to straighten her skirt and smiled with a sideways glance.

"I'm your humble servant." Approaching Andy's driveway, Trevor said, "I'm going to be bold and ask if I may have your digits? I believe that's what the kids are saying these days."

Andy snorted. "You make yourself sound ancient. What are you, forty?"

"You flatter me, which makes my ancient heart dance." Trevor flashed a cheeky grin. "I'm forty-seven. Tell me that's not ancient in the ears of a twenty-something girl."

"I'm thirty-something and no, forty-seven doesn't sound ancient. I don't have a phone, or I would certainly give you my digits." Gesturing at the tin roof of the carport, Andy said, "I can walk from here."

"Nonsense, I'll drop you safely at your front door. And Rachel has my number, promise me you will memorize it." Trevor took on the driveway, adding more grooves to his deeply scratched car, and parked in the clearing. He shut off the engine and twisted in his seat to face her. After a long, quiet moment, he said, "The moonlight becomes you, beautiful Andy." He cupped her cheek, touched the scar on her jawline with one fingertip and caught her eyes when she flinched. "If you are ever afraid, I can help." Leaning closer, he gently kissed her lips. "Call me for any reason, day or night." His low, husky voice turned playful. "You wait right there with that exact look on your face."

He ran around the car, opened the passenger door with a courtly bow and held out a hand for her to grasp. Using their linked hands, Trevor pulled her close, and rested his other hand on her waist. "I have an ulterior motive for helping you out of the car, as you can see."

"Ulterior motive? Elaborate, please." Andy parted her lips and slipped her hand around the back of his neck. That was all the encouragement Trevor needed to wrap her in his arms and kiss her until she gasped for air.

Leaning back, she rested her hands on his shoulders to look in his eyes. He was a good height for her, around five-nine or so. She didn't have to strain her neck to look at his face like she did with Laz. *He doesn't kiss like Laz.* Andy gave her head a tiny shake. "I'm sorry we missed the play."

"No need to be sorry, darling, each moment with you is a treasure." Trevor gave her one last kiss before reluctantly letting her go. "Sweet dreams, beautiful Andy." He waited until she went inside before leaving in a rattling rumble.

Andy desperately wanted to talk to Laz, but their bedroom door was closed. She had no idea what time it was...*we need a damn clock in this house*...but it seemed early for them to be in bed. *They're having sex, dummy.* She was too wound up to sleep and didn't want to hang out in her room where she possibly could hear fucking noises. Andy swapped her date clothes for shorts, grabbed a blanket and went out to the clearing with her water bottle. She shook the blanket out on the ground and laid down with her arms crossed behind her head. The image in her mind of the men running past the restaurant window played over and over while Andy tried to convince herself it was ludicrous to think that her not-too-bright husband and his knucklehead friend tracked her to San Sebastian. The notion was absurd, and she wanted to hear Laz agree.

He materialized in the open front door as if she had wished him into existence. Andy sat up and watched him from the corner of her eye, waiting tensely for Rachel to follow. Her rigid muscles relaxed when Laz closed the door behind him. Keeping her eyes averted, she tried to still her stupid heart as he walked to the edge of the blanket. Neither spoke for a long moment.

"You're home early," Laz rumbled, looming over her. "How was your date?"

"We had a good time. Trevor is very nice." Tilting her head to see his face hurt her neck—and her heart; he looked sleep-rumpled and Rachel-warm. Andy fiddled with the top of her water bottle. "A funny thing happened." She glanced up, and looked away with a sharp laugh. "We were having dinner at La Lupita and when I looked out the window, I swear I saw Dustin and his pal Jarrett running after a tour bus."

Laz squatted to bring his eyes level, carefully staying off her blanket-marked territory. "How sure are you about what you saw?"

"Not very. I had too much to drink and I only saw them for a second." She leaned forward, her eyes intent on his. "That's crazy, right? Mexico is huge, how could they track us here? Who knows about your connection to San Sebastian?"

"Rachel has discussed her travels with her mother, but San Sebastian is one of a dozen cities she's visited in Mexico. It's possible someone is checking each of those towns." He lowered himself from a crouch to sit on the dirt, wincing, and pulled a rock from under one bare thigh.

"I'll share my blanket, unless you think Rachel would disapprove." Andy refused to look at him, twisting the cap on her water bottle back and forth. Her pulse thudded faster when he moved to sit beside her. She closed her eyes and inhaled deeply, filling herself with his warm, spicy scent. Even tainted with Rachel's smell—something floral and gagging—waves of want pulsed red flashes on her eyelids and butterflies tickled low in her belly.

"She's sleeping," Laz said. "I was going to sleep in the living room so she could be more comfortable, but I saw you outside." He tilted his head and waited to speak until Andy looked at him. "It probably wasn't them, and if it was, you saw them leaving town so that's a good thing. They didn't find us."

"Maybe they went to tell the police?"

"Why would they be on a tour bus?" He rubbed her knee.

Andy hadn't felt his touch in days, they were so careful in front of Rachel. Her heartbeat quickened and she laid her hand on his for a brief squeeze. He rolled his hand palm up and cupped her small hand in his large one, positioning himself where he could see the house and their cradled hands were hidden by his body.

"Did something happen with Trevor? He's very pushy."

"He's a very nice man. I like him." His hand curled around hers was a poor substitute for the feeling of his body spooning her, but his closeness gave her something she had been missing, filling an urgent need. "Are you happy, Laz?" Andy regretted her words when he pulled away.

"I'm trying to be happy. Rachel and I are learning about each other. Big picture, we still want the same things. It's living together that takes work and compromise." He circled his knees with his arms. "Rachel's happiness is as important to me as yours."

"More important, you mean. She's practically your wife and she's carrying your child. Her happiness should be vastly more important than mine."

"Rachel chose this life. I forced you into it."

"I *chose* it. Maybe I had less time to think about it than you and Rachel, but I chose this life. You don't get to take credit for everything." Andy stuck her tongue out to lighten the mood. "I'm glad I'm here and that's the truth. Stop beating yourself up on my behalf."

"I know it hurts you to see me with Rachel."

"You're such an asshole. Get over yourself, I have." Andy rolled out of her tailor's pose to lie on her back. "Stargaze with me and be quiet or go back inside."

Without another word, Laz rolled to his back, stretched out full length and laced his fingers behind his head. The night quieted with only the sound of bugs calling to each other and a breeze up high that shimmied the treetops. In the clearing surrounded by jungle forest the air was thick, calm, and fragrant with summer-heated green.

If she shifted the slightest bit, their skin would touch. So close, but so far away. Andy knows how his body would feel—hot and humid, hard and soft, hairy and smooth. The curls on his chest would be damp with perspiration. She knows how he would feel under her cheek, she knows his smell and the taste of his sweat. Shifting a millimeter away, she concentrated on the night sky, making up her own constellations. Like watching clouds, she picked out shapes in the stars. A runner, a horse, a guitar. She closed her eyes and saw the stars on her eyelids, listened to the sounds of Laz breathing, his heartbeat and the rush of blood in his veins; she heard the pulse in his throat and remembered how it felt on her mouth.

Andy sat upright. "I'm going to bed." He stood when she did and picked up the blanket. She took it from his hand and shook out the dust.

"This was nice," Laz said in a husky whisper. "We should do this again."

"Sure, next time invite your wife." Andy forced herself to walk slowly back to the house, slowly to her room, even though she wanted to run. *I don't trust myself around him.*

Standing at her bedroom window, she undressed by the cold light of the moon. A movement in the clearing caught her attention and her heart skipped a beat, then galloped. Laz was outside, watching her through the window. Andy could feel his eyes on her naked body, his gaze carried weight, brushing across her breasts, a caress, a tickle across her belly. She grabbed the curtains and yanked them closed. *He would take me because he could, because I would let him. But he would still be Rachel's.*

* * *

"Can I use your phone to call Trevor?" Andy asked Rachel over coffee in the morning. "He says we can borrow his crew to till our garden and I want to get started on that today."

Rachel pushed her phone across the table. "I thought you had a phone?"

"Where is that phone, Laz?" Andy asked.

"Still in the car. Do you want me to get it?"

"If you give me the keys I'll get it myself."

Andy squeezed into the passenger door of the Civic, found the phone and charger in the glove box and glanced into the well between the front seats. She was surprised to see the gun was there, having assumed Laz had hidden it somewhere in the house. Checking that the safety was on, Andy set the gun on a shelf in plain sight with a mental note to tell Laz she had moved it. Strangers weren't likely to come into the carport and if one of them needed the gun, they may not have time to search for keys.

* * *

Trevor was quick to send help; four men and two mechanical tillers were breaking up their garden soon after breakfast. Trevor chatted with Laz and watched the work outside while Andy and Rachel baked banana bread with every door and window open to allow the heat to escape. They made a big batch so they could send a fresh loaf home with each of the workers.

Rachel washed dishes, gazing out the window. "Trevor sure is cute, isn't he?" She wrinkled her nose as if she were oohing over a puppy.

"He's gorgeous," Andy agreed, drying a plate. "And very sweet. I like him a lot."

"I'm glad you're having fun. I know how much Laz worries about you." Rachel said over her shoulder as she turned to the stove.

"Yeah, well, he can just stop worrying and stop burdening you with his stupid worries."

With her back turned, her voice halting between syllables, Rachel said, "Sometimes I think he talks about you to make me jealous." She flashed Andy a quick smile before turning back to her project. "It's awful to think this but sometimes it feels like he wants us to fight over him, like he doesn't want us to be friends."

"Too late," Andy chirped. "We're friends. And Laz is doing what all ridiculously handsome guys have done since cave man times. Manipulating women with their dreamy eyes and promises." She tried a hearty belly laugh but the truth was too close, and the sound was hollow.

"Men!" Rachel raised her hands to the sky. Still avoiding Andy's eyes, she added, "Laz can be a jerk, but he really is very sweet and loving, too. He worries that you're not happy."

Andy touched her arm and waited until Rachel looked her in the eye. "I'm happy. I don't know how many ways I can tell him. Next time he starts yapping to you about me, slide him a note that says 'shut the fuck up'. I'll even write the note for you."

Rachel threw her head back, laughing a bit too hard. "Do it, I want him to see it in your handwriting." She sobered and looked at her with smiling eyes. "I knew we would be friends. I'm going to hug you, even though I know you hate it."

Andy hugged her back with all the sincerity she could muster. It was the least she could do.

*   *   *

"This must be what heaven smells like." Trevor walked in the kitchen and swooped Andy off her feet, twirling her in a circle while she shrieked and squirmed. "My angel, the most beautiful baker on earth." He set her gently on the ground and pressed a firm kiss on her lips. "I warned you, I'm a terrible scoundrel, taking liberties."

She pushed him away, laughing. "Take all the liberties you want, but I prefer my feet on the ground. I might need to run." She caught eyes with Laz as he came in, before Rachel wrapped him up.

"I must make you love me so much that you will never have a reason to run." Trevor kissed her hand, his blue eyes twinkling.

"Love?" Andy sputtered. "Silly man. That's exactly what I would run from." She deliberately made eye contact with Laz before turning a playful smile to Trevor. "If I didn't know you were such an outrageous liar, I might be afraid."

"I shall never give you reason to fear me." Trevor kissed her hand again, his lips lingered on her knuckles. "My love is as true as it is shallow and fleeting."

"Shallow and fleeting," Andy said with a straight face. "Just the way I like it."

*   *   *

They walked outside together to look at the future home of the dream-garden. After a long day of dirt, dust and sweat, the marked plot of earth was tilled with a rich base of organic compost mixed deep in the freshly turned soil. The four workers piled in the dented old truck, each left with a paper-wrapped loaf of fragrant banana bread. Trevor said that his crew was paid an ample salary, but Laz slipped each of them a tip and thanked them in Spanish. Rachel and Andy thanked them in English. The men grinned as they drove away, waving out the open windows.

Laz slipped an arm around Rachel's waist, and they stood by the garden, heads close together, smiling at each other. Watching them, Andy felt a tightness in her throat, she closed her eyes with a grimace.

"You have a distinct fondness for your cousin." Trevor's posh accent was smoothly sarcastic, with an emphasis on 'cousin'.

"I have a fondness for you." Andy laid a hand in the middle of his chest, looking into his eyes. "Can we go to your place? I'd like to demonstrate my fondness."

He scanned her face with a serious expression, then his lips quirked in a half smile. "That sounds intriguing, my sweet. Do we need to say goodbye?"

"They'll figure it out." Andy slipped her fingers in his shaggy blond curls and tugged him close for a kiss full of promises.

*   *   *

Sex with Trevor was better than she had dared to hope, without all the pain-filled, mixed-up feelings that came with Laz. Trevor was lean, smooth and fair. Laz was big, dark and hairy. Laz was smoldering and rough. Trevor played Andy's body like a harp, delicately plucking every nerve with gentle confidence and patient exploration. Sex with Laz was animal heat and madness. Love with Laz was guilt and pain and rage and shame. Trevor was uncomplicated and they enjoyed each other's bodies with respect and warm affection. Her longing for Laz was muffled, if not silenced.

CHAPTER TWENTY-SEVEN
I'M NOT THE ONLY ONE

Laz drove the Civic to town for supplies and Rachel and Andy rode along with him; it had been days since they left the property and the town square was a welcome change of scenery.

"I need to stop in the candy store before we go home," Andy said.

"Yes!" Rachel exclaimed, touching Andy's arm. "I've been dying for Natalia's coconut candy."

"You two go ahead, I'll get us a table at Los Arcos," said Laz.

* * *

Natalia greeted them from her perch on the high stool. "Buenos dias, la Dulce, Andy is here for candy? Hola, Jennifer Aniston!" She motioned for the women to come closer and leaned in to whisper, "Two men were here a few days ago with your picture."

Rachel's face went still as she struggled to keep her carefree mask. She tinkled a brittle laugh. "*My* picture? Surely not. People tell me all the time I look like someone they know."

Andy heard dim voices through the roaring in her ears, and bright spots floated in her wide-open eyes. Mouth dry, her body fluctuated from icy cold to fiery hot to numb in a flash. *It was them. I'm not imagining things. Dear gods in all the heavens, how did they find us?*

"They said the woman in the picture was called Cindy Moore but I told them it was Jennifer Aniston." Natalia winked. "I've never heard of Cindy Moore."

Rachel let loose another shaky peal of laughter. "Nope, me neither!" She turned to link her arm with Andy's. "How about you, Dulce? Ever heard the name Cindy Moore?"

Andy pursed her lips as if in deep thought. "Doesn't ring any bells for me. Did the guy say why he was looking?"

"He said she was a missing girl and her mama is worried." Natalia rolled her eyes. "I said mamas worry, no matter what. And the girl in that picture is a grown woman." Her expression went briefly serious before bursting into a big, wrinkled smile like a sunburst on her brown skin. "How is your little bebe?" She touched a light hand to Rachel's belly. "How is Rachel Green Junior?"

"Ha! Laz calls the baby Junior but he insists it's a boy. Are you saying it's a girl, Tia Natalia?"

"Yes, and I have a fifty-fifty chance of being right. Story of my life." Natalia lightly touched Rachel's belly again. "Girl, boy, who cares. Any child born into a loving family is blessed." A flock of tourists converged on the tiny store. "Take some coconut candy and go, you pay me later. Give a kiss to that handsome man of yours. Dulce's cousin." Natalia added another wink.

Rachel linked arms with Andy, hurrying across the plaza. "Shit, shit, shit. It was Dustin and Jarrett that you saw. I need to call my mother. She needs to call off the hounds."

Laz was waiting at a table on the patio; he rose from his chair with a smile that faded as he took in their expressions. "What? What happened?"

Before they could answer, a waitress came with chips and salsa and took their drink order. When she walked away, Rachel glanced around and leaned close to Laz to whisper, "Natalia said two men showed her my picture a couple of days ago."

Laz made his own quick scan of the room. "And Natalia told them what?"

Rachel replayed the conversation, pausing while the waitress brought their drinks. Andy sat numb, silent, Rachel's low voice washed over her ears with only a word here and there making sense. Cindy Moore. Jennifer

Aniston. Mother. Andy rubbed her temples and tried to concentrate on the fiercely whispered conversation.

"I need to contact Mom and tell her to stop looking for me and tell people Andy is safe."

"How?" Laz laid his hand on top of Rachel's. "If you use a phone, they'll trace it. Even email, the IP address will show her where we are."

"I don't want to talk to her on the phone, she'll just start an argument." Rachel twined her fingers in his. "Can we drive to Vallarta and find a public computer? Is it safe in the Civic?"

Laz flicked his eyes to Andy and back to Rachel. "I could ask Trevor if I can use the VW."

"What will change if you tell people we're safe?" Andy leaned in. "If you tell your mother you're safe with him, I'm safe with him, then we're accomplices. I understand you don't want her to worry, but I'm not sure that telling her you're okay is going to change anything. The cops will still arrest us because of the money." She leaned back. "Whatever you want to do, I support you. But it's a four-hour round trip on bumpy roads. Is that really the best thing for the baby?"

Rachel dropped her cold hand on Andy's arm. "You're so smart, I didn't think of that. Laz, can you go by yourself? I'll give you the password to my email."

"If it makes you happy, I'll email your mother," said Laz, looking resigned, and unhappy.

*　*　*

Rachel wrote down what she wanted him to say, with a compromise to not mention Andy:

Mom,
Please stop trying to find me. I am safe and happy. I will contact you when the baby is born.
Love,
Cindy

"I know it probably won't help, but it will make me feel better to try," Rachel said, arms around Laz for a goodbye kiss. "Thank you for doing this, babe."

* * *

Rachel and Andy spent the day staying busy and pretending not to worry. They worked in the garden and tended the chickens. They baked a vegetarian lasagna with handmade noodles. Cleaning the house, Rachel only whined a little about not having her maid. Andy pretended to commiserate, while hiding her relief that Laz talked Rachel into sending the maid to Trevor's for a job. They expected Laz to be gone four hours and the time passed quickly; they didn't start to worry until he was an hour overdue. When he was two hours overdue, fear sank in like claws.

"Goddammit! Next time he takes a goddam phone with him." Rachel paced and cursed.

"Don't get yourself worked up, Rach, it's not good for the baby."

Andy stood watchful at the window until she couldn't stand being inside another second. She went outside to admire the garden, proud at how much they had accomplished in a few days, distracted by the prickle of anxiety that had her thoughts in a worst-case-scenario loop of dread. *What if he never comes back?* She kept the words inside her head, she couldn't say them out loud, not even to herself. *Bandits could have him. The police could have him. He could be hurt or broke down on the side of the road.* What would her life look like if Laz never came back? All her visions of the future included the three of them, four when Junior was born. Maybe five, for as long as Trevor sticks around. But not two. Not just Andy and Rachel. That isn't the plan.

* * *

When he finally rattled down the driveway—over three hours late—Rachel ran outside crying. Andy waited by the garden, giving them reunion time before joining them. Laz made shushing noises and stroked Rachel's hair. Over Rachel's shoulder, he mouthed to Andy, "I'm sorry."

"I'm sorry, I'm sorry," he said to Rachel. "Yes, next time I'll bring a phone. I didn't think about you being worried. I'm not used to people worrying about me. Rachel, shhh, calm down."

"What happened?" she sniffled. "Why were you gone so long?"

"I thought I should wait a little while to see if your mother would reply to the email and I started browsing the internet, looking for news about us. I wasn't paying attention to the time."

"Seriously? We imagined you murdered by a drug cartel and you're just surfing the web?" Andy said with a steely edge in her voice. "Well? Did she reply?"

Laz shook his head. "No, and I'm sorry I was gone so long for nothing."

Rachel shook her phone at him. "Why did you wait? I can check my email from here."

"I know but you can't reply. Remember that, okay? Because she's going to say something to piss you off and you'll want to reply. If she believes we're in Puerto Vallarta, that's fine. People are easily lost in the big city." Laz grabbed them both by the hand and led them to the kitchen. "I did find some interesting news." He motioned towards the table. "Sit, let me bring you a cold drink. Maybe this news will make you like me again." He brought three beers and popped each one. "Let's have a toast." The women raised their cans, shooting each other confused glances. "Here's to Dustin and Jarrett in jail." He took a drink while laughing and coughed a few times before continuing. "I was flipping through a local newspaper and saw their pictures. They were arrested getting off the tour bus."

"They're going to tell the police everything." Andy put her face in her hands.

"They were arrested two days ago. If the police thought we were here, we would know by now." Laz patted her shoulder. "They believed the locals who said they didn't recognize Rachel's picture. We don't have to worry about Dustin and Jarrett anymore. We're safe."

* * *

Life settled into a pattern. Andy, an early riser, had her first cup of coffee with Laz, who slept on an air mattress in the living room after Rachel complained he took up too much space in their double bed. Andy would tiptoe past him to the kitchen and usually his blankets were on the floor. *The best part of waking up is seeing Laz in his underwear.* She checked the internet for news while waiting for the coffee to brew. Two days after Laz went to Vallarta, she found an article in a San Francisco newspaper, an interview with Detective Lyle Cooper who said he would not rest until he found Adrienne Berg. Seeing her deadname in print was like reading about a stranger, Adrienne Berg was just one more missing woman among the dozens of women who go missing every day. The media agreed, consigning the article to page eight. With no new facts, no salacious details, the content-churning media monster had moved on in search of dirtier laundry.

Laz usually waited until the coffee was ready before he wandered into the kitchen—fully dressed. Since Andy started seeing Trevor, their morning conversations had become stilted and awkward. No lingering looks or stealthy touches. No intimate whispering, sometimes they did not talk at all. Rachel typically yawned her way into the kitchen around the time Laz and Andy started their second cup of coffee. Laz would ask how she slept and how she was feeling, fussing over her, bringing her vitamins and crackers for her morning nausea. Someone would start breakfast, someone else would clean the kitchen. They would all go outside to take care of the chickens and the garden, continuing their careful planning and planting. Laz added another big black bag to their shower arrangement so the angst over hot water lessened.

Seven nights in a row, Andy walked down the overgrown driveway to meet Trevor by the road and together they walked to his hacienda. Three of those nights, Rachel and Laz joined them and they played in the swimming pool. Five of those nights Andy and Trevor had sex, amazing, astonishing, fun, sexy sex. None of those nights included Andy sleeping over. After twice imploring her to stay, Trevor didn't ask again. She demanded that he allow her to walk home alone but he followed her anyway, so she held his hand, and he walked her to the door. Andy was secretly glad to have him by her side, and only mildly alarmed at how much she missed his attention when they were apart.

The rains came, and at first, they were ecstatic. The garden needed water and without an irrigation system in place, each drop had to be carried; this welcome summer rain would bring relief in more ways than one. They dug a trench around the rows to drain off the excess water, hoeing and shoveling and laughing in the rain. A gentle, constant rain. None of them owned rain gear but the days were warm, so they worked barefoot in wet clothes. After five days of gentle, constant rain, nerves were on edge. Without the sun to dry their clothes, everything was damp. They paced and stalked the house like caged animals. While in town for groceries, Andy dashed into the drugstore and gave Mr. Aguilar her phone number so he could call when her thyroid pills were in stock. She bought Rachel vitamins and Tums before she ran through the rain to where Laz and Rachel were waiting in the Civic, loaded with supplies.

On the eighth day of rain, a heavy mudslide buried the main road to San Sebastian. Authorities assured the town council that as soon as the rain allowed, the road would be repaired. Someone tried to leave by way of Santiago de Pinos—the nearest town and located on the only other road out of San Sebastian—but the road was too muddy to cross in a four-wheeler, too narrow for a four-wheel drive. San Sebastian was cut off from the world.

When Andy was down to her last seven thyroid pills, she broke them in half.

CHAPTER TWENTY-EIGHT
WATCHING THE DETECTIVES

Cindy's mother forwarded the email allegedly written by her daughter to Detective Cooper who requested that she not respond. The IP address was traced to a coffee shop in Puerto Vallarta with public computers; the popular and very busy coffee shop didn't have cameras but the OXXO across the street did. Cooper studied the frenetic comings and goings on the grainy security footage, searching for Cindy first, beginning from the email timestamp. Forward an hour, back an hour. After searching three hours before the email was sent and three hours after, Cooper concluded Cindy didn't send the email. Or she lived in the coffee shop. Or she used a back door. He called the shop and confirmed that yes, they have a back door, but customers were strictly forbidden. And if a six-foot-tall American-model-looking woman had trespassed through the back room to use the forbidden door, someone would remember.

Cooper started at the timestamp again, this time searching for Gabriel on the video. Lorenzo Navarro had given the detective a photo of Gabriel from his time in the service—clean-shaven young Gabriel in his white officer's uniform. Cooper kept that photo on his desk, along with the Lazaro Cardenas passport photo provided by Mexican authorities where Gabriel looked very different: auburn hair, dark brown eyes and a scruffy goatee. The sheer number of tall, thick, swarthy men passing through the doors of the cafe was mind-boggling. Cooper's eyes crossed after only a few minutes, imagining Navarro with a beard, without a beard, with a hat, without a hat, with sunglasses, without sunglasses.

A man caught his attention on the video almost three hours after the email was sent. A big man, wearing an orange San Francisco Giants baseball cap with the logo nearly camouflaged by dirt, his black beard full and untrimmed. The man glanced down the street before crossing and the OXXO camera caught a clear shot of light-colored eyes against dark skin before the man slipped on sunglasses. Cooper studied the photo of Gabriel in uniform, his face deeply tanned, light hazel eyes blazed directly into the camera. Hawk's eyes: pale green-gold with a look of stubborn pride. Cooper played the few seconds over and over, comparing the man's profile, the shape of his eyebrows, the flip of his dark hair from under the cap. The scar on his top lip wasn't visible, but the crooked nose looked correct. Cooper picked up the phone to arrange another interview with Austin and Berg. Those fools knew more than they were telling.

*   *   *

Berg and Austin were more interested in talking to Cooper today, although they were not speaking to each other and could only agree on one thing: life behind bars was not a good fit.

"Let me get this straight," Cooper said. "Fife sent you to Mexico to search for Cindy Moore and you ended up on a tour bus to San Sebastian because Cindy mentioned she liked their coffee?"

"It sounds pretty stupid when you put it that way," Jarrett said, his face sullen.

"I'm going to hate myself for saying this, but I'm impressed by your field work." Cooper massaged his neck and grimaced. "Mrs. Moore gave a list of places Cindy had visited and San Sebastian was on the list."

"Don't bother," Dustin said, with a flip of his chained hand. "We showed Cindy's picture to everyone. No one in town recognized her."

"No one in town *admitted* they recognized her," said Cooper. "There's a difference. If police show up there asking questions, locals might remember better. The only road into town is under repair right now and it's not high on the list because it doesn't seem like the kind of place Cindy would choose to live. She likes to shop and party from what I've been told."

"She's not shopping and partying in San Sebastian. That place is stuck in the eighteenth century. Party like it's seventeen ninety-nine." Jarrett chuckled at his own wit. No one joined him.

"We're working another angle. Adrienne had a prescription for levothyroxine in her bathroom," said Cooper. "There were only a few pills left. According to the doctor, there should have been at least six weeks of pills in that bottle." He glared at Dustin. "Do you know what happens if Adrienne runs out of pills? Long story short, she could die. If there's anything else you're not telling me, this is the time to talk."

"I swear, we told you everything. She can't run out of medicine. She can't die because of me." Dustin groaned, holding his head in his hands.

"Fortunately, and unfortunately, in Mexico you can buy that drug over the counter. We're checking with the main distribution centers to see if any pharmacies started purchasing the drug that hadn't stocked it before. It's more than a long shot, it's a needle in a haystack, but worth following up. I will find your wife, Berg." Cooper heaved a frustrated sigh. "I only hope those women are with Navarro willingly, and they're safe."

"We know Cindy is willing," said Dustin. "She's probably guarding Adrienne while her boyfriend runs her errands."

"Maybe. If so, I hope they're keeping her supplied with medication. We've alerted area hospitals to contact us if anyone is admitted with a thyroid emergency. Again, a long shot but I don't have a lot to go on."

"How long are you keeping us locked up?" Jarrett demanded. "Fife doesn't want to press charges and you're more than halfway convinced that Adrienne is an accomplice and not a hostage so you can't charge us with kidnapping."

"Is that what your lawyer says?" Cooper asked, eyebrows raised.

"Our lawyers are worthless," Dustin said.

"And we can't get bail because they say we're a flight risk," said Jarrett, indignant.

"You didn't report your wife missing for two weeks, Berg. Until I speak to Adrienne and see with my own eyes that she is safe, the DA is willing to charge you both as accessories to kidnapping. As for Fife, I'm told he's left the country for good, turned over control of the company and is now living somewhere in the Caymans." Cooper chuckled. "He said he understood why Cindy wanted to live in a different country than her mother."

"Fife is basically giving us that money, so I want to press charges against Gabriel for stealing it." Jarrett tried to cross his arms but his chains were too short.

"Shut up, Austin. This case is already a pain in my ass." Cooper gathered his notes and drained his coffee cup in preparation to leave. "Fife won't press charges. If Gabriel didn't kidnap anyone, there are no charges to be filed and everyone gets off scot-free with three million cash? No way, no fucking way. Do you have any idea how much time and money has been spent chasing down all you idiots? Someone will pay." He stormed out of the room.

* * *

Back in their cell, Jarrett and Dustin resumed their cycle of petty squabbles. Starting with a rehash of the interview with that jerk, Lyle Cooper.

"We need to hire a real lawyer." Jarrett clicked a pen as he paced the cell, clicking and clicking the pen faster and faster.

Dustin wanted to stab him in the throat with the pen. Instead he rolled over and covered his head with the pillow. He yelped at a poke in his back and sat up. "What?"

Jarrett pointed at him with the pen. "Why aren't you listening?"

"I'm tired of your whining. They won't let us out until they find Adrienne and spending money we don't have for a lawyer is more stupid than stealing the money in the first place." Dustin poked Jarrett hard in the shoulder with his finger. "Listen, jackass, if we're extra, extra lucky, this will be the only time we spend behind bars. Pray they find Adrienne, pray she's healthy, and they drop all charges. We could be out in a few days without even a trial. So can you please, please, *please* shut up?" He rolled over and covered his head with the pillow.

* * *

Cooper checked in with the team and after much fussing, the department spared four officers to comb the streets of Puerto Vallarta with photos of the three missing Americans. The road to San Sebastian was expected to be passable in a few days and they would check there, too. Only because Barbara Moore insisted Cindy had raved about the town; Cooper thought it much more likely that Cindy was in Puerto Vallarta, a city of 500,000 people where she could be invisible and have all the comforts of her privileged upbringing. The budget was creaking, administration was complaining, and Fife refusing to press charges was the second-to-last straw. It would only take one piece of evidence to prove Adrienne was a willing participant and they would call off the search.

His phone rang with an international prefix. "Lyle Cooper speaking."

"Detective Cooper, this is Officer Julio Garcia with the state of Sonora police department. I'm calling about a missing person case you're working on, Adrienne Berg?"

Cooper sat up straight in his chair. "Yes, Officer Garcia. Did you find something?"

"Two men were shot on the side of the highway near Hermosilla. Witnesses saw a car with a flat tire in the same area, a black Honda Civic with California plates."

Cooper clenched the phone, pressing it harder to his ear. "I'm listening."

"Two people in a black Civic with California plates bought a tire in Guaymas. A big man with a young boy. Our commander briefed us a few days ago that the Americans are looking for a big Latino man and a much smaller man traveling together."

"The description of the people and the car match what I'm looking for. Do you have any sighting of them after the tire store?"

"A woman in Mazatlán reported her license plate stolen and her neighbor said he saw a black car with California plates cruising the area. That stolen license plate popped up on a scan of Pemex security camera footage. The station is in La Encinera. After that is nothing but wilderness until you reach San Sebastian."

Leaping from his chair like he'd been tasered, Cooper barked, "San Sebastian? Are you saying the people in the black Honda are wanted for murder?"

"They are wanted for questioning but let me be clear, detective, the murder investigation is a formality. Do you have any idea how little Mexican police are paid? We have more important cases than two dead bandits. I am calling you because there is a reward for your missing person. If you find them in San Sebastian, I get a reward, yes?"

After Cooper ended his conversation with Officer Garcia, booked the next flight to Puerto Vallarta. He would go to San Sebastian himself.

CHAPTER TWENTY-NINE
THE VISITORS

"I'm bleeding."

Andy and Laz froze at the kitchen table, their shocked eyes on Rachel. Her face was white as chalk, and she clutched her rounded belly. She was over five months along and they had all felt Junior's sharp elbows and knees through Rachel's skin, the roundness of the skull as the baby rolled inside. Her obstetrician owned a sonogram machine, but Rachel did not want to know the sex of the baby they called Junior, randomly using she/her or he/him depending on the mood of the moment.

"I'm bleeding," Rachel repeated, more sharply.

Laz jumped to his feet. "Do you need to go to the doctor?"

"You should be lying down." Andy bustled to Rachel's side, herding her across the living room. "Laz, call Dr. Gonzalez and see if she will come here. Rachel shouldn't be bouncing down cobblestones. How much blood, Rach?"

Inside the bedroom, Rachel pointed to a pair of stained panties lying on the floor. "That much blood. And whatever I wiped when I peed just now." She sat on the bed and lowered her face in her hands. "It's too much blood, something is wrong."

Andy rubbed her back. "Lie down and relax, Laz is calling the doctor. Try to stay calm. I'm getting some water, okay? I'll be right back." She passed Laz in the hall, grabbed his arm and stood on tiptoe; he leaned down so she could whisper in his ear. "It's a lot of blood." Andy gave him a serious look. In a louder voice, "Getting Rachel some water."

When she came back to the bedroom, Laz was crouched on the floor by Rachel's side, holding her hand. Andy set the water on the table by the other side of the bed. "Did you call the doctor?"

"I left a message," Laz said, without taking his eyes from Rachel's face. "She's with a patient but I told them it was an emergency, and I should hear back from her soon. How are you feeling?" He fleetingly caressed the rise of her belly, like a butterfly landing and flying off. "Are you in pain? Any cramps?"

Rachel's eyes filled, and a tear dripped down her cheek. "Maybe a little. I always feel something, you know? Something is always pinching or poking or aching."

"Is that normal?" Laz asked, frowning.

"According to the doctor, yes. My body has to make a lot of adjustments for another human to move in." Rachel clutched at his hand. "Can you call her again? Tell her to hurry. I don't want to lose our baby." Her voice cracked and she rubbed at her face with both hands.

Feeling useless and in the way, Andy went to the kitchen to call Trevor. "Sweetheart," she began. Ever the chameleon, she had effortlessly slipped into his habit of using effusive terms of endearment, and he really was a sweetheart. "Rachel is having some troubles and her regular doctor is busy. You wouldn't happen to have an extra obstetrician on your list of local friends?"

"I do know a doctor, my love. He's not an OB but I'm sure he can help. Can I call you back in a few minutes?"

"Please, thank you. You're the best." Andy smiled to herself as she ended the call, but her smile faded as she considered the reality of their circumstances—San Sebastian is the wrong place to be in an emergency. Especially now. The sun had reappeared with a vengeance, filling the air with steam, but the local roads were a swampy mess, and the main road was still under repair. San Sebastian was effectively an island. There were plenty of fresh fruits and vegetables, meat and eggs, but supplies were running low on anything that wasn't produced locally.

Andy began noticing symptoms of her lowered thyroid hormone around the fifth day of her half dose—sensitivity to cold, fatigue, brain fog. She had planned to talk to Laz and Rachel about her symptoms but now they had more critical issues.

*   *   *

Trevor and his doctor friend arrived quicker than expected, splashing through puddles in a vintage Jeep so covered with mud, dents and scratches it was impossible to tell what the original color might have been. Dr. Simon Bechtel was another British expat, retired after forty years in socialized medicine and he had seen a bit of everything. His formal manner— requesting a chair, refusing to sit on a patient's bed—contrasted with his wrinkled Elton John concert t-shirt and baggy corduroy shorts. His head was smooth as an egg, pale and speckled. "Do you want anyone to stay while I examine you?" he asked.

"Andy?" Rachel's voice quavered. "Would you?"

"You want me to stay?" Andy perched on the side of the bed near Rachel's shoulder, her eyes on Laz's worried face as he left the bedroom and closed the door. Rachel grabbed her hand, Andy blinked hard and bit her cheek to hold back tears—Rachel's hand was white and cold as a marble carving. She gripped Andy tightly and squeezed her eyes shut while the doctor examined her.

"I can't do a thorough examination in these conditions, but my advice is go to a hospital." Bechtel gently pushed Rachel's knees down. "The big hospital in Vallarta should have access to a helicopter."

"A helicopter!" Rachel's voice was hoarse and choked with sobs. "It's that serious?"

"The road is out, remember?" Andy's hand pulsed in her tight grip, feeling Rachel's heartbeat in her palm. "Do you want me to get Laz?"

"Not yet." Rachel let go of Andy's hand to blot her face with the sheet. "Doctor, can you give us a minute?" After he closed the door, Rachel held the pillow over her face and howled.

Andy flailed her hands helplessly. "Please, Rach, you have to relax, you're making it worse." Through a lump in her throat, she said, "What can I do? What can I do?" *What would Rachel do?* She stretched out on the bed, pulled the pillow from Rachel's face and wrapped her arms around her. Rachel grabbed on and cried into Andy's hair. She was saying words but crying so hard Andy couldn't understand her. "Shhh, shhh, hon, seriously." She pulled away to look in Rachel's swollen, wet eyes. "You must calm down," Andy said sternly and put a hand on either side of Rachel's face. "Look at me. Breathe in for four counts, out for four. Ready?"

Rachel blinked several times and shuddered before she nodded and pursed her trembling lips while Andy counted off one Mississippi two Mississippi...in and out until Rachel's body slumped and she said in a hoarse, choked voice, "Don't let Laz choose the baby." Her chin quivered, she inhaled deeply and tightened her jaw. "If the doctors ask Laz, he'll choose the baby's life over mine. You know he will."

"Rach, it won't come to that. You're flying to the hospital and they'll fix you right up."

"I hope you're right." Rachel closed her eyes and laid her head on the pillow. After a pause, she said, "I'm not coming back here, Andy. This is a horrible place to have a baby." Words, jerky and shuddering, tumbled out. "It's not magical. It's primitive. I can't live like this. I don't want to raise my child here." She pinned Andy with a steely gaze. "When I get out of the hospital, I'm going to my mom's house. Don't tell Laz." Rachel firmed her trembling lips. "I'll call him when I get home. Don't worry, I won't tell anyone where you are."

Andy was stunned, speechless and frozen with shock. Her thoughts were already racing with the ramifications of a helicopter coming to their hiding spot, and Rachel being found out as Cindy Moore. If she and Laz had to go to jail to save Rachel's life, to save Junior's life, so be it. The Universe giveth and the Universe taketh away. But to just give up? Willingly return to that mess in the 'normal' world? Not without a fight.

"The hospital will know when they send the helicopter, hon, but that's okay. We'll figure it out. You just stay calm." After a long silence, one broken by the rumble of male voices from the other room, Andy said, "Are you ready to see Laz? Yes? Okay, I'll send him in. Tea? I'll bring some chamomile." She did not recognize her own voice or these nurturing noises coming from her mouth. Andy felt like she was playing a role, although this performance came more naturally than some of Adrienne Berg's acting efforts.

"She wants you, Laz," Andy said. "Did the doctor mention a helicopter?"

Laz brushed past her without a word and stalked to Rachel's bedroom.

Andy frowned at his back, turned to give Trevor a tired smile. "I'm so glad you're here."

Trevor enfolded her in his arms. "Precious angel, how many times must I beg you to call me in your time of need? My friend Leroy lives in Puerto Vallarta, and he owns a helicopter."

Andy's heart leaped with hope. She leaned closer. "Can you ask the pilot not to tell anyone about this place? We don't want people to know we're here."

With an appraising look, Trevor cupped her elbow. "Come, darling, show me what you have to offer a parched man. Bechtel, a drink?" Dr. Bechtel waved a negative response. Inside the kitchen, Trevor turned on the faucet and they stood close together at the sink. He spoke in a low voice, a serious voice she had never heard before, a deep tone with no trace of banter. Even his accent turned harsh, street. "Andy, I am serious. If you're in trouble, please tell me. I can help, please let me help. I know you and I tease and play but I do love you. You must know that." His grave expression carved the lines deeper on his face.

She stared at him, weighing his words, choosing her words. "We've done things." Her voice low and even, "Things they put people in prison for doing."

Trevor's intense stare stayed with her as he turned off the water and pulled her to his chest. "Darling, you're trembling," he said in his posh accent. "Don't be afraid. Keep your secrets if you must and I shall keep you safe as best I can." He tilted his head down and tipped up her chin with one finger. In his street voice, he said, "I can keep you safe if you let me."

Dr. Bechtel said he would wait until the helicopter arrived and if he had room, he would go with Rachel. He and Trevor sat on the heavy chairs in the living room and arranged pillows under their butts and behind their backs while reminiscing about Mother England. Andy stared blankly out the front window, hugging herself, absently rubbing her arms. An involuntary shiver shook her body like a dog with a rag.

In a flash, Trevor was by her side. "Are you cold?" He scanned her face, curious, and touched her arm covered in goosebumps. "How can you be cold? This room is like a sauna. Are you sick?" He pressed a palm to her forehead. "Doctor, do you mind looking at Andy?"

"No, please, don't get up." Andy waved her hand at the doctor. "I know what's wrong. My thyroid hormone is low because I'm rationing my pills. But the road will be repaired soon and there's a shipment of meds coming." Brain fog, that sense of her synapses not firing correctly, was more disturbing than the chills. "Doctor, do you know if there is a substitute? Some alternative medicine available here, now?"

Dr. Bechtel rubbed his whiskery chin. "There is but you won't like it." At her questioning look, he went on. "Pig thyroid. People used that for years before synthetic thyroid. Still do. You dry it and put the powder in a pill, but I imagine you could get it down some other way."

"I'll ask Leroy to pick up some medicine for you." His smile was sweet but all the flirt had left Trevor's voice. "You and your secrets." He pressed a firm kiss on her forehead. "Beautiful Andy. I told you to be mysterious, but you could have talked to me about this."

"I had it handled. Who knew the road would wash away?"

Trevor called the pilot. "He's already in the air but he's contacting the hospital for someone meet him on the helipad to take Rachel inside and he'll ask them to bring some of your medicine to the roof." He glanced at his phone. "He should be here in about fifteen minutes. Do you want to see if Rachel needs help packing a bag?"

"I'll check." Andy stood on tiptoe to kiss his cheek. "You really are the sweetest thing." She kept her face carefully neutral, while wondering what Rachel would pack if she was never coming back. She cleared her throat as she neared Rachel's open bedroom door. "Hey, girl, the helicopter will be here in a few minutes. Can I help you pack a few things?"

"I can do it." Laz rose from his seat at the edge of the bed. Worry and fear had aged his face.

Rachel tugged on his hand. "I want Andy, please? Can you go hang out with the guys?"

He looked both relieved and hurt. After Laz closed the door, Rachel swung her legs over the side of the bed. "Help me, Andy." She pulled a backpack from the closet and directed Andy through her things, stuffing the backpack with her laptop and padding around it with clothes. "The rest of this stuff you can have. Don't you dare cry, this is already hard enough." They hugged and sniffled. "This was a seriously insane way to meet a friend, Andy, but I'm glad we met. Someday I'll bring Junior here to meet you."

"You better," Andy croaked. "I hear the helicopter. Are you all set? Here, lean on me."

"Oh, no, he's landing right on the garden," Rachel moaned.

"It doesn't matter," Andy said. "Don't worry about anything but you and Junior."

Laz took over for Andy and helped Rachel out to the helicopter, splashing through soupy mud; Doctor Bechtel crouched and slopped in the muck alongside them. After a quick conference, the doctor gave thumbs up and clambered onboard. Laz ran back ducking under the whirring blades and running with an athlete's grace. They gathered by the house until the helicopter whooshed over the treetops.

"Godspeed, dear Rachel and Junior," Trevor said solemnly. He studied Laz's face. "Lazaro? Should I stay or do you want to be alone?"

Laz rubbed his eyes with both hands. "Please stay. At least until the doctor comes back. I'd like to be with my friends if there is any bad news." He turned to Andy, his eyes drowning in distress. "What do you think? Do you think they're going to be okay?"

He didn't want an opinion, he wanted reassurance. It was the least she could do. "They are going to be fine," she said. "Rachel and Junior are going to be fine."

CHAPTER THIRTY
LITTLE LIES

"We should check on the chickens," said Andy. Crossing the clearing was a game of leapfrog to avoid the worst mud puddles and the money didn't cross her mind until she caught a warning glance from Laz. A low barrier of sandbags and straw bales surrounded the chicken coop area in a blocky rampart; the money was wrapped tight in plastic but was it enough to hold off this kind of water? They were in no position to dig it out and dry it so they could only hope.

The garden was smashed to smithereens by the landing helicopter, and the chicken's fenced exercise area had been blown clean by its whirring blades. The birds had probably been more upset while the helicopter was doing its thing, but they had settled to disgruntled clucks and pissed-off struts. Andy opened the storage box for their feed, more mindful than ever about the money buried beneath it with Trevor at her side, feeling the cash as a looming and sinister presence. Guilt weighed on her shoulders, and the burden of so many secrets.

"What a lovely home you've made for your chickens." Trevor gestured at the barrier. "An absolute fortification." He smiled at her, one of his new serious smiles.

Andy smiled back and scattered feed, clucking at the chickens and disregarding Trevor's intense scrutiny. She felt off balance at the shift from 'just-having-fun-Trevor' to 'I-love-you-Trevor'. Keeping him at arm's length was becoming more difficult and she caught herself opening up to him, even while suspecting Trevor had his own secrets. She assumed something like tax evasion or a messy divorce. White collar crime at worst. At best, he was a sweet-talking serial monogamist who would scramble for cover at the first whiff of serious intentions. *Who is he? And do I want to know?*

Adding to her uneasiness around Trevor was a sick, dark part of her thinking *with Rachel gone, Laz and I can be together.* A slithery, sly voice that hissed *the baby could die.* Andy wanted to slap herself, drag her fingernails down her cheeks and tear at her flesh for allowing this selfish, evil voice in her brain. Rachel and Junior will live, and they will always be the most important people in Laz's world, wherever that may be. If Rachel returns to California, if she goes back to being Cindy, Laz will take his punishment as Gabriel. To be in his child's life he would give up his own. *Laz would give up this place, and me, without a second thought.*

*   *   *

Bechtel said he would call when Rachel was taken off the chopper. The flight was supposed to take less than twenty minutes and over thirty minutes had passed since the helicopter left the clearing. Anxiety increased with each passing moment. Andy, Laz and Trevor alternated pacing with staring out the windows, no one spoke. When Trevor's phone rang, they all froze.

"Hello, Bechtel, what? Rachel what? Sorry, Simon, I can't hear you. We'll talk when you land." Trevor huffed a noise of frustration and tucked away his phone before resting a hand on Laz's shoulder. "I caught the words Rachel is in good hands. And it sounds like the helicopter is coming back. The doctor can tell us more when he arrives."

The news didn't diminish Laz's worry lines. He nodded at Trevor and walked into the kitchen, leaned over the sink and stared out the window.

Andy followed and rested her hand on his forearm. "They will be fine."

"I want to run to her," Laz said. "There's nothing I can do."

She slipped one arm around his waist, intending a quick squeeze but Laz turned to face her and enveloped her in a hard, humid embrace. Tension rose from his body in hot waves and he shook from the effort to hold on to his tears before he let go.

"What have I done, Andy? This is all my fault. If Rachel dies, if Junior dies, it's my fault. More blood on my hands. It should be me, not them."

She had no words to comfort him. Because he was right. If he had insisted that Cindy come back to the States, she would have come back. If he hadn't stolen the money, they could have gone back. If he hadn't taken a hostage, they could have gone back. Dustin and Jarrett would be in jail or lounging on a tropical island. And Adrienne would be painting or reading or writing or gardening alone. Andy stroked his back. *I have no regrets. Laz has enough for both of us.*

The distant throb of rotating blades caught their attention, the sound thickened to a roar and they headed outside to watch the chopper come down. The pilot landed long enough for the doctor to jump out and he was off in the air again with a brief flick of his hand. Dr. Bechtel crouched and dashed across the muddy clearing with his sandals in his hand.

"Let's rinse off this mud again, we don't want to mess up Rachel's clean house," Laz said in a falsely bright tone. He smiled at Andy. "I mean, *our* clean house." He stopped at the outdoor shower and pulled the spray nozzle down, chattering as he sprayed his feet. "I want it to be nice when she comes back. Couple days or so, doc? What do you think?"

"Let me catch my breath, Laz," the doctor huffed and puffed. "Pour me a drink and we'll talk."

*   *   *

The four of them rinsed off the worst of the mud from their feet and gathered around the kitchen table. Laz brought out the hard stuff—a local small batch blue agave raicilla. He poured four shots, and they made a toast to Rachel and Junior's health.

Bechtel sighed heavily, pressed his lips in a grim line and gave them each a hard stare before he spoke directly to Andy. "You might have warned me that the police are looking for you."

Andy struggled to compose herself, avoiding Trevor's sharp, inquiring eyes. "What happened?"

"We got Rachel on a gurney, then I asked about the thyroid pills." Bechtel narrowed his eyes at Andy. "The police had an alert at the hospital for anyone with a thyroid emergency, they were instructed to contact some detective. They asked where Rachel came from." He took a sip before continuing, "I convinced the doctor to give me the pills and we got the hell out of there. I've no interest in chatting with your American detective." He pulled a box from his pocket and dropped it on the table. "I didn't tell them anything and Leroy didn't say anything, but he is livid." Bechtel pointed at Trevor. "I would not have expected this from you, amigo." Amigo should have sounded funny in his proper British accent, but no one was laughing.

Andy laid her hand on the table with a light smack to get his attention. "Doctor, please don't be mad at Trevor. He's as much in the dark as you."

"Leave me in the dark." The doctor slammed back the rest of his fiery liquor and set the clay shot glass on the table with a clunk. "Some detective comes sniffing around my place I can tell him I don't know a thing and it will be the truth." Tapping the box, he said, "Take three tablets now and back on your regular schedule tomorrow." He rose from the chair. "Call if your symptoms don't improve."

"Wait, doctor," Laz said. "I can never thank you enough for your help, you must let me pay you for your time." He hurried to Rachel's bedroom and came back with a folded sheaf of hundreds. The doctor eyed his outstretched hand. "It's clean money," Laz said. "I swear. Please, take it."

"Give it to the church," the doctor barked and turned to Trevor. "Clarke, keep me posted on the woman's condition, would you?"

Trevor walked the doctor to the door. "I will, Simon, and thank you. I am forever in your debt."

"That makes us even." Bechtel added a grim smile, tipped a one finger salute and sloshed barefoot to his Jeep.

Trevor stood at the open door until the Jeep disappeared. He closed the door gently and turned around to face Andy with an inscrutable expression. Another chill shook her body, but Andy held his eyes without flinching. "I prefer not being left in the dark, my love." He came closer, ignoring the defensive posture Laz took up at Andy's side. "Tell me what I'm up against." Trevor flicked a glance at Laz. "I'd like both of you to enlighten my darkness."

Laz opened his mouth to speak but Andy cut him off. "Trevor deserves to know." She tossed back her three thyroid pills with a shot of raicilla. "My husband embezzled three million dollars. I found it in his closet and asked Laz to help me steal it." She kept her eyes on Trevor, resisting the urge to look at Laz. She would not admit her shame to Trevor, that she had fallen madly in madness with the man who abducted her. That the man who cut her face and recorded her screams also made her come screaming and howling like an animal. That she wanted to fuck him the first time she saw him and that didn't change even after he put her in handcuffs and drugged her. The past was between Adrienne and Gabriel, it had nothing to do with Trevor and Andy.

Trevor dragged his gaze from Andy to look Laz up and down. "Why him?"

"What do you mean?" she said.

"You found three million cash and needed someone to help you move it. Why this man?"

"He heard Dustin talk about it on the company plane and he asked me if it was true." Andy knew she was floundering.

Trevor crossed his arms and gazed at her through half-closed eyes. When he finally spoke, he used his light-hearted-flirt voice. "Sweetheart, if you two were having an affair you can tell me. I won't be upset. I never believed you were cousins." His voice was soft but his smile was stiff and he watched Andy's face intently.

"Not an affair, more like a one-night stand." It was a superhuman effort to not look at Laz.

"Two-night stand as I recall," Laz said gruffly. His eyes slid across hers and landed on Trevor. "We're friends now. Just friends. I'm committed to my family, to Rachel and Junior."

Trevor cocked his head. "Andy, my love, I don't care that you had a fling with this handsome beast. I am *not* a jealous man. Now about this money..."

Laz's reaction to that was an abrupt stiffening of his spine. "What about it?"

"I don't want any, if that's why your hackles are up. I want to know who is after you. The mob? Drug cartel? Or just this American detective?"

Apparently, Laz wanted Andy to continue spinning her web; he remained silent and picked at a callous. "Rachel's mother had a private detective looking for her. Dustin and his friend. Maybe the FBI, whoever prosecutes embezzlers. Don't worry, it's not drug money or mob money."

"Dustin is your husband? Dustin Cardenas?" Trevor raised one eyebrow and knocked back the dregs of his shot. "Cardenas isn't your name, is it?"

"Don't make me tell you lies," she said in a low voice. *More lies.* Before he could reply, the phone chirped. "It's Rachel." She answered, "Hey, girl, how are you?"

"The baby and I are going to be okay," Rachel slurred. "I have to stay in bed a few days. Mom is chartering a plane to bring me home."

Andy let loose the breath she had been holding. "That's good news, I'm glad you and Junior are okay." She gave a thumbs up to Laz who was motioning for the phone. "I heard a cop was hanging around, have you talked to him?"

"Not yet. The doctor told him to come back tomorrow and they would check on my condition." Rachel croaked a sharp laugh. "I plan on being in no condition to talk to cops ever."

"Good plan, Rach." She wanted to say more but Laz was scowling and making that imperious hand gesture. "Hold on, Laz wants to talk to you." He took the phone and left the kitchen. Andy watched him stride across the living room, go into Rachel's bedroom and close the door. Only then did she turn back to Trevor.

"I'm sorry for involving you." She could not meet the full force of Trevor's scrutiny; his crystal blue eyes seemed to piece her skull and see into her brain. Andy's gaze skittered from her hands to the floor to the window. "I understand if you want us to move out, if you don't want to see me anymore. I understand."

He rested his hands on her waist. "I'm not going anywhere," he said, gravel-voiced. "Neither are you, whatever your name is. If your husband shows up here, he will be handled. If the police show up, what crime did you commit? Your husband stole the money. You found out and left him to come to Mexico and live with your cousin and his girlfriend. That is not a crime."

Andy offered a weak smile. "I hope the police see it that way."

CHAPTER THIRTY-ONE
WE HAVE ALL THE TIME IN THE WORLD

With little to do besides drink and worry about Rachel, they performed these tasks at the kitchen table with a sunbeam slicing a knife edge across the scuffed wooden floor. After a few awkward attempts at light conversation, Andy suggested they check the wreck of the garden and see what could be salvaged.

She scooted off the chair to stand next to Trevor. "You can supervise, sweetheart." Kissing his cheek, Andy said, "I don't expect you to play in the mud with us."

"Tell you what." Trevor said with his playful smile and serious eyes. "I'll go home and ask cook to make something delicious for tea and return around six-ish with food and wine. How does that sound, darling?"

"Sounds lovely." Andy attempted to mimic his posh accent, and she was no better at that than her Spanish accent. But she made Trevor laugh, a real laugh, and the tension eased. She walked him to the edge of the clearing and watched until he exited the green tunnel. The air was as heavy as a wet wool cloak, muggy and full of steam. Andy walked slowly back to the house, almost dragging her feet. She was alone with Laz for the first time in a long time and her secret that Rachel wasn't coming back flashed a guilty neon behind her eyes. Stopping at the shower to rinse her feet, she heard Laz shout over the water.

"Why are you washing? Let's go to the garden."

Andy turned off the shower and peered around the edge of the enclosure. Laz faced away from her with a beer gripped in each hand. He didn't turn when she took a can from his hand. "Bossy," she teased but he didn't respond, it was as if she had not spoken.

Laz didn't speak or look her way as they leapfrogged puddles to the mess formerly known as their garden. Dozens of starts had been donated by neighbors: corn, tomatoes, peppers. The rows of freshly planted green things had been smooshed into the mud where the helicopter landed.

"I have to stay busy." Laz waved his arms at the garden, beer sloshed and foamed out of the can. "She says she's okay but they want to keep her for days and that doesn't sound like she's okay." He stopped at the first row of squashed tomato plants and spun around to look Andy in the eye. "Did she tell you anything? Tell me the truth. Is she really going to be okay?"

She tried a one-arm squeeze to avoid looking in his eyes. Hugging his stiff body was like hugging a tree, rigid and unyielding. "Rachel told me what she told you. She needs to rest for a few days. They will be fine."

He cupped her chin, searching her eyes. "I believe you." He looked to the sky and blew a harsh breath. "God, if you let me keep my family, I'll never do another wrong thing in my life."

He raised his beer to the sky for a toast and took a sip. Andy didn't join him. She had never made a deal with a deity before and saw no reason to start now.

*   *   *

They spent several silent hours in the garden, straightening smashed rows and replanting the vegetables that looked like they might survive. Not long ago, Andy would have thought of nothing but how to get Laz to touch her, and he would have gone out of his way to make that happen. But the connection they shared was frayed. She watched his muscles move, watched his shirt darken with sweat and dirt and he never glanced in her direction. *He's thinking about his family.* Andy's mind was on her secrets. Secrets from Laz, secrets from Rachel, secrets from Trevor. The sun lowered to the treetops, and they called it a day. Laz offered her first shower, went to his bedroom and closed the door.

Andy showered, slipped on a sundress and combed her hair with her fingers. It was almost as short as the day Laz cut it, only now it was neatly trimmed and a light ashy brown, a shade she had not seen since she was a teenager. She padded barefoot past Laz's closed bedroom door without pausing and paced the living room, straightening pillows that didn't need straightening. She checked the phone, no new calls. Would Rachel call again before she flies home? Or wait and break the news after she's safely across the border? At the kitchen window, watching birds duck and dive for bugs, Andy heard Trevor's VW rattling down the driveway before she saw him roll into the clearing. He opened the passenger door and pulled out a cardboard box.

Opening the back door, she called out, "Do you need help?"

"Thank you, my love, if you could please hold the door open for me, thank you, I'll just set this on the table." Trevor bustled past her without meeting her eye and chattered on, "Cook made us a lovely chicken piccata and I've paired it with an herbal sauvignon blanc. I'll just pop this salad in the fridge until Laz joins us. Let me see now, where are the wine glasses?"

Andy noted his quick, jerky movements, the false cheer in his voice, and his lack of eye contact. The moment Trevor's hands were empty, she grabbed one. "What's wrong?" He attempted a charming smile, but she frowned and repeated, "What's wrong?"

He took her hand in both of his and a serious expression deepened the lines in his face. "I've lied to you, kitten." Trevor kept his unblinking gaze on hers. "I *am* a jealous man." He half closed his eyes and peered at her through his caramel-colored lashes. "Tell me again that you and Laz are just friends so I can free my imagination of what happened here after I went home today."

Laying her other hand on top of his to make a tight bundle, Andy said, "Laz and I are friends. We worked in the garden. That's all. We didn't even talk. Laz can't think of anything but Rachel and Junior."

"And you?" Trevor softened his face. "What did you think about?"

"I thought about the words you said." Andy looked at their clasped hands instead of his mind-reading eyes. "When you said you loved me. If I believe you. If believing you is a good idea." She raised her eyes to meet his intense gaze. "How can you love me when you don't know who I am? Are you who you say you are, Trevor Clarke?"

"That is the name on my birth certificate, love." He untangled their hands to cup his palms around the curve of her skull. "And I love who you *are*, I don't care who you were before we met. Keep your secrets or not, I only ask that you tell me what I need to know to keep you safe."

Andy slipped her arms around his waist and leaned against his chest, breathing in his scent. Smoky black tea and lemon, sweet and hot. "But you really don't know me, I don't know you. We only met a few weeks ago."

His voice rumbled against her cheek. "Do you care for me at all, darling?"

She jerked her head back to look up at him. "I care for you a lot, you know that."

Pulling her back to his chest, his deep voice rumbled, "Then fall in love with me, sweetheart, even if it's only for a short time. It feels wonderful."

Something unknotted in her chest, a tension that had been there always. The strain of holding herself tightly to herself loosened ever-so-slightly. 'Fall in love' finally made sense, the sensation was like that moment in your dreams when you fall from a high place and wake up gasping to find yourself safe, in a soft place. Andy stood on tiptoe to whisper in his ear, "Thank you for loving me."

"Oh, darling, the pleasure is all mine."

* * *

They were sharing steamy kisses when Laz walked in the kitchen, his hair damp from the shower. He sniffed the air and smiled. "Hola, Senor Trevor, what is that amazing smell?"

"You guys have a seat. I'll get plates and forks," Andy said.

"You sit," Laz said, his eyes gentle on hers. "I need to stay busy."

While Trevor poured the wine and Laz set the table, Andy rode the waves of conflicting emotions that rocked her. Her eyes moved from one man to the other, imagining her life after Laz-then-Gabriel goes back to California. That was happening, another of those things she cannot change. *I think I could fall in love with Trevor. Gabriel can never be mine.*

They made small talk at the kitchen table, eating and drinking wine. Andy insisted the dishes could wait and they regrouped in the living room, playing cards until dark. Laz glanced at the cell phone so many times, Andy snatched it from his hand and set it on the windowsill.

"The ringer is on the highest volume. You would hear a phone call or text from across the room." She gave Laz a look filled with sympathy. "She's probably asleep. If I know Rachel, you won't hear from her until eight or nine tomorrow morning."

Laz rose to his feet in a smooth motion and took the phone back. "I'm going to bed." He went to his room and closed the door without looking back.

"That poor man, he's so worried," Trevor said. "Should I go home, love?"

"No, please stay. Stay the night with me." Andy pressed a soft kiss on his mouth.

"Take me to bed, darling." His voice husky and warm. "Although I won't promise that you'll get any sleep."

Sleep was the last thing Andy wanted; she embraced this new feeling of falling, and the feeling of being treasured. Holding nothing back, they made love for hours, drawing out the pleasure with intense eye contact and whispered words of adoration. She lay on her side, sweating in the moonlight, watching Trevor's chest rise and fall in the cool gray glow. Clouds scudded across the crescent moon, making abstract shadows on their bodies. Andy drew shapes on Trevor's skin, dragging her finger across his ribs.

He shivered. "Tickles," he murmured.

"I found a weakness?" She chuckled an evil laugh and moved in swiftly to kiss him in the same spot, to lick him, bite him, and blow across his humid skin. Andy drew on his ribs again, using her fingernail.

Trevor curled into a ball around her and snort-laughed. "Stop, stop torturing me. Is this how you treat a man after he's bared his soul to you?" When she wriggled to get free, he held her tighter. "Will you tickle me again if I let you go?"

Muffled to his chest, tears of laughter mixing with their sweat, she gasped, "Yes, but not today."

He released her. "Fair enough. We'll call this a temporary ceasefire but remember, love, all's fair in love and war."

"I don't want to battle you." She propped herself up on an elbow and pushed him to lie flat on his back. "I want you to guess what I'm writing." She stroked her fingers across his hard, flat stomach, just below his belly button.

"You have our undivided attention." He motioned to his penis, clearly rising to the occasion.

"Close your eyes." She drew shapes across his stomach with her forefinger.

"Once more," he said, his voice low and scratchy. After a moment he opened his eyes. "I love you, too, kitten. And I can't bear the thought of someone hurting you or putting you in jail. I can help. I swear I can." He sat up in bed and pulled a sheet over his raging erection. "Without distractions, I want to tell you something you should know about me. It's not much of a secret, darling, I simply don't mention it until I feel the need. Have you heard of Her Majesty's Secret Service?"

"You mean like James Bond?" Andy sat up in bed, cross-legged. Smirking at the look in his eyes, she covered her crotch with the sheet. "You're a secret agent?"

"Nothing so glamorous as Bond, but the same outfit. You've heard of MI6?"

"Vaguely. It's like the CIA?"

"In some ways. I gave my country twenty years and came away with a generous pension, plus a tidy return on a lifetime of investments. You see, darling, I'm a hedonistic man with no ties and gobs of money. I discovered this charming village and all its wonderful people some years back and came here right away when I retired. I do love it here, but I had always planned to move on when I became bored with the slow pace. You have given me reason to stay." He drew letters on her thigh in big, gentle swipes of his finger: I LOVE YOU. "I won't leave San Sebastian while you're here."

She grabbed his hand. "I need to tell you something," she said, low and urgent. "Rachel isn't coming back." His eyes widened and she hurried on, "Don't tell Laz. She doesn't want him trying to stop her. But when she tells him, he'll leave here to be with his family. Even if it means he goes to jail." She opened her mouth for another confession, clicked her teeth shut, blew a long, slow breath. "I need to tell you something else. Something bad." Her chin trembled and she clenched her jaw. "After I tell you, I'm afraid you won't like me."

He laid his hands on her knees. "That is outside the realm of possibility. Unless you're an alien? I hadn't considered an alternate species." Trevor struck a thinking pose, fingers resting on his chin. "It doesn't matter. I still love you."

She looked him straight in the eye and said without emotion, "I killed two men." Scrutinizing his expression in the shifting moonlight, Andy pinned him with her narrow, unblinking gaze. "Do you still like me?"

Tightening his hands on her knees, Trevor said, "I love you. If you killed someone you had good reason. I won't believe you kill for sport."

"Laz was changing a tire and two men tried to rob us. I shot them. I killed them. He didn't do it. If it ever comes to that, if anyone asks, it wasn't him. It was me." Andy's steady voice cracked, and she hugged herself.

Trevor grabbed the light cotton blanket from a rumpled heap at the foot of the bed and unfurled it over her shoulders like a cape. "Open and shut case of self-defense, my love." In his deeper, serious voice. "No one would put you in prison for that."

"We didn't report it. The law frowns on that."

"The law is different in some places. Not saying it's right or wrong, simply stating facts. Sweetheart, no one is searching for you because of two dead robbers. Unless it's to give you a medal." Clutching the edges of the blanket around her, he gave her a shake. "You must be a crack shot, old girl. We should set up targets and have a contest."

She shook with reluctant, silent laughter, then sobered. "Have you killed people?"

"I'm sorry, that's classified." His expression was somberly regretful. "I would like to be an open book but there are things I can never tell you."

"I understand." *That makes two of us.* Andy flung off the blanket and rose on her knees. "Can we play James Bond and Pussy Galore now?"

CHAPTER THIRTY-TWO
RUNNING UP THAT HILL

Lyle Cooper was fuming in bumper-to-bumper traffic between the airport and his hotel on Highway 200; if he squinted, it was as though he had never left the Bay Area. Smog. Low rolling hills on one side, and peeks of the Pacific Ocean between commercial buildings on the other. Idling at yet another red light, his private cell phone rang with an international prefix.

"Lyle Cooper speaking."

"Detective Lyle Cooper from Marin?" said a woman with a Spanish accent.

"Yes, ma'am, how can I help you?"

"This is Juanita Obregon, I'm the head nurse at CMQ Hospital. I understand you're looking for someone with symptoms of thyroid hormone deficiency."

Cooper whipped his head around, looking for a place to park. "Yes, yes, do you have a patient?" He muscled his way across the next lane, enduring flipping fingers and angry honks. "Hold on one second, please, Nurse Obregon, I'm driving."

"Hang up and drive, sir, I'll call you back."

"Damn it!" Cooper shouted to no one. He found a break in traffic and scooted into a hotel parking lot, stabbing at the recent call with one hand and sliding off his seat belt with the other. He left the rental car running and the a/c blasting—Puerto Vallarta in August is a tropical hell. His call went straight to voicemail. "Juanita, it's Lyle Cooper. Please call me back. I'm parked safely now." He hung up and dug out his notepad, pen poised and waiting. "Come on, come on." After forever, the phone rang.

"Juanita?"

"Nurse Obregon returning your call, Detective Cooper."

"Yes, ma'am, Nurse Obregon. Thank you for calling. How can you help me?"

"We received a request from a private helicopter pilot to land on our helipad. He had a pregnant woman in fetal distress and asked for levothyroxine to be brought to the roof."

Cooper paused, letting this sink in. "Do you have the patient's name?"

"When she checked in, she told us her name was Rachel Green. But when we asked for a passport, it said Cynthia Moore."

"Where did the helicopter come from?"

"She refuses to say."

"Refuses? Are there phone records or a video from the helipad that can help me find the pilot?"

"I'm not sure but I can check. Are you coming to the hospital?"

Cooper opened the map app on his phone. "I'm looking at the route now, see you in twenty minutes?"

"Have me paged."

* * *

Thirty minutes later, Cooper was still looking for a place to park; even the hospital's valet parking was full. He rumbled down cobblestone streets, cursing creatively, and finally found a spot ten sweaty blocks away. He entered the lobby wiping his forehead, inside was blessedly cool and smelled like hospitals everywhere—disinfectant, boredom and pain. At the front desk, he asked them to page Nurse Obregon and was rubbing his tired eyes with both hands when a middle-aged woman in a nurse's uniform approached him.

"Detective Cooper?"

"Yes, hello, Nurse Obregon. Thank you for taking time to meet me."

"Ms. Moore cannot be questioned today." She held up a hand to stop his interruption. "Her condition is stable but she needs calm and quiet."

Cooper stifled a frustrated growl. "I should call her mother."

"She spoke to her mother on the phone soon after she was admitted."

"Good, good. I'm sure Mrs. Moore was happy to hear from her daughter. She's been missing for nearly three months."

"Missing? Or hiding?" Nurse Obregon said with an almost imperceptible smirk. "I also spoke with Mrs. Moore."

Cooper had to chuckle. "I don't envy you that conversation." His smile faded. "Did you learn anything about the helicopter?"

"I'm passing you on to our information office." She gestured for him to follow. "You can try talking to her tomorrow but to be honest, detective, I don't think Ms. Moore wants to talk to you." Nurse Obregon stopped at a closed office door and turned to look at him. "And unless you have a warrant, we can't force her to see you."

"I understand. And she's done nothing wrong that I know of," Cooper said. "Her mother just wants to know she's safe. But I believe the thyroid medicine is for a missing person, a woman who is connected to Cindy Moore. I can get a warrant, but I'd rather not. If you could pass that on to Ms. Moore with my phone number, I would appreciate it."

Opening the door, she motioned for him to enter. "Ask for Jimmy, he can help you with the phone records and perhaps the roof video as well. Good luck, Detective Cooper." Nurse Obregon offered a vague wave and hurried down the hall.

Jimmy couldn't help with the video, he suggested the security department, but he found the phone number in their records. Cooper called from the hallway.

A wary voice answered, "Hello?"

"Sorry to intrude, sir. I understand you're a helicopter pilot." Cooper waited but no reply seemed forthcoming. He went on, "You transported a woman to CMQ Hospital in Puerto Vallarta." The silence continued. "I need to know where you picked her up. I'm a detective from California looking for a missing person and I would appreciate your cooperation."

"I don't know about a missing person." The British-accented words were issued with reluctance. "A friend asked for a favor and a woman needed help. She's in the hospital, talk to her."

"I can get a warrant."

"Go ahead," the man said and ended the call.

"Son of a bitch," Cooper spat. He stomped down the hallway to security where they set him up with a computer to watch the brief video; from the time the helicopter landed until it took off was less than five minutes. The chopper was splattered with mud and half the registration numbers were illegible, no matter how he zoomed and focused. He saw some arm waving from the medics with the stretcher, as if they told the pilot to shut off the blades, but the blades continued spinning. Hospital staff lifted Cindy to a stretcher and rushed her out of view. Cooper paused the screen at a clear image of a man in a white coat holding out a box and a bald man in the helicopter reaching for it; the video did not have audio but it looked like a screaming match and the bald man won, taking the box from the white-coat and slamming the chopper door.

* * *

Cooper trudged back to his car and programmed his app for directions to the hotel; he would have to wait until daylight for the drive to San Sebastian. He ran a hot bath, opened the bottle of coconut Tequipal he picked up at the airport and poured the sweet, creamy liquor over ice before sliding into the scalding water with a hiss and a throaty, "Ayiyiyi, caliente." Adjusting a rolled towel behind his neck, he closed his eyes and exhaled long and slow. The instant his muscles turned to jelly, the phone rang shrilly, vibrating on the back of the toilet. Cooper bolted upright, sending a splash over the side and the rolled towel into the water. He rubbed the top of his head to dry his hand before answering the phone. "Hello?"

"Detective Cooper? This is Cindy Moore."

"Cindy, thank you for calling. How are you feeling?" Cooper climbed out of the tub dripping and used a towel to dry himself one-handed.

"I'm not well, detective. I understand you want to talk to me?"

"I'm looking for Adrienne Berg." Still wet, Cooper struggled to slip on his robe, shouldering the phone to his chin.

"Sorry, I don't recognize that name."

"Andrew Cardenas? Andy?"

"Nope, I don't know that person either," Cindy replied. "Sorry I can't help you."

"We know you're with Gabriel Navarro and he's traveling with Mrs. Berg."

"You don't know jack shit, sir," Cindy snapped. "Gabriel was supposed to meet me weeks ago and he never showed up. He said he wanted to raise this baby with me and instead he abandoned us. Typical damn man, disappears when there's baby he doesn't want." She spoke rapidly, her words rising in anger.

Cooper dropped on the edge of the bed, his face a mask of disbelief and frustration. "They went to San Sebastian. That's where you live, isn't it?"

"Gabriel never showed up in San Sebastian. You say he's traveling with a woman? I don't know where he is but when you see him, give him a kick in the nuts for me."

The sound of silence greeted him next. Cooper lay back on the bed, spread-eagle. "This can't be true. She's lying. This cannot be true." He jumped up and paced, his robe untied and billowing behind him, the mini-split blasting his damp skin with frigid air, talking to himself, "They got gas in Encinera, they had to be going to San Sebastian. Unless something happened before they made it to town." He made some phone calls to local authorities, but no one could give him a clear answer of how far along the road repairs were and at this point it was irrelevant; even if he had to walk the last few miles, he would be in San Sebastian tomorrow.

*   *   *

Cooper was five miles away from the village, according to the map app, when the narrow road changed from pot-holed blacktop to cobblestones. His teeth clicked together, and his spine cried out for mercy. Slowing to a crawl, he let loose a stream of profanity, no doubt the ancient road had been the target of these words and worse over the decades. He winced and yelled when he bit his tongue on an especially aggressive bounce. The road climbed in altitude and degraded in surface; cobblestones changed to rutted, muddy earth to gravel and back to cobblestones. He saw a sign that said 'Road Repair Ahead' and beyond the sign, an enormous chunk of the hill covered the road in earth, boulders, and displaced trees. Some progress had been made clearing the landslide, but right now not a person, tool or vehicle was in sight. He had no cell signal to check exactly how far he was from San Sebastian, but Cooper calculated the town was less than three miles away, and he wasn't turning back.

Parking the car on the shoulder, he left a note on the dash with his cell phone number and grabbed his daypack. He had a file with photos of Cindy, Adrienne, and Gabriel, a full bottle of water, and a granola bar. Cooper inched around the slide to the muddy road beyond, setting a jaunty pace down the center where it was higher, drier and studded with grasses and weeds. "This should take less than an hour." He tipped a raven on a wire fence a cheeky salute.

* * *

His good cheer faded as the road transitioned to cobblestones with less mud and more ankle-twisting opportunities. The higher elevation wasn't as hot as Puerto Vallarta, but it was still a steamy jungle. Sweating and stumbling, after a long interval of nothing but overarching branches and encroaching greenery on both sides of the narrow lane, Cooper rounded a corner to see four cows in the middle of the road. They looked too sleepy to bother with him, but he kept a careful watch on the animals as he scooted around them; this was the closest he had ever been to a cow that wasn't behind a fence. Several minutes later he passed a farmhouse and barn, set far off the road behind fields of corn, one of the few signs of life. There might have been signs of civilization, but Cooper kept his focus mainly on his feet—to avoid tripping, and to avoid snakes. This place was bound to be full of snakes.

* * *

After almost ninety minutes of walking, Cooper came upon Villa Nogal and a few meters further, a sign welcomed him to San Sebastian. Ten minutes after that, he bought a cold bottle of water and sat on a bench in the shady plaza with a gusty sigh. He chugged water and picked up the tail of his Hawaiian print button-front shirt to wipe his brow. A passing woman, sunbaked and at least eighty, glared at his bare belly. Cooper covered his offending skin and mouthed "sorry" at her, then in Spanish, "Lo siento." She harumphed and tottered by.

He sipped water, appreciating the cool shade, resting his feet and observing the activities of the town square. In a perfect world, Adrienne would simply appear before him; his feet were throbbing, and he still had to walk to his car before dark. With a stifled groan, Cooper heaved himself off the bench and began making the rounds of shops in the square. No one at Los Arcos recognized the people in his pictures. He tried El Fortin, the drugstore, the market, the bars, the jewelry store, each business that lined the square was run by people who shook their head at the photos and mumbled negatives at him in Spanish. Until the candy store.

The woman seated on a high stool smiled widely at Cindy's picture. "Jennifer Aniston!"

Cooper forgot about his tired feet. "You mean Rachel Green?"

The woman's face paled. "No, no, she looks like Jennifer Aniston."

"She looks nothing like Jennifer Aniston." Cooper narrowed his eyes. "If you know Rachel Green, please help me."

The woman continued to shake her head. "Sorry, sorry, I don't know. Excuse me." In a rare move, Natalia slid off her tall chair and scurried across the store to help a customer.

Cooper stomped his feet on the way out. "Everyone knows her, dammit. They are all protecting her." He started for his shady spot on the square and saw two old men sitting on the bench. "Buenos dias, senors. Were you here yesterday when the helicopter came?" Cooper made his voice bubbly and his expression one of excitement, as if he marveled at seeing such a thing.

"Oh, si, it landed at Senor Trevor's hacienda," said one man.

"Callate viejo tonto," grumbled the other man.

"I'm not an old fool and I don't have to shut up. It's no secret Senor Trevor has a friend with a chopper." The man waved his arms in the air, gripping the cane, looking nothing like a chopper.

"Yes, Senor Trevor. He gave me directions to his house but my phone is dead." Cooper waved his perfectly live phone. "Can you help me?"

"He lives on the road to panteon antigua, the old cemetery." The man twisted on the bench and pointed to the main road. "Walk out of town, you'll see the sign."

Cooper left the village the way he came in and soon found the sign indicating a right turn would take him to the ancient cemetery. He walked on tender feet, ouching on the uneven cobbled road with no sign of humanity until the sun glinted off corrugated metal, nearly obscured by tangled vines. A break in the green revealed a narrow path of freshly churned mud drying in clumps. Crouching, he unsnapped his ankle holster and palmed the gun before starting down the trail.

CHAPTER THIRTY-THREE
YOU KNOW MY NAME

Trevor and Andy took care of the chickens in the morning and made breakfast. Laz emerged from his room grumpy and withdrawn, moping over his coffee because Rachel hadn't called. Andy talked him into waiting until at least noon before calling her.

"She needs her rest. And I know you texted her." Andy raised both eyebrows at Laz's hangdog expression. "Did she text back? No. Because she's resting, her body needs rest. Find something to do. The jungle is encroaching on the far side of the chicken coop. Go out there with the machete and work out some frustration."

Laz gave a twisted smile. "Bossy. I'll do it because I want to stay busy, not because you say."

"I'll get the rake and clean up behind you," she said.

"And on that note, I'll be running home to do my chores," Trevor said. He pressed a firm kiss on Andy's lips. "Do call me later, sweetheart. I miss you already."

*   *   *

Laz and Andy carried the tools they needed to tackle the vines and bushes that constantly threatened to overtake the clearing. Several silent, sweaty hours later they had a pile of green ready to become compost.

"Time for a break, Laz. Want some lunch?"

"You go ahead." He tossed her a wave. "I see one more spot I want to rip out real quick."

Andy trotted across the clearing and was inside the shower enclosure rinsing her dirty feet when she heard a deep voice shouting. She shut off the stream of water.

"Gabriel Navarro!" the voice shouted again.

Bladder and bowels clenched, and Andy's heart thudded to a stop, leaving her breathless and dizzy before it switched to racing madly, pounding against her ribs. She eased the door open a crack, holding her breath. A strange man stood halfway across the clearing with a short, ugly gun in his right hand, pointed at the ground. She slipped out of the shower, holding the door so it didn't bang behind her, and heard Laz say, "You have the wrong man."

A coldness washed over her and steadied her frantic heartbeat. Andy dashed to the carport and grabbed the gun. She ran back to the edge of the clearing behind the stranger, slipping off the safety and loading a round in the firing chamber with a sharp snick. "Leave him alone!" she screamed, straight-arming the gun. The man whirled around, keeping his gun pointed at the ground. Andy widened her stance and yelled, "Go away and leave us alone!"

"Adrienne Berg?"

She shouldn't have been surprised, but hearing her old name out loud was startling. Tightening her grip on the gun, Andy barked, "Who are you? What do you want?"

"Detective Lyle Cooper, Marin police department. You are Adrienne Berg, aren't you? Are you hurt? Is he holding you against your will?"

"You can see I'm fine," she said. "He hasn't done anything to me."

Cooper held out his free hand. "I'm laying my gun on the ground and reaching into my backpack for a photograph. I want to make sure it's you." He opened his pack as he spoke and pulled out the folder, talking low and slow as if soothing a spooked horse. "I don't want to shoot anyone and I don't want to get shot, okay? Just trying to solve a case, just doing my job."

Andy kept her gun centered on his chest, watching his every move with an icy calm and steady hands. Laz remained on the other side of the clearing, gripping the machete, looking poised to hack his way through anything. Cooper stood upright and came close to getting a bullet in his chest when Andy saw the sun spark off black metal in his hand and her trigger finger flinched.

"He hasn't done anything to you? How do you explain this?" Cooper turned on the recording of Adrienne's screams. Her shrieks and howls filled the clearing and echoed off the thick tangle of forest. "He kidnapped you. I know he did. And you went along with him to be safe. I understand. Everyone will understand. But he hurt you and he should pay for that." Cooper hit Play again and turned up the volume, her screams sent the birds reeling from the trees.

From the corner of her eye, Andy saw Trevor charging down the driveway. He also held a gun, his eyes wild as he took in the tableau in the clearing.

"Andy! My god, I heard you screaming. What's going on here?" Trevor moved to Andy's side with his gun trained on the strange man in a flowered shirt. "Who are you?"

"Everyone needs to calm the fuck down," said Cooper. "I am not getting shot over this bullshit. Just tell me the truth and I'll leave. Did that man kidnap you?" Cooper looked Andy in the eye and pressed play on the tape recorder.

Andy held his gaze, face blank as her past-self screamed in pain, rage and terror. "I was acting," she said with a flippant shrug and a smirk. "Fooled you. I should get an Academy award for my performance."

Cooper kept his disbelieving eyes on her. "You are lying." He stared at her unblinking for several breaths, scrutinizing her face before he dropped his gaze, grimacing as if in pain. "I know you're lying." He knew in his guts those screams were authentic. But what could he do? The Mexican authorities would not help him extradite. The embezzlement victim would not press charges and the American authorities may not care enough to prosecute. What was a paltry three million in the days when elected lawmakers were stealing billions? Adrienne claimed to be a willing participant in a crime that had become not-a-crime. Add two dead robbers to their score, according to the Mexican police, also not-a-crime. And she was alive, safe, he saw with his own eyes, so technically, his mission was accomplished. Cooper dangled his gun by the trigger guard. "I'm putting this away. It would be great if the rest of you would lay down your weapons." Without waiting for a response, he knelt to tuck the snubnose in its ankle holster. Shoving the recorder in his daypack, he stood, looking from Trevor to Andy to Laz. His eyes paused on Laz. "This was all you," he said calmly. Cooper waved at the house and garden. "Your paradise is going to be lonely without Eve."

Laz tightened his grip on the machete and moved closer. "Are you talking about Rachel?"

"Cindy is going home to her mother. She didn't tell you?" Cooper gave shocked Laz a look of wide-eyed innocence. "Sorry, I assumed you knew." He shouldered his backpack. "I don't suppose one of you could give me a ride to my car? No? I'll see myself out." He paused and gave each of them another hard look. "I really fucking hate it when the bad guys win." Down the overgrown tunnel of green, Cooper stomped. "Goddammit! Someone will pay. Austin and Berg will pay. I'll find something to charge them with. Someone is going to pay."

Andy followed the muttering Cooper to the end of the driveway, as if in a dream. She watched the detective limp down the cobbled lane towards town with her arms wrapped tightly around herself; she felt like she might fly apart. Avoiding the moment when she would have to face Trevor. Wondering what Trevor and Laz were doing. *Are they talking about me?* Andy touched the scar on her jaw. *What an actress I am.* Even when she could no longer see Cooper's back, when nothing was left to look at, she stayed where the driveway met the road and waited to see who would come to her. The crunch of footsteps did not compel her to turn, but her heart leaped like a startled rabbit. A hand on her shoulder...*hazel eyes or blue?*...and she turned.

"Blue," she breathed.

"Did you say boo?" Trevor's expression was sleepy-eyed and affectionate. "I'm the one who should say boo, dearest. Did you not hear us walking up behind you?" He nodded at Laz standing a few feet away and peered into her eyes. "Do you need to sit down, darling?"

She looked him in the eye. "Do you still like me?" Her voice only shook a little.

"Kitten, I love you." Trevor cupped her face, kissed the tip of her nose, looked into her eyes for a long moment and said in a calm, gentle voice, "And I also like you just fine." He pressed a warm kiss on her mouth. "Now let's go inside and have cocktails." He scooped her in his arms and carried her, ignoring her shrieks of protest. "I can't remember ever being so thirsty. Laz, be a sport and pick up my gun, thank you so much. Oh, and Andy's gun, you don't want to leave that lying around."

"It's not my gun." Andy pushed at him to set her down and opened the back door. "And just because you *can* pick me up, doesn't mean you should. I like my feet on the ground."

"In case you need to run." Trevor gave her a rogue's smile that crinkled the corners of his sparkling blue eyes. "Not your gun? You handled it with remarkable ease." He pulled out a tall chair and motioned for her to sit.

"It's my gun." Laz paused in the middle of pouring shots to look Trevor in the eye. "If anyone asks."

"But I know how to use it," Andy hurried to add. "Trevor knows, Laz. I told him. I told him everything."

Trevor tapped her earthen mug. "Surely not everything, love. Save some juicy bits for later."

"Did you know, Andy?" Laz held his cup against hers, pushing. "Did Rachel tell you she wasn't coming back?" His eyes were fierce, and wounded.

That sick, dark part of her was fiercely satisfied to see his pain and helplessness. It was a small part of her, but it was there, a giddy, gleeful gladness. *He deserves to suffer.* "She's scared. A scary thing happened, and she feels lucky that it wasn't worse. You can't blame her for wanting the baby to be safe."

"I don't blame her, but she could have talked to me. You could have talked to me." Laz drained his shot and slammed the mug on the table with a loud crack.

"Turn it down a notch, my friend," Trevor said evenly. "You're scaring my girl."

"Andy's not afraid of me," Laz growled. He turned back to the bottle and poured a healthy shot. "You know I have to follow them." His pale eyes drilled into hers. "She doesn't want to talk to me now but at some point, she'll call me. We'll work this out." He tipped back the fiery brew and shuddered. "I should have asked Cooper to arrest me and give me a free ride back to California."

"Free ride? You have money," Andy said. "The passport could be a stumbling block."

Laz shrugged. "If they arrest me, I get a ride home. But when Cooper said sometimes the bad guys win, he was talking about us. We won. No one is after us."

"We're not bad guys," Andy said. *Everything we did seemed reasonable at the time. We didn't want to hurt anyone.* "I don't feel like a bad guy."

* * *

One Year Later

"Alexis, my beautiful wife, how are you liking Lisbon?" Trevor smiled at her from across the tiny metal bistro table. The terrace where they enjoyed morning coffee had a view of the Tagus River, the 25th of April Bridge, and the statue Cristo Rei offering blessings to the city at his feet.

"It's fabulous, sweetheart." The woman formerly known as Adrienne Berg smiled at her handsome 'husband'. "I could stay here forever." When her retired secret agent boyfriend suggested a new identity—a fresh passport and a new life—she didn't have to ponder it for a second. Andrew Cardenas is now a ghost. Alexis Clarke is her name, for now—no one knows what the future will bring.

"As you wish, dearest, but can we take vacations from this spectacular city to visit more of the world? There is so much I want to show you."

"Show me everything." Alexis-once-Andy rose from her chair and straddled him. "Take me around the world and back. In between our travels we can stop in San Sebastian to visit Gabriel and Cindy and Junior."

Cindy told her mother in very few words that if she wanted to see her grandchild or daughter, Barbara had no choice but to make peace with Gabriel; he was now a part of Cindy's family although they made their interactions brief. San Sebastian was their home and Gabriel was learning to be a stonemason. The stolen money was slyly inserted into the economy with the help of friends in high places. The Navarros kept a helicopter at Trevor's hacienda, so Puerto Vallarta was only minutes away.

"The child has a name, Lexy-love, and a beautiful one. It means little queen, you know. Very fitting for her royal highness."

"Reinita will always be Junior in my heart." Gabriel didn't discuss this with her before announcing his child's name and so far, they still had not discussed it. Alexis tried to understand that giving his daughter this name was Gabriel's way of honoring their time together, the secret time the two of them had shared. But hearing Gabriel say his daughter's name, his words and voice filled with deep love and affection, felt like the stab of an icepick to Alexis's heart. She did not want to hate him for altering the memory of something she would never forget, but she hated him a little. Keeping that tiny burning thorn of hate alive was a thing she nurtured.

They kept their friendship with Gabriel and Cindy alive and stayed in touch as Alexis and Trevor traveled. Alexis lived as if her new normal would end abruptly; this could not possibly be her real life. Flying first class, staying in luxurious hotels, eating and drinking the best of everything, and meeting people all over the world that Trevor knew from his days in service.

Alexis loved Trevor the best she could. Another tiny thorn she nurtured was one of ice. Her instinct for self-preservation would not allow her heart to fully thaw. Through her life, every time she allowed herself to believe she was no longer capable of feeling pain, someone she cared about proved her wrong. It was the way of the world. Only a crazy person could love another with their entire heart. Alexis didn't believe anyone who claimed they did.

But this feeling she had with Trevor was an unshakable confidence that he would not hurt her, and knowing his first instinct was to protect her. He made her feel like a treasure. She would be the first thing he saved in a fire, even if he died trying. This made her want to protect him, treasure him, treat him like a prize. Surely that defines love. If so, Alexis loved Trevor. If someday this feeling of being loved and treasured goes away, the loss will be bearable. To have this for even a short while was worth any price; she had hurt more and received less from others who claimed to love her. If Dustin had treasured her the way Trevor does, Adrienne Berg would have fought to the death to return to him.

Thoughts of Gabriel sometimes brought a wave of longing that engulfed her, a sick, dark pain that left her breathless. She believed when that happened, it meant he was thinking of her, that they were connected, and their souls cried out for each other. Even though that could not be true. Even though life with Gabriel was never possible, and a thing she no longer wanted, he lived in a corner of her heart and she nurtured that, too. Their past was undeniable. He was a force that had swept through her life and devastated the landscape as carelessly as a tsunami, an earthquake, a meteor. Powerful and inescapable.

THE END

ABOUT THE AUTHOR

When not writing, Cheri Krueger can be found reading, traveling, or indulging her Scrabble obsession. Married with two grown sons and a grandson, she lives in the beautiful San Joaquin Valley where she enjoys local music, craft beer and playing with puppies.

NOTE FROM CHERI KRUEGER

Word-of-mouth is crucial for any author to succeed. If you enjoyed *The Abduction of Adrienne Berg*, please leave a review online—anywhere you are able. Even if it's just a sentence or two. It would make all the difference and would be very much appreciated.

Thanks!
Cheri Krueger

We hope you enjoyed reading this title from:

www.blackrosewriting.com

Subscribe to our mailing list – *The Rosevine* – and receive **FREE** books, daily deals, and stay current with news about upcoming releases and our hottest authors. Scan the QR code below to sign up.

Already a subscriber? Please accept a sincere thank you for being a fan of Black Rose Writing authors.

View other Black Rose Writing titles at www.blackrosewriting.com/books and use promo code **PRINT** to receive a **20% discount** when purchasing.

Printed in the USA
CPSIA information can be obtained
at www.ICGtesting.com
JSHW021407220923
48800JS00001B/54